SMOKING HOPES

by
VICTORIA N. ALEXANDER

THE PERMANENT PRESS
Sag Harbor, New York 11963

To my father

Copyright © 1996 by Victoria N. Alexander

Library of Congress Cataloging-in-Publication Data

Alexander, N. Victoria, 1965–
   Smoking hopes / by Victoria N. Alexander.
      p.   cm.
   ISBN 1-877946-69-9
   I. Title.
PS3551.L357714S63   1996
813'.54—dc20   95-19557
                                                             CIP

first edition, October—1500 copies

Manufactured in the United States of America

THE PERMANENT PRESS
Noyac Road
Sag Harbor, NY 11963

1

Charlie Dean

The view from my apartment on Thirteenth Alley describes the backs of buildings along Fourteenth. Below, my neighbor's three-year-old, a gorgeous ink-eyed Peaseblossom, crayons on the front stoop. Slouching next to her is an older, untroubled, much envied, promiscuous sister. Caveman, the building super, gingerly walks his rat-sized Chiquita around a homeboy slalom course while a boom box plays hiphophouse. Farther down, a sidewalk party features neon-clad kids splashing in a wrench-opened Hydra while "papis" sit in crippled kitchen chairs around a hibachi, watching broken chickens turn from ocher to black. As a white girl passes, trailing a cellophane banner of dry cleaning, they cry "mami" and ask God to bless her. It's August at night.

The apartment house overlooks the street with uncurtained windows like many televisions for viewing (mine is the fifth from the left, Caveman glances up, catches my eye). Noises filter out through fly screens. Snatches of neighbors' answering machines, double-you-be-el kicking S FM, the wail of shark-toothed toddlers, and National Public Radio swirl together with fried odors and exhaust in the airshaft. It's a good sound, an important sound. It's got flat notes and minor characters, melodies, squawks and cat howls. It's got bottom, but no rhythm.

Living in an uncurtained apartment I've become indifferent, more or less, to being watched, to watching. I occasionally glance out the window over the sink, while washing seventeen coffee spoons, at the redhead in the next building who stares into her refrigerator, thinking. Then she seems to forget, whatever it was, and closes the door. I watch her do this.

Imagining my own audience when I walk naked from the tub I hold in my gut. I put my panties on before my bra and roll my stockings on with pointed toes. Just little things. I'm both actor and slightly reluctant audience to every outtake, mistake and scene. I manipulate the medicine cabinet mirror so that its view holds the other mirror on the adjacent wall. I stand transfixed by the unfamiliar view of myself—a view to which others are privileged but is rare and strange to me. Is this how others see me? Is this how I am seen?

I move around my apartment alone as if someone were watching me. An omniscient narrator in my head has taken His place, narrating my life silently in third person and even employing adverbs to embellish my actions. In the center of my mind, just under Wernicke's area, I deposit acquaintances, even loves, into Dickensian categories. Encumbered with metaphors, similes and epitaphs, which are as gaudy as costume jewelry, I maneuver theatrically throughout my days.

I don't like to leave the neighborhood, but it's past due time to make some uptown money in order to blow it in the downtown shops and cafés. The new job will be temporary. My finances observe mysterious cycles. The conclusions of my sporadic bank statements leave me indifferent, leave me in a wake of receipts, crumpled bags and hatboxes, cash withdrawal slips, and returned checks. I can't account for it. I spend most of my time reading, looking out the window, being looked at, and listening. But the bill pile on my Frigidaire keeps growing, and the landlord has been leaving messages on my machine. So I'm on my way to the upper avenues of money.

Hailing from Avenue A, hand raised for a cab, I hear the usual, "Yo! Hey Blondie, need a ride?"

I "invite" this. I'm conspicuous, and as unreal as animation, so exaggerated I frighten with my tall, celluloid presence.

I've been air-brushed and touched-up, surgically altered. I've had everything done. Occupational hazard. Having been an erotic performer for three years altered my perception of my own body. Once you make that initial violation of nature, you realize being happy with what you have is not at all necessary. You can change your body like you can change your hair style or tailor a dress. What is good can be made better, and bigger, or smaller till it ceases to be what it was.

Often I was exposed to the scene of Joe Customer wrangling a gulp from a Bud, swallowing and burping into the back of his hand saying, "Yeah, I like you tits. They nice. Stand up kinda on they own like, but not too stiff like some of them other silicon jobs. No, I like you tits. You got good tits. And legs too."

Joe, I didn't mind. He was insecure and understandably vicious, a paying customer whose insults were sneakily posed as compliments. In defiance of the fact he had to pay for our friendship, he folded his money into the shape of a bird or, instead of money, gave initialed tokens of love, bracelets, lockets and rings.

In any case, he was grateful for the chance to have a look at me, and I did what I could to attract more men like him. My body was my livelihood, and upkeep and renovation were tax-deductible. Modest saline breast implants were first—the most basic of accessories in that line of work. Firm and cool aqueous balloons adorn my incongruously slight torso. They worked! I drew the attention of more customers and made more money. I re-invested. Thighs were liposuctioned, ribs removed (that'll confuse a forensic team some day) to give me an incredible Barbie waist.

I had collagen injected to give my lips an impish snarl, nay a negroid swell. I inserted lapis lazuli eye contacts which were custom-made in a slightly larger circumference than is natural, except to wide-eyed small animals. Walt Disney draws people with eyes like mine. I had hair extensions put in, real human hair. No doubt some Cambodian woman spent ten years growing it, cut it and traded it for an egg. It was processed to an Anglo shade, braided and glued to my head. For this service I paid Paulo nine hundred dollars and can expect the extensions to last about three months. I had a stroke of eye-liner tattooed on. I had my nose sculpted into a work of art, minuscule, dainty. My cheekbone implants extend to the same plane as my nose so my preternatural profile is more than slightly suggestive of a feline's. My chin implant speaks strength.

Happy with all the improvements I sought even more happiness. I enlarged my breasts again, and I made even more money, so I enlarged them again, and I made even more money. If the pattern continued, I'd soon have had two asses.

Finally, I quit, had to. I'd begun to want really bizarre things done, like any rich fool. It's insufficient at this mental locale to be most beautiful in the classic sense; to be extraordinary is the goal. I thought about having my teeth sharpened like African Mbuti girls. Then I considered having my navel removed. I could imagine. A Helen of Troy, not born of a human. At first the customer would be excited with wonder, "There's somethin' about that girl, can't figure it out. Yeah, I . . . Oh my God! What? D'she hatch?"

Thank God that job ended and the money ran out.

But that was only a few months ago, and this new job uptown is only a little different. Ever since my husband, Gottlieb, left me, I have found myself in "morally ambiguous" forms of employment. My American Express bill is the pet excuse, but honestly I think I simply like it.

"Yo! Hey Blondie, need a ride?"

I turn around to face a goateed Puerto Rican kid riding a bicycle-built-for-two. Why not? I jump on the back seat, sidesaddle. I'm wearing a blood-red strapless with matching cocktail hat with a veil which casts artful shadows across my brow.

With the extra weight the kid must stand to pedal. We sway side to side, threading our way through the traffic. After a few blocks, I hop off in front of the Korean fruit stand for cigarettes. The bicyclist drills on.

A sign in the window says, "No dog allowed." I reckon I'm all right to go in. I pick up some diet gum (blue Trident) and diet "marbles" (Marlboro Lights) and request an extra book of 540-HOTT matches.

Outside the stand is an off-duty cabby leaning on his opened door. "Hey, need a ride?"

Why not? "Going uptown?"

"Fifty-ninth Street."

"Close enough."

Why not? is only a rhetorical question. Women like me don't fall victim to random killers. I will never be strangled by a stranger and dumped into a ravine. My death will be my own undoing.

I climb in the front seat and the cabby stamps his boot on the accelerator and slaps the shift lever into drive. We buck into traffic.

"Just gettin' off?" I ask, feeling obliged, as his guest, to make polite conversation. His personal effects are in view: doughnuts, notebook, his shoulder bag, made of Pleather. The strap is torn. I look away.

"Yeah, and you?" He nods to the traffic in front of him.

"Just going in. I'm no good for a day shift."

The cabby is working days now so's he can spend more time with the wife.

"What are you giving girls free rides for with a nice wife at home?"

"Oh, I seen you jump on that bike, y'know what I'm saying? I thought you'd appreciate me keeping yous outta trouble for a while."

This is strange: self-preservation should be my responsibility. With a sigh the girl in the red dress supposes so.

"Where do you work, all dressed up like that?"

"Japanese Piano Bar."

"Oh man," he slaps the steering wheel. "Watch out for them places. Once me and my wife was eating at a Japanese restaurant." Cabby turns and gestures apologetically, "I try different things sometimes, y'know. During dinner, my wife she gets up to go to the toilet, y'know what I'm sayin'? Only she accidentally goes through a wrong door. After she don't come back, I go looking for her, and I hear her yelling through the back door." He raises his voice an octave, "'What are you doing? Let me outta here!' I had to go in and get her out. Had all these women sittin' around this big lounge-like place. Some Chinese guy, Japanese, whatever you call it, thought she was one of the geishas and was trying to get her to work."

Hmm, this job might turn out to be more exciting than I thought. "I haven't experienced anything quite like that yet. So far everything's been on the up and up, merely lighting cigarettes and pouring liquor."

"I'm tellin' you watch out. Those Japanese want to buy America, even our women!"

It was perhaps to some extent a curiosity for phobias which gave me the idea to work as a hostess in a Japanese club. We have all heard the fearful whispers. They're buying up all *our* real estate! They're winning all *our* college scholarships! They think they're better than us!

I don't have xenophobia like the cab driver, but I may have xenomania. I like to examine Japanese, which may be as dehumanizing as fearing them. It's fascinating, the phenomenon of Japanese Man being served by American Woman, inimical types engaging in polite conversation—one a precarious king, the other resentful, and paid. You don't find so often these days such gender-specific roles.

The cabby drops me off at Fifty-ninth. As I'm getting out of the car I check his license. "Thanks Akis," I say, and Akis's cab goes barreling over the Queensborough. I click crosstown on pave-worn heels. Ever since I was a toddler, my steps have been heavy far beyond my weight. Vengeful steps—I'm determined.

As I walk through the swank neighborhood, a man swaggers out of a restaurant with garlic-scented jowls, noisily digesting an expense-account-paid dinner. I catch his eye. We have a silent understanding. I want Essential Bio-Tech shampoo and fresh roasted Guatemala Antigua coffee. I want elaborate bath supplies and that ninety dollar hat on The Hall between Third and Fourth. Why? Spite, tempered with fun, makes me viciously happy, desperately secure. I'll tell you about it someday. For now I have to concentrate on the money meanness in my heart that obscures my philanthropy.

Don't think bad of me. You haven't got the complete story yet. You will. First, my name is Charlie Dean.

2

Club Kiki

Of course, Charlie Dean isn't the name that appears on my birth certificate. I rechristened myself a few years ago for convenience. Every new job demands a new name. When I walk up Club Kiki's weirdly small staircase, ring the bell marked mysteriously in spidery characters and cross the threshold, I'll assume yet another name, Angel.

Inside the club it is cool and dark. Flowers are set out on the coffee tables. A dozen leather sofas and love seats form six discreet "living room" areas. The glasses are polished, and bottles with customers' names written on the labels sit waiting. To my left is red-haired Belladonna, a ballet dancer from Russia with an extremely high hairline and excellent posture. She sits, chin up, looking down her nose, waiting. Ultra, across from me, couldn't be thinner, have larger breasts, bluer eyes or longer hair, not without ceasing to be human. She looks like an Old Movie Star, pale, fabulous and mythical. She holds men in utter contempt. At each break she reapplies her cherry lipstick in the dressing room and is furious that they, those men, actually think they could have *her*. Gigi is American, from the Midwest, black-haired, white-complected; blood is the color of her lips. She is quiet, unsure, but determined not to be, and she has the craziest lime green eyes. There are three soft-spoken Japanese women, my friend Lola and others with ridiculous names. We are alike in many ways. We all wash our lingerie out every night and hang it in the shower to dry. We eat at expensive Village restaurants more often than we can afford. We let gay salesmen sell us outrageous dresses. Several of us want to be models or actresses or curators. Most don't have green cards or are in some other way restricted. I'm the only one here by choice, I think.

The door bell chimes three times rapidly. By now I've learned that the "playful" sounding ring indicates customers at the door, not one of the employees. I roll my eyes up at the closed-circuit monitor above the bar. The fizzling blue video describes the tops of two heads, whose I can't recognize. Two of the Japanese women, Yoshiko and Kazuko, lazily sweep their cigarette packages and lipstick under the table. Jun san, the fastidious manager/waiter, claps his hands twice in the air, and we stretch magazine ad smiles.

Two young American businessmen blunder in, with probably just enough Japanese to have gotten them through the door. The sign by the bell says in Japanese, "Ring three times." The waiter, Jun, is flustered and suspicious because seldom do American men find their way in. One man is mustached and has a double chin, the other tan with clean brown hair. Jun tries to discourage them. "Japanese club. It custom to talk to girls." But they insist. I hope, for their sake, they have their gold cards. Still suspicious Jun applies questions. Are you members? How did you hear of us? Which Japanese firm are you gentlemen associated with? Finally, they produce a note which contains instructions to Jun in Japanese. He bows promptly. They return awkward bows to Jun, to indicate: "Yeah, we've been to lots of places like this."

But no, they are out of their element and nervous. Any American in a Japanese hostess club is a faux pas waiting to happen, myself included. I feel sorry for them and want to, as a fellow American, tell them to leave before they make fools of themselves.

I know how I felt when I crept in for my interview. I had stumbled or trespassed upon a way of seeing that my cultural conditioning hadn't prepared me for. Here, they use a social language understood by a neglected side of my cerebrum. Idle, elegant ladies sit shoulder to shoulder in a sumptuous sofa, looking vaguely amused at absolutely nothing, waiting to serve. Who would believe pseudo geishas in America? Most New Yorkers would never dream places like this are as common as wasps' nests in barns, located right above the uptown side streets we walk on every day.

Jun bows pigeonwise and directs the Americans to a distant sofa by the piano. Meanwhile Todo and his usual crew stroll in and grab the table near the front.

The "Mama san" comes out from her lair in the back and bows to her guests. Her hair is exquisitely piled on her head, secured with a onyx comb. Ringlets of hair tickle her neck and mislead one to see a kind of softness in her. Her nails are sculpted, red and long; especially long are the thumbnails. She walks back to my table in a furious rustle of satin. "Ladies go!" she says and snaps at Lola and me. In Japanese "Lola" is pronounced as if you had a mouth full of ice cubes, "Row-ra."

Vulgar jokes on stereotypes come easily here. I'm trying to wriggle out of that skin of thought, but it is so hard here where two cultures meet in awkward transaction. To them, I'm another stereotype. Lola and I are "blonde babes," of unusual interest to homogeneously dark Japanese.

We are seated with customers. There are four men at our table and four women, seated boy, girl, boy, girl. I perch next to Todo on a small round cushion, which is lower than his seat, an appropriate prop because "The customer is king" is our motto. Jun san brings a tray of steaming towels. I unfurl one and offer it to Todo san, laid flat across my upturned palms (prescribed towel method Geisha code 5 sec. 004). He asks the usual, "What's your name?" I answer, "*Watashi wa Angel desu. Onamae wa okikase kudasai?*" I speak the kind of Japanese learned from outdated textbooks, awkward and overly polite for: "I am Angel. Let me hear your name please?"

"Where are you from?" he asks as if he hasn't before.

"New York." I lie. Last time I said Texas.

"Ah so," he says, turning to Gigi.

"Wyoming," she pauses, "Cheyenne."

"Oh," he brightens up, smiling, showing his bicuspids that

11

slide across each other like shears. He turns to his colleague. "She's cowgirl."

I'm already nodding my head in agreement because I know the colleague will ask, "Gigi one of . . . cheerleaders?" I quickly confirm, and he seems satisfied; Todo seems proud. But then the conversation lags, so Gigi asks them if they've just come from dinner and what they had. It's usually something weird, like poison blowfish, and she can go into her conversation on "Strangest Foods Ever Eaten." This leads into her rattlesnake fry story. They love that stuff. She's sure to mention Stetson hats, sharkskin boots, greased-pig-catching contests and rodeo clowns.

They seem pleased with her story, as if they understood it, and quickly get to the next question. They want to know her race. Todo seems overly obsessed with this. She tells him Danish. He nods approvingly.

The necessary small talk transpires: Hobbies? Ambitions? Blood type? Do you have a boyfriend? Do you want a boyfriend? A Japanese boyfriend?

Lola tries a feeble joke, which ends flatly with a wheezy insecure laugh, mine. I smile. Silence. A nervous laugh. I discreetly wipe the corners of my mouth for smudged lipstick. Another nervous smile. Faked smiling makes me dreadfully tired, and my eye and the corners of my mouth begin to twitch, not altogether attractive. I'm getting paid for this. "So."

"So," answers Todo.

Silence.

Then my auto flirt kicks in, the dumb blonde giggle, the accidental palm of his thigh, the teasing shove.

"Won't you teach me Japanese?" Giggle.

"What do you want to learn first?" Smirk, smirk.

Giggle, giggle, shove his shoulder, "Oh, you know, stuff." "Stuff?"

"Oh, you! Stop that," giggle. "I mean important stuff like, 'thank-you and good morning.'"

"Good morning, thank-you? He, he, he. You can thank me in morning."

Feigned surprise, palm over O-shaped lips. "Oooops, I didn't mean it *that* way!" and so on and so on.

SMOKING HOPES

Soon, however, I tire of this script. "You say modern Japanese are not religious, but wouldn't you agree that the chauvinistic social structure imposes moral restrictions with godlike execution?"

Todo is a bit startled at the suddenly well-turned diction and adjusts his tie. But he does answer candidly. "By that do you mean social structure has place of American church?"

"Yes, except that secular ethics are not usually as rigid as religious ethics."

"But you think our ethic seem as rigid?"

"I don't know enough to say. I'd like to know your opinion."

Across the table, Gigi, probably in an effort to keep herself awake, suggests a word game to learn some more Japanese. "What's the Japanese word for meow?" inquires Gigi.

"And cock-a-doodle-do?" adds Ultra.

Soon they've got the table howling like a Nippon barnyard, well-dressed, rigid, staid Japanese replicating hog and cow sounds. While Jun san tries to flatten his grin, he takes Gigi's glass of expensive cognac and surreptitiously replaces it with tea.

Meanwhile Lola watches the table with the concentration of a chess champion. It's her job. As soon as Todo stamps out a cigarette she empties the ashtray into a napkin and wipes it clean. She tops off each drink, observing the prescribed ritual of adding one ice cube, a dash of liquor, a drop of water and stirring daintily with a crystal rod.

I tend to get involved in conversation and forget to push the liquor. I let the glass empty, stare at the unlit end of a cigarette as it dangles from a client's lips, answer truthfully.

One of the guests finishes his rendition of *Moon Liver* at the mike, accompanied by George san on piano, and Jun, Lola and I drop our flaming matches, crystal stirrers, and conversation to do an earnest bit of clapping, golf tournament style.

It is part of the procedure to rotate the hostesses every half hour or so because small talk tends to peter out quickly. Mama gives Lola and me a signal to move to the table with the Americans. We jump up to leave. Bye Todo. We're moving on. He sits stunned mid-sentence, as if his meter had expired.

At the Americans' table my fearful symmetry shocks them.

13

They are befuddled for the obligatory few minutes. Soon they accustom themselves, or at least conceal their wonder and manage to tell us their names.

After having conversed in limited English with the Japanese girls, our American friends are confused. One asks me what hostesses do. I explain the customs and demonstrate how we pour the drinks and wipe the ashtrays. "That's it," I add.

Drunkenly, one gets his cigarette to his lips and leans my way. He offers to "complete the transaction" without Mama san, later, his hotel.

At one hundred dollars per guest, it's beyond him to doubt that he's in a brothel. Americans couldn't imagine having to pay a girl for small talk and easier chain smoking. Whereas these Japanese seem glad to pay for silly services. Of course, I don't understand the fun of this either, but that's why I'm here, to learn.

Later, Lola and I stand at the door seeing our customers off. She whispers, "*Mota kite ne,*" which translates into "Come up and see me some time," but which Lola doesn't understand herself.

Mama san hands out our money. I count mine: only sixty dollars, not enough to pay Amex, Visa, Bloomingdale's, and New York Telephone. We run down the stairs and decide who's sharing a cab to the Village. A familiar cab driver waits for us in front.

As we drive downtown, since I'm somewhat new to the business, I ask the others if Mama san wants them to call customers at their offices and invite them in. I feel funny about this. It's a little too personal for me.

"Ultra" says, "Don't worry. When you call them at work they're so surprised they giggle, 'he, he, he.' I say, 'this is Prima'—or whatever. I really want to thank you for the lovely time I had at Club Kiki the other night. Please come again tonight. They go, 'he, he, he,' and I hang up. Don't think about it, just do it; it's just a job."

Everyone has bailed out by Third Avenue, and I get into the front seat. I notice the Pleather bag, torn in the remembered spot. The cab driver doesn't even bother to look up at the street he is turning on to. He eyes me sidewise in the seat, and we and a flanking police car go swarming up Thirteenth Alley.

"Whoa," I say, "three quarters of the way up the block, right where that fat woman is doing the salsa in tight pink shorts."

He brakes and my head bucks forward. My purse slides down my legs to the floorboard. "Thanks," I say, noticing the meter has been switched off since Third.

"Hey," he says, clipping my knee bone with his index and thumb, "C'mon, why don't you show me if you're really a girl."

I roll my eyes and get out of the car. I guess he figures he's allowed to say that since he gave me a free ride. I don't think he expects much, just hope really. A lot of men I know pay out large sums for hope.

"Damn," I say aloud climbing, like a high-heeled mountain goat, up my steep stairs. "Why didn't I simply pay the cab driver? Always accepting favors. Someday someone is going to try to call in my debt."

I fumble for my keys, and I get an eerie feeling that things are not quite right, like I've stepped onto my double's set instead of my own. When my key doesn't turn in the lock I realize I'm on the fourth floor not the fifth. "Oops." I dip my head, and look to see if anyone saw me. What other silly things did I do tonight? Oh yes, the bicycle guy. By the time I got to work I'd forgotten about it. What a waste. The girls would have had a nice laugh at me over that one.

I find my keys still fit in my door, and I go in. "Hi Self." Every time I greet my empty apartment this way I have in mind the men who have said with astonishment, "You live alone? A beautiful woman like you?" On the heels of this discovery comes the proposal: "I would marry you."

My worst fear.

Self is the temporary designation of my nameless pet cockatoo. He stares at the pealing mad hermit who feeds him, beseeching, "Charlie?"

I bought Self, or I rescued him rather, from Wadsworth's, where he'd spent much of his life in a cage half the length of his tail. The shop girl had giggled, "I thought no one would ever buy him. He's been here almost a year!" This vile girl had watered and fed him with no more compassion than she might have for a goldfish. I'm sure Self is quite mad. Yes, Self is mad. We make splendid roomies, he and I.

He flexes his wings and bobs his head crazily. "Charlie!"

I unzip my dress and it falls to the floor. Grabbing the rim of my loft bed, I swing my feet up and under, pull myself over like a gymnast mounting the uneven bars, smash my face against the sheets and drag the rest of my body up. I'm sure the process looks quite absurd. I'm going to have to get myself a ladder before I have anyone sleep over. When I first built the bed I had Lola sit on top and watch me climb up. "Watch my face, this must be funny," I said. She watched me groan and struggle till at last I had pulled myself up. But she simply said, "No, you look all right," as if criticism might have hurt my feelings. I want people to recognize the ridiculous. We can't be serious about ourselves all the time. We'll go mad.

I situate the phone under my pillow, and don't dare look at the clock. I can count on Rocco to wake me up in time for our sitting (I do a little nude modeling for an Italian painter on the side). During the night I doze, unaware that I'm sleep-listening to a live symphony broadcast filtering through the open window. In my sleep I hear vague applause. I roll over, extend my arms straight out and politely clap. I roll over again and fall back asleep.

This is the difficult part. I have nightmares. When I finally beat my insomnia, I have to watch these terrible reruns, featuring a me very distant from this Charlie Dean me. Here is the first of the series. It's the pilot on which the long running tragic sitcom is based. The dream begins when I wake up with a start in the Hotel Carlton in a suite called the "Holiday Room." Rolling, warped floorboards are painted hot pink, and the table and chairs are zebra-striped like the stairs in the main hallway.

I actually lived in that very room outside of my nightmare about six years ago, right after I took up with a man called Gottlieb, who is now my Dream-Director, Omniscient Narrator and estranged husband. As always in the dream he has gone out, hours before. I am waiting for him to come back, waiting, waiting, waiting in that suite in the Hotel Carlton.

Suddenly I'm in the bathtub—dreams lack transitions—

16

but there isn't a plug, so I have to stuff a plastic bag in the drain and hold it with my toe. The big porcelain tub is chipped and stained with rust. The water has become uncomfortably cool. The windows are open and the coarse curtains are flapping into the blue night. I keep thinking someone is in the room watching me. But I am alone, feeling very alone, suddenly. I dry off with an absurdly small towel and get into the bed between sheets that are too short for the mattress. Whereupon I fight insomnia till I wake up on Thirteenth Alley.

Awake or asleep, things are much the same, always waiting for Gottlieb.

3

Rocco Says

I am still asleep when Rocco DaVinci's voice comes through the answering machine, "Good morning Sweetheart. Sorry I'm late."

I scramble to pick up the receiver and when I do feedback whines in our ears. "I'm sorry, did I wake you?" he asks.

"What time is it?" I ask because his answer will determine mine.

"Eleven, I'm sorry. I realize we were scheduled for ten. I'll pay you for your time I've wasted." He chuckles. "I'll go round and purchase some croissants and cappuccino and be over momentarily. Do you find that agreeable dear? I'm not too early?" He chuckles at his own politeness.

"Of course not. See ya bye . . . Oh, Rocco wait!" I remember the buzzer is cross-wired again, and consequently my bell rings in the apartment below me. But, I'm too late. He's already hung up. I lie in bed awhile. I stretch back on my feather-stuffed futon and feather pillows—all Japanese-made. I smile a drunkard's sugary smile at my cockatoo, who is pulling at the hem of the sheet. The heaviness in my body, the ache from sleeping is a joy really. I arch my back, spine crackling, then slump back in bed with a sigh. "It's a good morning, Self, think so?" He yawns and smacks his beak in agreement. After a while, I dismount to draw a bath. No showers, no compromises here, a good long hot bath with expensive Japanese cosmetics creating a riot of iridescent foam. I have all the unnecessary accoutrements one could want in the bath: a pillow, a jet spa, a tray that rests across the tub filled with sponges and scrubbers and oils. I drink my coffee in the tub and say "ah" after each sip. The bath extension rings.

"I buzzed, darling. Didn't you hear?"

I respond incredulously and swear I'll go down and let him in myself.

I spray my body with scented oil, wrap myself in my new silk kimono, apply much too much red lipstick and skip bare-foot down the unevenly worn, shallow stone steps. Rocco is waiting in the foyer with his back turned as usual, practicing some rite of politeness. He means to look as if he's entertaining himself with the view of the street (at what, the chucked washer/dryer?). Accompanying his polite forms, he is hand-somely dressed in a forties suit, fedora and cane umbrella, carrying a large pad of drawing paper, a bag from Dean & Deluca's and a briefcase. He smiles.

Rocco showers me with compliments, "Don't you look lovely this morning." He kindly refers to my sleepy look as "sweet eyes." On the way upstairs, I ask, "Can I help you with your bags, take your coat?" and he unnecessarily thanks me again. Thanks me for letting him carry all his own things, thanks me for allowing the use of my tiny apartment—even though he has a large studio in the West Village. I am too lazy to travel. He knows he's doing me all the favors. Why, he sketches me while he quotes the likes of Tacitus and Cicero as if they were his best friends, and feeds me Italian pastries and coffee, and pays me for it. It's one of the easiest jobs I've ever had.

I open my door, and after several volleys of, "No, after *you*," one of us gets in and the other follows, profusely grateful.

My apartment is done in Off-Broadway. The walls are a deep soporific green which ends abruptly in a jagged line right below the ceiling seam—like a hurriedly painted stage set. On the back wall is a backdrop on which is painted a picture of a long hallway leading to luxurious, vaguely crooked and mutely colored rooms. My furnishings are props, picked from the wings of closing shows, unreliable pieces; the antique chairs have false bottoms and the tables weak legs. Rocco and I drink our coffee on the floor, on Japanese cushions.

"Ah, more Japanese furnishings," says Rocco and politely does not inquire after the source.

"The Japaneseness, it's like sand in a beach house, pervasive. It gets gritty in between my toes."

"Be careful, dear. Be careful." Rocco has witnessed, in the past three years, my rapid transformation, physically, internally. My eyes are a brighter hue, but look at him dully. My breasts are fuller, but they are cold to the touch. I am sexier, yes, but aloof. Of these things Rocco is silently aware, too polite to mention them, too polite to express alarm or ask the obvious questions. What is Charlie doing? Working in some kind of exotic brothel? As a prostitute? Geisha? What? Instead, he hovers nearby with a mixture of anxiety and fascination, and, no doubt, a gentleman's semi-erection.

Rocco says no thank-you when I offer him some of his own pastries.

"Do you mind if I sharpen my pencils?" That's Rocco's way of saying, "Take off your clothes."

I let my kimono fall while Rocco's head is lowered. He sharpens his pencil points. "There," he sighs, which is code for: I'm looking up now. Are you decent?

"Your skin against the dark green reminds me of a painting—*The Death of Chatterton*—of a young man who, upon sipping a vial of poison, dies. He is otherworldly white, milky pale."

I like the image, but I'm somewhat self-conscious of necrolatry. Suicide is an embarrassing topic for us. Rocco must have forgotten and let the comment slip. Now he is uncomfortable and looking for a way to change the subject. You see, I met Rocco three years ago when I showed up at his studio doorstep and volunteered to be his nude model. I had noticed an artist-in-residence plaque on his door. I was a complete stranger. When he showed me in, I stripped in the foyer. He led me to a mattress in the studio. I lay down. He put a clean canvas on his easel and began to paint.

Immediately, I fell asleep because, prior to ringing his bell, I had swallowed ninety Benadryl tablets. He must have noticed the change in my skin color. I woke up in the hospital alive.

He found a note clutched in my sweaty palm, instructions to send the painting to Gottlieb. The event would have been quite dramatic if I had died, but as it turned out, I was simply an overly emotional fool. For a time, I harbored the fantasy that at least Rocco might have taken me while I was unconscious. But now that I know Rocco, I know that was not the case.

I find the taped toe marks over on the floor and adjust my feet accordingly. Rocco suddenly says, "I read a poem last night in a book on the Gnostic Gospels . . ." Then he drives into an extended discourse citing works found in the Nag Hammadi Library collection, and we are saved from recalling that embarrassing episode.

While he talks, I only half-listen. The sun hits three p.m., reaches into the airshaft for its daily moment, and throws a wedge of light on the wall and begins to withdraw again. My eye twitches. I look at Rocco. He tells me to look away. I think he feels women are prettier when they're being seen, not seeing.

"The poem," Rocco reminds me, "was found in fragments, buried in Egyptian sand. A woman is the narrator, and she is a powerful speaker. Some would say blasphemous." Rocco always comes round to women and how they got their infamous reputation.

"Many ancient civilizations," says Rocco as my mind begins to wander, "were originally ruled by women."

Forget what I said about nude modeling being easy work. Remaining still is a kind of sensory deprivation. My mind races while my body grows weak.

"We have a great deal of literature to support that theory. This poem is one example. It's called, 'The Thunder, Perfect Mind,'" says Rocco in a thundering voice.

My belly, exposed, is a vulnerable thing, a soft spot, unprotected by any bone.

"As I said, the poem is narrated by a woman, and it echoes a famous declaration. I think you'll recognize it."

Even when I'm sleeping I never leave my belly uncovered.

Rocco quotes the poem, "'For I am the first and the last . . .'"

I twine my sheets around me.

"'. . . I am the honored and the scorned one. I am the whore and the holy one. I am the wife and the virgin.'"

I want to hug myself for comfort.

"Need a break, dear? You look tired," says Rocco.

I say no I'm fine, like a good Roman, but actually it feels as if portions of my body are expanding as I imagine he's working on them. I feel like a Picasso.

"It's an old poem, early A.D. It ends, 'I am the utterance of my name.'"

My left eye twitches again. Posing is easy enough for the first few minutes, but a slight tilt of the head becomes strenuous work when sustained. I feel like my head is held in a vise used for daguerreotype photos. My skin is sweating where it touches between my thighs and where my hand rests on my hips. My underarms burn, and a pearl of sweat crawls down my side.

"Ah, beautiful," he says, making a mark.

I relax and adjust. My left leg is a wooden club. Rocco turns his back while I put my "frock" on.

I examine the drawing. I'm glaring over my shoulder at an intruder, eyes full of disdain, perhaps bored.

Rocco replaces his pencils in their case.

"You do like women a lot, don't you Rocco?"

"Oh, I adore them." He laughs and shakes his head.

Rocco's gone. Left me more money than I deserve and apologized for it. I took a nap, then decided to read *The Rise of Modern Paganism*. While reading, dreamily I wander. My thoughts hang on the tidbits of neighbors' conversation. I hear a telephone installation man ask the redhead where she wants it. I slip my hand inside my skirt.

I've imagined the house-calling workman bit a lot lately owing to the experiences of the past few days. Monday, the phone repair man was over because the lines were down. Tuesday, the Con Ed man came to read the meter. A carpenter fixed a door jamb. And I so like the way laborers wear those heavy tool belts on their hips. A second Con Ed came to check a possible gas leak at the vacant apartment next door, which happened to be locked and inaccessible. He called in the fire department, and I eagerly volunteered to let them use my window to get to the fire escape. Four of them came in, clumsy in all their gear, rubber raincoats and hats, knocking over a lamp, stepping with their big dirty boots on my bench to open the window.

Reclining on the sofa, I watched, sipping a Remy in the middle of the afternoon, wearing my short kimono, with the tie "carelessly" knotted.

Nothing happened. It never does. And at the time, I'm not really interested. But later, for instance now, I think of how it could have gone. Since the verb "to be" has come to mean "to be seen," I become my own audience. I picture myself calling in a false alarm. I open the door, as I had done, with my kimono hanging loose. Four bulky firemen enter and immediately sense that there is no fire. "You reported a fire, Miss?" asks the captain, smiling because he knows. The fourth closes the door behind him. I take a step back, and they fill my little room, all that equipment, all that gear. The captain picks me up and perches me on my window sill and parts his rubber raincoat.

The phone rings. I get myself to the good part, computing my time; the machine is set on four rings, and the length of my outgoing message is a minute or so. When my machine finally picks up, I hear Lola's young voice yawning into the tape. I imagine she's just woken up, rolled over and called me.

"'ow are you?" she asks when I pick up.

"Oh, sitting here playing with myself."

"Right, darlin', 'ow is your bird?"

Lola and I arrange to meet. I will eat my lunch and finish my book, and she will show up in time for coffee.

I sit at the Sidewalk Café, located on the corner of Sixth Street and Avenue A, or "The Hall" as it is sometimes called. The Sidewalk Café is an old sluggish East Village institution which has gone on endlessly, unforgivingly, like the Pyramid Club opposite where transvestites dance on the bar for tourists. The waitresses here are a repertoire of skinny girls in black mini-skirt aprons. My girl has the most beautiful translucent skin and a sharp nose. But her gray eyes are too dull and get lost in her pale complexion. A little eye-liner and lipstick would do some good. She would be a beautiful blonde—I can see tender dull blonde wisps under her arms when she reaches across me for the cream—but her hair has been dyed—about three months ago I would guess—an awful magenta and black. She has a large floral tattoo on the back of her calf and is wearing high-top sneakers. I'm as apathetic to this startling creature as I am now to a familiar Hitchcock film. As I watch her walk away, I think how her lovely skirt knocks about loosely. Then, all at once I take her in with an outsider's eye. My god, what this girl would do to an uptown restaurant. Yet, here she's a wallflower. I look around, everyone appears as if they've just rolled out of bed. Behind me is Donna and her husband, whose hair at the crown looks like it was matted down by last night's pillow. It must be laundry day; everyone is dressed in last resorts. The neighborhood's traditional black attire is threadbare, Swiss-cheesed, Chinese laundered gray, with faded indecipherable slogans about closed clubs and forgotten famous people. What's happened to the neighborhood? The East Village and I? Like an old married couple, one of us has taken the other for granted. I'm finally realizing my spouse has worn socks to bed for the last five years. Now I realize why the neighborhood atmosphere is so relaxed and cozy, everyone stoop-sitting and strolling up and down. No one has jobs. They're all homeless. But my waitress brings me an endive, dandelion and arugula salad with carrot dressing, and she's forgiven; we're all forgiven. I slouch in my chair and read, deferring the cappuccino till later with Lola.

4

Coffee

"Doesn't the neighborhood look ever so dreary today?" Lola sallies in, looking a bit bedraggled herself, and gestures to the people at the table next door. "It isn't what it used to be," she clichés on. "Gone downhill."

She seals her coral lips around a "fag." Lola likes to use English slang and has the faintest hint of an English accent, whether faked or a remnant from childhood I don't know.

"What a dreadful day. I've got a headache so." She puckers her lips and presents her forehead. "Have I got fever you think?"

I reach across to her warm damp brow. "A little maybe."

She sighs, satisfied with my response. "I've been working too hard, poor me." Lola seems sure she has my sympathy. "Had a good lunch, darlin'?"

"Yes, I had." She wants to know what I ate. A salad. Yes, it was nice.

"Good," she says.

She smiles, the kind of smile that comes after throwing back a shot of scotch, more a frown.

When our cappuccinos come, she pulls a reused Evian bottle out of her bag—the bag with several changes of clothes, cosmetics, four-inch high heels—and dumps whiskey into her cup. The milk foam slops over the side. "Want some?" she asks, while I stare at her lips.

"Oh, what? Sorry, no."

She's smooth, like cocoa, like coffee. She is rude and sexy. A man would not be embarrassed to ask her to do anything. She would do it, too. She has that special quality of, to put it nicely, availability and willingness which can be very attractive. Her skin is seductively pale, heavy earth-tones around her eyes, and her bone structure severe; her face, it's compelling, a wide sympathetic forehead. I've talked to Rocco about her. Rocco says to watch out.

I've made friends with her because Lola is a compellingly dangerous girl. I simply have to watch to see what she will do next. It's as if I've found a fire burning in my house and cannot flee to save myself. A burning room is a dramatic set. I survived a fire once when I was a young girl. I have repeated the exciting story on several occasions. Half asleep, I thought I heard a strange popping sound, which I later found was window glass exploding in the heat. I opened my bedroom door (the doorknob was warm, but I didn't think) and faced an orange wall. I ran, anyway, under a dropped ceiling of smoke. I became lost and hysterical and cowered in a corner, partly because I was confused and partly because (I won't admit this openly) I wanted to let the sturdy fireman do his job. I played my part too—rescued maiden in a night slip—even though I might have gotten out on my own.

"Gosh, I miss Gottlieb," says Lola.

Our lovers have the same name. And it's not a freaky coincidence. I am the estranged wife, and she is the estranged mistress of the same man. The interesting part is that Lola doesn't know who I am, as I pretend to be her friend. My secret gives me the unique opportunity to study the other woman up close. The situation has gone on this way for several months. Soon something will come of it.

"I don't suppose you've heard from him?" I ask.

"He'll come back."

"How do you know?"

"You're always so skeptical. Someone like you couldn't possibly understand, Charlie. You're cold, mechanical, bloodless. You don't know what it's like."

"I suppose 'it' means love."

"I hate the way you always pick at my words."

"I'm sorry. I only want to be precise. Let me describe it for you. You two were meant to be. He's your soul-mate."

"You make it sound stupid."

"Do I? You know it sounds to me like unconditional love of the supernatural variety; it sounds religious almost. Do you speak German?"

"You're nuts, Charlie."

"No, I'm exaggerating to make a point."

She stares dully for a minute before changing the subject.

"Are you liking the piano bar?"

"What?"

"I said how's your coffee." Beautiful blond Lola is frowning that peculiar smile of hers.

"Oh, all right. I appreciate the opportunity to learn a little Japanese. Sometimes the conversations can be interesting."

"Oh, I had a outlandish customer last night," says Lola brightening, "who starts confessing, in a coarse whisper that made my blood freeze, that he likes to feel pain."

"How did you get on that topic?"

"Oh, well he was trying to explain to me why . . . why he came . . . I don't remember actually. He must have led me into it somehow."

"Yes."

"He wanted me to step on his hand." Lola shudders.

"I can't believe a Japanese businessman asked that of you."

"Oh, he was American. I feel so creepy about it," says Lola, scrunching her nose.

"Figures."

"I did it too," she says, slowly looking straight at me, daunting.

"Why?"

"Forget it. Any mysterious strangers offer to whisk you away to Tokyo yet?" asks Lola.

Lola is referring, in her careless way, to a dream I have of going to Japan. But my desire is not as easily satiable as Lola might think. You see, I dream of sailing to Japan. Every day the sailing part becomes more important than the port. Lola, too, wants to go to Japan, but she doesn't care how she gets there. My desire to go to sea is a romantic one, a literary

27

one. I want to go to sea, with all the attendant metaphoric implications. Several years ago, I worked as a New York marine operator. Kilo, Echo, Alpha, Six, Nine, Three had been my handle. I had the night shift (insomnia was ridiculous in those days anyway), linking radio operators to telephone land lines. Sitting in a dim closet, various switchboard lights gently flickering around me, I listened to sailors, captains and pilots talking to wives, children, shipowners. I heard a man call for help as his small sailboat went down. "There're children on board," he explained. I told him to switch channels, to hail the Coast Guard, but he was too panicked to understand. I hailed the Coast Guard for him, but I couldn't give his location.

But that was Big Drama, and as important were the little dramas, the loneliness of those men at sea, the love they poured out to their disinterested wives, who often were not at home to take the two a.m. calls. I heard those sailors sinking, in a sense, too.

Something about being at sea that makes one vulnerable and purely human. What will I do there? Read. Think. Sleep. I won't have to worry about paying my rent or feeding myself. I imagine that sailors don't have these cares because the captain has seen to all that. In order to earn my keep, I will scrub, sand and polish. With aching shoulders, raw throbbing fingertips, I'll swing in the evening in my hammock, thinking.

A difficult, unlikely, impossible dream, seafaring will be on my horizon for a long, long time. But really, we merely have to want something in order to stay alive; we don't have to actually get it.

But why Japan as a port? That, too, is only an idea, not a real hope. You see, my husband is in Japan.

I answer Lola's question. "Plenty of men have offered, but they want to fly."

"You won't go but by boat?"

I nod. "A slow boat."

"You're weird," says Lola.

My Lola. You shake your head at a girl like Lola, but you find yourself watching her (you call it "keeping an eye on her"), as if she could teach you something.

Meanwhile Lola rambles on about Gottlieb. Just as he did to me, Gottlieb walked out on her, literally. He went to the deli for coffee one evening and never came back. Even though he's been missing a long time, he's on her mind as if he were about to walk in the door. In the interim, liquor and coke sustain her state of limbo. The first helps her pass the time waiting; the second gives her hope that there is something to wait for.

I imagine that her mind is constantly conjuring up memories of days and nights passed. Every street corner, late night diner and song reminds her of some moment, and it replays, replays. She stares vacantly ahead of the cup in her hand. I mention something about how lucky we are that we don't have to wake up early to work at Kiki.

"Yeah," is her vague reply. Her mind is not on the present. It's gone back to a memory which she has long since corrupted into a kind of low-budget video. She pauses a frame, examines it, looking at him, looking at his image of her. Reassured, she presses play and smiles.

In my mind, too, I see Lola's last morning with Gottlieb. I can hear the alarm clock beeping steadily, this particular morning for four nine-minute intervals of snooze. "Get up, honey," she says. "You have to go to work."

"Coffee," he says without opening his eyes, without waking, lying with his mouth open, head back, rattle in his throat. She's had only as much sleep as he, but she gets up to get his coffee, because it's the only thing that she can do for him. Standing at the hot plate, she's gently sway-backed, and her belly is round. She's tempted, because she worries about money, to use less coffee, but she doesn't want him to say it's weak and send it back. So she uses extra heavy spoonfuls. Spoonfuls that will help you, Gotty, wake up. She lies down on the futon while the coffeemaker is sputtering on the other side of the studio apartment. He can feel her cold skin slip under the sheet, dotted with cigarette burns, and he asks, "Coffee?"

"Not yet, honey. I'm making it."

She wants to help him wake up gently, easily, so she combs his black oily hair back with her fingers and strokes his cheek. Frustrated, he brushes her hand away. She sighs. She wants

29

to say she loves him, but he's fallen back to sleep, and she can't reach him there. She tries to wake him by rubbing his shoulders, but he continues to sleep as soundly as a child with his hands over his penis. The coffee maker is quiet now so she gets up to get his coffee. Her skin is goosebumpy as she pours in the cream carefully, imitating the way she'd seen him do it. She pours just until the cream rises up again from the bottom. She walks on a tightrope to the bed with the hot cup in two hands. "Here's your coffee." His puffy eyes look dull and weary, but they are finally open. He dogstretches and yawns. He coughs, exploding the trapped phlegm in his throat. He lights a cigarette, and his head nods to his chest. She watches him carefully. "Don't fall asleep again, honey. Drink your coffee." He obeys, but then closes his eyes again. The ash on his cigarette grows. She puts the ashtray under it and gently nudges his hand. The ash falls. He opens his eyes. He gulps half the cup. Then the other half. "Is it all right?" she asks and wonders if he can even taste the way she measured the cream. Do you, Gotty, even notice how much her actions say "I love you" in a way she cannot?

But Gottlieb thinks she means to say, "Look how much I do for you." He grunts in reply to her questions.

"How are you?" she asks, meaning are you unhappy with your life? Do you want to tell her how you no longer believe in yourself? Do you want to confide how your job makes your head ache and your feet stink and pays enough to keep ahead of the notes, but not enough to keep the eviction notice off the door, and people don't look up to you anymore, the way they should? Do you want to tell her that you think you may have failed, and you're scared?

But she can only ask, "Can I do anything else?"

"More," he says and pushes the empty cup into her hands. Get him more strong coffee, with honest cream, sew the holes in his pockets that allow his dull coins to fall to the pavement and scatter. That's really all she could do for him. Get him more coffee. She couldn't help him, make him stop spending all of his time on cocaine and casinos, stop hating himself, though she tried. She could only get him coffee. It would help him wake up, start his day better. Maybe he'd have better luck.

I believe this is a reasonable scenario to imagine about Lola and Gottlieb. It is, in fact, my own memory of the last morning I spent with him. I recognize myself in Lola. I can only recognize what is myself in others, and still learning takes time. I've seen rerun after rerun, and still I'm surprised at the turn of the plot. Hard as I try not to suspend my disbelief, when the lights are lowered, I believe again that Gottlieb is real, that love is real.

Lola pops a slice of bright blue chewing gum into her mouth, kneading it noisily with open lips. "Look, it's the Dog Man."

We turn to watch Dog Man walk up St. Marks with his eight black bitches on leashes and a posse of puppy clones. The famous Dog Man, famous for being poor and homeless and having dogs, is, sadly, a much-written-about East Village personality and tourist attraction.

I pay the check with my American Express card. I hadn't felt like gathering change from my ashtrays, but I have to give my girl a ten-dollar tip in order to get the bill up to the charge minimum. Bills will soon arrive with determined ferocity, but I will be equally ferocious in my determination to remit.

On our way uptown to the Union Square subway, we make a few purchases: the hat I wanted, and a couple of outrageous silk dresses for work tonight. After buzzing us in, the salesghoul (face of white pancake and lips outlined in black) sits behind the counter ignoring our obnoxious presence while Lola and I torment her with questions: How much are these dresses? She licks a black lacquered finger and, turning the page of her *Details* magazine, says, "Two" (translation: two hundred dollars). After having inconvenienced her so, we feel pressured to buy, and we wrestle the mannequins to the ground and strip them of their dresses. The girl does take the time to take our money. My green Amex, so flattened from overuse, barely makes an imprint.

Back out on The Hall we eye, disinterestedly, the street vendors' stolen and found merchandise that's arranged with department store finesse on carpets and blankets. I pick up a paperback for three dollars from a man with skin the color

31

of wet clay wearing a grey sailor's cap and a salty beard who also offered to throw in a half a pack of Newports.

We arrive at the subway in plenty of time to get to work. Lola and I descend the subway escalator and pay our tolls. On the platform, Lola and I see a scoliosis-shouldered, bare-chested man in dirty Farah slacks, plastic tennis shoes, sock-less. He's not an unusual sight. We're not afraid yet. Routine and Danger wear the same head around here. It's not that we're oblivious to the danger, the insanity, simply fine-tuned to it. All day through open windows and thin walls we hear babies wailing and fathers banging. We have to learn to distinguish between crisis and loud television before we dial 911.

We wait now, Lola and I, dangerously beyond the "Stand Clear" line.

Farah Man twitches.

We don't want to overreact by running up the stairs to safety, so we wait nonchalantly. "Perhaps we should stand back a bit, get out of the danger," I mention reflectively.

There is a pause from Lola. The impatient air of the tunnel begins to sigh. The train thunders in. Farah Man screeches. Now everyone is glancing at one another exchanging silent plans of action. A heavy man in paint-specked clothes and skin with a frightened shine looks at us as if he were about to say, "Watch it girls. Protect yourselves." A father amateurishly maneuvering a stroller (with deluxe padded arm rests and wheel wells) looks at the housepainter as if he wants to say, "Watch my back, and I'll hold on to the kids here." Lola holds my hand. The train thunders in. Farah Man lurches forward, grabs a copy of the *Post* out of the garbage, flings it at the thunderous head-car, and the newspaper splatters. Wrecked leaves flutter helplessly and land on our indignant heads. But that's all. We're safe; we get on the train and fight for seats and pretend that nothing almost happened, that none of us almost died, that we hadn't planned to save one another. Even Lola pretends. We ride in silence with eyes darting like marquee lights as they take in the sequence of blurred passing stations.

5

It's Happening

One night at Club Kiki, the conversation lags because there is no point to it anymore; its value as a means to get to know the hostess had been inappropriately assessed. Nothing is left to be said—where she's from, what she eats—because it was all empty foreplay to get to this, to this part, when each word has absolute meaning, no ambiguous subtext.

It is silent. The last uttered word dissipates insignificantly. It is as if a light rain had long since stopped, and suddenly realizing it you close your umbrella.

The hostess's low-cut dress slips slightly lower. Slowly, a nipple becomes visible through the lace of her slip. The customers draw heavily on their cigarettes and leer at her breasts. Their senses slowly confirm their hopes. And her hand, placed lightly at her throat, slides downward, slowly, surely, finally moving the strap off her shoulder, letting the dress fall wonderfully down.

The pianist stops playing. Karaoke was simply an excuse to get to this. Jun lowers the lights, and Mama san is not to be found: her function is complete. The workings of the Kiki machine are moving with well-oiled, comfortably warm friction. Then the six men at her table leisurely reach inside their breast pockets, withdrawing checkbooks, scribble obscene amounts with zeroes like hundred-eyed monsters, and drop the checks on the table next to the now useless stirrers,

33

matches, napkins and glasses. It's happening. She cups her breasts in her hands and uncrosses her legs, which up to this point in observation of house rules, have never been untwined. She leans back casually and lifts her skirt over her stocking hem. Her garters. Her panties. She moves her panties aside. It is time. The men unzip. Each steps back, forming an unconnected semicircle. Now, she says, for ten dollars more, in cash, one of them can enter, once. One man, lucky enough to have the small change handy, takes a crumpled bill and drops it on her pale belly. He leans over her and slides himself in once, for one warm moment. Now, she says, someone else for five this time. Just once. Another man takes his turn, while the others, with frantically shaking fists, watch. Each takes his turn and finally the last goes for free, and he gets to go, not once, not twice, but he gets to stay till the end, because it's happening. It's happening now all over the club; every hostess is bare-bottomed, bare-breasted, littered with swamp-green currency. Then the slow throbbing inside her, the pulse beat in her ear against the pillow, and it's over. Mama san smokes wickedly in the back.

It stops there, because there is no reason to go on. It stops there and consequently, it never happens. Upon reaching the signified, the interpreters, embarrassed, turn.

6

Homo Hostess Rhetoricus

Everything is exactly as it appears. Pretty girls pour drinks, light customers' cigarettes and make small talk. What this reality signifies, however, is left to the mind of the interpreter. The imagined possibilities for future nights are left to he who thinks about them. That the hostess's vision of the future differs wildly from that of her customers does not make the present reality a lie. For example, "I enjoyed speaking with you tonight. Please come back real soon," when said by a waving hostess at the door, does not mean: "I like you; let's date," particularly if she's said it in memorized Japanese. However, it does represent a Club Kiki Truth. She really does enjoy talking with him (because she is paid well for it), and she really would like him to come back (so she can draw ten bucks' commission). Hostesses simply do not lie.

The only law a hostess is guilty of bending is the law of probability. There are two answers: Yes and No. Although the customer's chances are not fifty-fifty, this is the hope that colors the air. Possibility makes fools of us all. We sit clucking, incubating dubious eggs, because against all reason we come to *expect* something simply because the possibility exists. If a Kiki customer flips a coin ninety-nine times and each time it comes up heads, when he flips it that hundredth time his chances are still no better than fifty-fifty. The clients' chances with hostesses don't improve with attempts either. Nonetheless, remote possibility begets cruel hope, which is fueled by a belief in (1) good luck (2) his own personal charisma—in other words, superstition mated with egoism. This hope is woven with the hostess's vague responses: She says, "Thank-you for the invitation—but not this week, some other time, perhaps," and so the customer begins to believe in the fabrication of possibilities himself, at once inventing and performing the role of hero. Although this role is merely not impossible, it has been interpreted as likely on the stage Mama san has set.

The hostess never says what she will not do. She never asks what he hopes his money will buy. Therefore, she's not actually hustling the fool. Ah, you object? What sort of girl is such a sophist? What sort of chameleon finds justification in any well-phrased explanation? What kind of girl insists: "I was only following orders. They knew the risks"? If you have the history can you understand? Excuse?

At Club Kiki each girl has a history; several have crossed paths along the way, and thus they recognize old friends smoking in the dimly lit lounge. Their stories sound the same. Each started within the parameters of innocence—or was it ignorance?

Take Belladonna, for example. Take Lola or Ultra or Gigi. Anyone will do. When Gigi was sixteen she got a job delivering singing telegrams. Her costume was really skimpy anyway, so when the company expanded to include a strip-a-gram department, she was easily persuaded to fill bra and panty orders: "Most of the people who want strip-a-grams give them to their friends as a kind of joke, you know, to embarrass them on their birthday or whatever. It was almost always done in a public place, restaurant, office, VFW hall. I got a lot of fiftieth wedding anniversaries. Women and little kids were there, strictly PG. I didn't even take my bra off, merely stripped down to sexy lingerie—or g-string later when I started doing bachelor parties. Money was good. A hundred for fifteen minutes of dancing. And for only five minutes of that was I down to bra and g-string. You know, I'd arrive in a police costume and pretend to arrest the client. I'd spend ten minutes unbuttoning, flash a little cheek and run. Then one day, a client requested that I wear a kind of see-through bra. The restaurant, or private club, would be pretty dark anyway, and they would pay an extra fifty dollars. No problem. Eventually, I started going topless—so long as no one touched me or anything. But finally I went to the bachelor party that turned out to be four guys in a back room. I had noticed there was no cheese dip or crackers, but I didn't think. I put a tape in my beat box and climbed up on a wobbly table. When I finished dancing I found they had stolen my clothes. I got away though, but I had to hail a taxi naked—except for my heels. I really felt a lot safer when I started working in a topless bar, where they have bouncers to protect you and all."

Gigi eventually came to Club Kiki.

She exhales, staring at the smoke. Never had she laid out all the events like that. That was how it went. "You know how it is and all, don't you Angel?"

"Sure, I know," I admit.

It is ten-thirty and still no customers, so we sit around and smoke like dragonladies and chat. Belladonna strikes a match and stares at it before she touches it to her cigarette.

Gigi is not quite willing to let go of her story. It seems incomplete and horrible the way she's said it. But it has all its fingers and toes, hasn't it? That is the way it went. But something about the tale is malformed. An aborted memory is trying to get through the anteroom door. Gigi can't imagine why a vision of her mother has flashed through her mind. (What's she doing in this memory?) If she could remember, she would see very clearly her mother sitting on the pearl green sofa, television off, kids in bed. The gritty noise she makes grinding molars doesn't wake the kids, ever, even if she does it till three or four, waiting for Daddy to come home. "Mommy, what are you doing awake? Can't you sleep?" asked a sleepy Gigi. (Of course she was operating under a different name then.) But Mama didn't answer because Gigi already knew; Gigi obviously couldn't sleep either. It had reached her, too. Gigi was holding a dirty dress-shirt, belonging to her father. It had been her habit then—those times when he was seldom home—to sleep with something of his. Retrieved from the laundry basket, it smelled of him, sweat, cologne and smoke. Perhaps she was becoming superstitious, which is to say sentimental, passionately holding on to something that represented him because she felt his existence less and less powerfully. "Where's Daddy?"

"Perhaps he's dead, or he simply doesn't care," Mama said bitterly. But Mama was so pretty, wasn't she? Yes, she was pretty, had long black hair. Most of the other mothers were older and had cut their hair short, but Mama still had young hair, and wore cat-eye make-up which was too sexy for a mother—Mom said the neighbors whispered this behind her back. Her lipstick was always kissed off early in the day and never reapplied. Yes, Mama was very pretty. And Mama waited and hoped Daddy was still alive and loved her. Then Gigi and her Mama found a cocktail napkin in the pocket of the shirt that Gigi was holding. In gold lettering the napkin said, "Chez Pussycat," and in Chanel red lipstick it was imprinted with a kiss, a name (something ridiculous, like a pet's) and a telephone number. This pet-woman, she must be so much prettier than Mama, but Gigi quickly hid that ugly thought and developed a more satisfactory one: she was disgusting, gross, and we (Gigi and Mama) hated her.

Gigi no longer had any room for this thought. *She* was this pet-woman now. Wives waited for her lovers.

"*I* used to be a receptionist," Belladonna says, shaking the match. The law firm hired her because she "looked good at the front desk" and "had a nice voice." Belladonna met Kazuko at her next job. "It paid a lot better."

Kazuko says timidly, "Yeah, last month we work for one of those phone sex lines. I had to say lot of strange thing."

I think we all had a general idea of what those things might be. Most of the hostesses nodded.

Kazuko continues in her timid English, "No, I had quitting. I had pretending to be a five-year-old girl most of time. Yeah, I starting worry I might be make perverts to commit sex offenses. That's why we coming here." Hostesses nod again.

Belladonna says nothing but remembers an awkward pleasure, unnatural, yet familiar.

"Lola, didn't you and Angel work at the Chez Doll?" Ultra asks. Perhaps Lola hadn't wanted me to mention it because she doesn't respond right away. She dismisses the whole business by saying she earned four hundred dollars a night.

"What did you do for four hundred a night?"

Nothing, she insists.

The ensuing quiet is worse than anything Lola could enlighten them with, so she continues with a shrug. "It's all innocent. Champagne hustle. That's all. I got commission to sit with a customer and a bottle of sparkling wine that cost him two hundred."

"In a private room in the back?"

"In a booth with curtains." Lovely Lola's breasts and cheeks flush.

Officially, that is all. But the price makes for a bit of confusion.

It's just a job, says Lola, and with this brilliant cliché seals the whole matter up as if what is done for money is excused, unlike something done for, say, honest pleasure.

In sum, our accessibility should appear dubious, even though we have only one answer: a long protracted unchanging "maybe." Don't believe it. The customers don't either. My job is to create doubt. With doubt comes uncertainty. With uncertainty comes hope. With hope comes anticipation, excitement, a good story. These places couldn't exist without a hope which is endlessly deferred.

An opened door throws slanted light across our faces, and we fall silent. The cold swish of Mama san's taffeta ball gown is heard as she strides toward us. "All right ladies, no talking. What do you think this is?"

I have my theories.

"I've got business to run here." She sits in her overstuffed chair across from our table and clicks on a reading light. "You know it really make me mad, that you girls don't care about business. You have to be good to customer. I don't want any of you tell them you have boyfriend. That's not what I pay you to say. You have to say you're single and looking for boyfriend. You got it ladies? Lola, you got that?"

No one responds, but Mama san, undaunted, continues, "It's ten-thirty, and no men yet. I can't afford to pay you ladies to sit around. You have to call up customer and invite them in. Did you call your customer today, Angel? Belladonna, give me list of ten customer you call today. Everyone, you have to call ten customer."

No one moves except Yoshiko, who lights a cigarette.

The door chime rings, rings, rings. Mama san jumps up. "Now smile ladies, smile!"

A posse of four wobbles in, heavy with drink, dinner and the uneven weight of their briefcases, stumbling to a table in the rear. George san has already begun to play a popular Japanese song.

"Oh no," says Yoshiko, "it's the Mad Dancer."

"Who's Mad Dancer?" I want to know.

"You never met Mad Dancer? He really makes you work," says Lola smiling.

I would like to discover what "work" here really is. I doubt the way I can pour an ounce of Chivas is worth the money I'm paid, but some customers do stress the importance of this. Last week an evil shipping magnate with a goatee stared me down because his cigarette had been hanging limp from his reptilian lips for minutes. My god! He glared, and I innocently smiled back in bad Japanese. I realized my faux pas too late when Belladonna, noticing the situation, all but shrieked and scrambled for a matchbook. I made a half-confused attempt to strike a match, but apparently I'd mortally offended him; he curled his upper lip in disgust the entire night.

Not expecting him to return, I'm surprised to see him in the Mad Dancer's group. In fact, "he requested Angel special," according to Mama, who croaked this in my ear as she shooed me to the seat next to him. I guess he assumes I was sufficiently horrified into submission. Ohno is his name, pronounced in English, "Oh no!"

Well, Mr. Oh no! takes out a cigarette and hands me his lighter. I don't know what's worse, a man who thinks money will make me like him or a man who thinks his hostility will. Ohno sits without speaking. He is, in a way, attractive. I mentioned the goatee. He is also completely bald and rather tall.

"Why are you so quiet, sir?"

He smiles at my formality. "I know Japanese men probably seem strange to you. This is just a job, I know that."

I smile. "You're right, but I sometimes like my job."

He smiles at me. Perhaps he's not evil at all, simply cool,

maybe cynical like me. He puts his cigarette to his lips. Noticing it right away, I light it for him. "Good," he says.

"Do I get a treat?" I ask; he laughs.

"The reason," he pauses to exhale, "I seem to stress importance of your lighting cigarettes and pouring scotch is to make it easier on you." He looks at my blank expression and continues. "I'm paying a lot of money to have you sit next to me. You know that."

"Yes."

"If you think you've done your duty with these little tasks, you won't feel obliged beyond that." Ohno has well-mannered speech and a clean smell.

"That's nice of you."

"My colleague over there," he points to the Mad Dancer, "likes to give a lot of money to the hostesses 'for nothing' he says. It's his way of putting them in an awkward position."

"Nothing can be done to make this arrangement comfortable."

"You still feel obligated speaking with me?"

"Yes."

"I like honesty."

"I like talking to you, but I don't know if I would continue if I weren't getting paid."

"Can we try experiment?" He puts out his cigarette and reaches in his breast pocket.

"This is fun," I say, rather like a gleeful child.

He takes out a hundred dollar bill and lays it on the table. "Now," he says, "if I give you this will you agree to meet me for lunch tomorrow so that we can become better friends?"

"I'll agree to it, but I won't show."

"Why?" eyebrows and voice raised.

"Well, I would agree at first because right now I enjoy talking to you, but when I get back home I'll start thinking that I have a lot of reading to do and . . . "

"I see."

"And," I continue even though I can tell maybe he doesn't want to hear it, "I'll begin to rationalize that it's okay to keep the money because you shouldn't be so foolish as to try to buy my opinion."

"You know I don't care. Take my money, and set me up."

41

"Stand."

"Huh? Here, have it. Here's my address." He hands me the hundred and a card. "No wait. I keep this." He takes back the card, returns it to his breast pocket saying, "If I give you my card, I give myself hope."

I wanted to see his card. I'd heard he was in shipping. "Aren't you in shipping?"

"Does that interest you?"

"Very much. Could you tell me about it? Have you ever been to sea?"

"Certainly. Often. I love being out to sea. I love being alone. I'm afraid I don't like to socialize much, having some trouble making myself understood."

"Your English is very good."

He smiles. "Thank-you, but that is not what I meant."

"Of course it isn't. I'm sorry. I know what you mean."

"Why are you here?"

"Besides that I like exotic part-time jobs, I want to go to Japan."

"That is easy. How much do you need for ticket?"

"I want to sail there."

"Sail?"

"Sail, or cruise. In my own ship."

"Now, what will you do with a ship?"

He is amused with me. Good. "I read a notice about a Coast Guard lightship for auction."

"Lightship!" (laughing).

"Yes, I'm being honest. I hope I don't sound silly."

"Yes, you do."

"Actually, it's probably a good buy. There are only thirteen lightships in existence. Most of them have been converted to museums. This one can be got fairly cheaply. It was sunk once and damaged, but not badly. It would make a good private club."

"Sounds like too much trouble."

"It's worth it for the romance," I say smiling.

"Which paper?"

"*The Times.*"

Ohno nods. "It's more than you can afford?"

"Silly question."

"No backers? No interested parties to help you with this venture?"

"Not yet."

"Why not apply for passage on cargo ship?"

"I've done that already. I'm waiting to hear back from them."

"It sounds like you're on top of things. I can't offer you much better advice."

"Does your shipping line take passengers?"

"No, but perhaps you would like to join the crew. Can you chip paint and sand?"

"Boy, can I ever."

"I wasn't serious. You would cause too much trouble among the crew."

Then unfortunately Jun san comes up behind me and indicates that he wants me to "rotate" to the Mad Dancer. I get up reluctantly. Mr. Ohno seems to regret it too. I shake his hand before leaving him and move next to his colleague.

The group of men made up of Ohno, the Mad Dancer and two others begin to discuss business in Japanese, and more or less ignore us. This is traditional behavior. Ultra, Lola and Belladonna begin talking too, each to each; like Eliot's mermaids they do not sing to men. On the table are some little snacks for our customers. There are some pretzel-like objects, which I found to be like dry expanding bits of fish-flavored Styrofoam, which attached to my tongue and peeled off the skin. I have never been hungry enough to sample the dried minnows. The Mad Dancer eats handfuls of the little silver bodies like popcorn. Occasionally, he whispers slightly obscene compliments in my ear, smelling vaguely of Korean barbecue and distinctly of dead fish. The men complete their discussion. Then, with a fish eyeball staring at me from between his two front teeth, the Mad Dancer asks me to dance.

After flinging me about the room and twisting my arm out of the socket, Mad Dancer requests a waltz. Mr. Ohno watches angrily as the Mad Dancer presses my body against his and thrusts his Elvis pelvis out. With his average Japanese height, his groin area fits under mine. To avoid this kind of contact, I stick out my rear end a bit. He compensates, and

I have to sway my back more, not only to avoid his marauding hips, but also to keep my implants from being painfully smashed into his collar bone. I hold my chin over his shoulder to avoid eye contact, but this makes it possible for him to breathe hotly on my nape. I could look at him face-to-face, but as I've already mentioned there is his breath problem, also the cross-eyed problem at this distance. I feel inclined, therefore, to withdraw my head and shoulders as far as possible. This gives me a bit of a double chin and a disdainful frown.

As the Mad Dancer glues his body to me like a leech, I feel slightly taken advantage of. God knows what's going on inside his pants, and there I am smiling, still being polite. Under normal circumstances, you understand, I do not let strangers rub their pelvises against mine.

In the nick of time, Mama rotates me to Hiro's table per his request. "Thanks for saving me," I say sitting down.

"Nice to see you again."

"Nice to see *you* again," I say, although I do not recognize him.

"Thank-you for calling and inviting me back tonight."

I had called ten customers at random to make Mama san happy. I do not remember which ones. I quickly look him over for some distinguishing characteristic to help place him: short, Japanese, black hair peppered with gray, brown eyes. No luck. I do recognize his "short" Hope cigarettes on the table, a very popular Japanese brand. "Well, I'm honored to see you again."

"*Hai*, thank-you." He bows his head with his palms on his knees. "*Hai*, usually I don't enjoy myself at piano bar, but with you I am very comfortabre." He nods/bows again.

I bow. "Thank-you. I am comfortable with you too."

His egoism allows him to take this as a full-fledged compliment. "*Arigato!*" (bowing). "I remember last Friday as I was leaving you said, '*Mota kite ne*,' and I asked if you really meant it. You said you did, and I believed you."

"Well of course I meant it!" I have forgotten what *Mota kite ne* means.

"Yes, and then when you called today I said, 'Hello.'" He demonstrates how he answered the phone by putting his fist to his ear. "And you said, 'May I speak to Mr. Hiro please?' and I said, 'This is Hiro.' I already knew it was you, but then I asked, 'Who is it, prease?' and you said, 'Angel *desu*,' and I said, 'Oh, yes Angel san!' and you said, 'I really enjoyed speaking with you last Friday, the fifth. Won't you please come back again tonight?' and think I laugh a little here because I was little nervous, but then I said, 'I think I may be busy tonight, but thank-you for calling.' Actually, I had plan to come tonight anyway, but I wanted to surprise you."

"Oh, and what a nice surprise it is!"

Again he mistakes my politeness for sincerity and bows. I begin to feel a bit guilty that I inadvertently inspired him to total recall. I would like to remind him that it's my job to be nice, and he shouldn't take it the wrong way. Hiro spends the rest of the hour recounting the boring conversation we'd had the week before.

Later, Lola and I are in the back brushing our hair and trading lipsticks. Yoshiko is stripping out of one of the company gowns, a loaner, a very fancy affair with white lace and silk.

Yoshiko is small, a made-in-Japan doll. Her voice is so soft and apologetic. Her whisper frustrates the customers over the obligatory few inches between them. They are reminded of their own pubescent daughters ("I starting to think family shouldn't bathe together anymore"). Todo's business card and several twenty dollar bills fall out of her brassiere, and she laughs like a hag. "Did you have him? Mr. Todo? I think he have spore disease." It's his worst fear, to be the butt of this beautiful girl's joke. Some of the men really seem to think the whole business is sincere. It makes me wonder. It makes me sad.

I look down at my dress. How did I get so wrinkled?

Lola looks at me and winces. My pretty new silk dress is all turned, crunched and pleated in impossible directions. Then I remember the human steam press. "Oh yeah, it was Mad Dancer."

"He dances like that creature in *Alien* might, doesn't he, all stuck on you like. Give you a tip for it, did he?"

"He gave me a fifty to let him rub against me till he reached

45

orgasm." I try to flatten my skirt out with my hand. "Just joking of course."

The joke is getting old though, isn't it?

I take a cab home alone. I actually pay the driver. I'm tired. I don't feel like praying anymore. I'm not having fun. I can't sleep for hearing Hiro san's narrative replay in my head. I try to recite the nautical alphabet backwards, instead of counting sheep, but I get stuck on 'H.' Hero? Hope? I can't help but regret hustling a fool that is hoping for something like love, but a good hustler can't afford to imagine how her fool feels.

7

How I Imagine My Hero

On Hiro's way up from Battery Park, as train approached Union Square, he remembered he didn't have to be back at home until ten. He suddenly had to get off. He had to see Angel. She'd told him she lived in Village.

Hiro's Rolex read, "Eight one," as train conductor announced train would be bypassing Fourteenth Street Union Square due to police emergency. A little annoyed but still committed to his plan, he got off at Forty-second Street and took local train back.

There was green spire above Tompkins Square Park where Angel lived. He could see it from Fourteenth Street when he got off train. As he walks towards it, it seems to get farther and farther away. Hot and sweating now, he tried to hail taxi. As he stepped off curb, a manhole cover suddenly blew into air with loud exprosion, and the street became filled with running water. No taxi could get through. Luckily, bus had waited on the corner, and he boarded it. He didn't have correct change. The spire above the park in her neighborhood beckoned him. Hiro gave bus driver a twenty and was let on.

Due to the water main break, traffic was being rerouted down Broadway. The bus drove down Ninth Street and Hiro got off at Avenue A and St. Marks and began to walk toward Thirteenth Street. Angel had mentioned that she often ate at the cafés on Avenue A.

His watch said eight-thirty. What was name of Angel's favorite bar? Camellia, no. Chameleon, yes. That was name, but was it "A Chameleon," "The Chameleon," or simply "Chameleon"? Every time he used English noun he struggled with this question. There seemed to be no definite rule. As he walked he looked around, and there it was, The Chameleon! He walked past Sidewalk Café and into Chameleon on Sixth Street. He was only customer inside small white bar room; however, bartender ignored him.

Hiro pulled out twenty dollar bill and slid it across bar.

"Wha' can I get you?" the bartender asked in English accent—Hiro noticed.

"Information!" Hiro said confidentry smiling.

Bartender's expression didn't change.

"I'm looking for a blonde girl, lady," he smiled. He hoped that he would excuse his error. "Named Angel." He felt his face redden as he realized "Angel" was probably not her real name. "I think name is Angel. She is blonde hair, and tall, and very pretty."

Bartender folded his arms.

"She looks like movie star," he added.

The bartender's face showed recognition. He obviously knew who Angel was.

"Sorry, mate can' 'elp you there. Ge' you a drink, though."

"Chivas and water," he said. The bartender brought it promptly. But Hiro do not intend to drink it. Before he left, Hiro took out cigarette (almost out of Hopes; he must get some more) and the bartender lit it for him. Hiro left a ten on the counter. It was polite thing to do. The bartender took money and called after him, "Hey, don't forget the matches. You might need them. Here you go mate."

The matchbook (which said 540-HOTT on cover) had the name "Charlie" and a number written inside. Wasn't that what Lola had called her? he asked himself. Hiro looked across street and saw pay phone. He dialed number and heard Angel's voice.

"Hello, this is Charlie. I'm not here right now. . . ."

It's Angel's number.

"If this is Lola, I'm out shopping. Later, I'll be at the Thai place. Meet you there. Anyone else, leave a message if you like."

Hiro was lucky man. He hung up phone, without leaving message (he wanted to surprise her). After asking around neighborhood, and parting with more cash, a salesgirl directed him to Thai place on Avenue A. It was across from St. Marks, surrounded by buddhas and clearly marked: Thai Palace. Hiro rebuked himself for not noticing it.

The waiter showed him table in back of the empty restaurant. Too early probably, only nine o'clock. Then he saw Angel. She was there with Lola. Her legs, so long, unfolded and refolded under table.

He sat quietly, not wanting to disturb her, merely to look. When waiter took his order, he asked him to send his Angel—and her friend—two of the biggest drink on menu.

After a while the waiter brought two of biggest drink he had ever seen, poured into coconut jugs, lots of fruits on the side, even a balloon and umbrella. Unfortunately, Angel's face was hidden now from Hiro view. Ah so! He waited.

* * *

Meanwhile on the other side of the Thai restaurant, behind huge drinks I say to Lola, "At least that's how I imagine how he thinks, in the role of epic romance hero."

"He thinks with an accent?"

"Probably. I can't imagine him without one. His language difficulties are part of his ordeal, part of what makes him uncomfortable and hesitant. I think it's charming, don't you?"

"I think you make him sound dumb."

"An accent dumb? That's your judgement not mine. Anyway, I'm sure that *is* him. Name's Hiro."

"Oh, I don't know. We meet so many like him," says Lola before sipping her fabulous drink.

"No, Lola, look. He's wearing the same tie."

"Right, that is the very tie the man named Hiro wore the other night. Ooh, how exciting."

I admit it seems too coincidental. "However," I say, "coincidences happen in real life, making it seem contrived."

"Yes, I can see that. Ooh, like an Aldo Giovanni film!"

"Hiro probably followed us here."

"You think?"

"Actually it's quite likely. He told me his deepest secrets, tedious stuff to me, but important to him. So he thinks we have something between us."

"And on top of that you make his penis swell," says Lola biting into a cherry while I noted her lips were exactly the same shade of red.

"Precisely. He hasn't been able to stop thinking about me since our first conversation."

"Still, his finding us here is incredible," says Lola, shivering on the word "incredible."

"You want to get the check?"

When the waiter brings the check, I notice he forgot to add in the drinks.

"Great!" says Lola. "Leave him a big tip."

We leave the restaurant, skirting through a crowd of pointy-breasted buddhas. Lola tries out her Thai on the hostess, waving and saying what she thinks is "thank-you" but is really "good luck." The hostess, confused, nods.

Speaking of coincidences which make life seem contrived like a film or novel, I must explain the incredible circumstances that allowed Lola and me to meet. After Gottlieb left, I grew obsessively curious about the other woman, this Lola. I knew she was a stripper.

There's some wisdom in the old adage: If you can't beat 'em join 'em. I wanted to discover what a girl like Lola had offered him. I wasn't necessarily looking for Lola herself, only girls like her. But topless bars are few in number, and it turned out that the Chez Doll where I got my first job had employed Lola for a long, long time.

It was my third day on the job, and I was talking to a man who happened to be one of Lola's regular customers. Jeremiah was his name, a retired sea captain—as chance would have it—round-bellied, blue-eyed, hoary-headed. Jeremiah stopped me when I mentioned my ex's name.

"Gottlieb?" he asked cautiously.

I said yes.

"Not too many with a name like that. Strange coincidence

because there's another girl here who's always going on about a Gottlieb. Gottlieb this. Gottlieb that. Always complaining mostly."

I still remember the pathetic look of anticipation on Lola's face when I approached her and asked, "Waiting for Gottlieb?"

"Yeah?"

"I used to know a Gottlieb," I said, and her expression turned to unabashed hope. Her eyes soon had tears hanging in the rims. One eyebrow was raised. I loved her right then.

I laughed and said that I, too, had a Gottlieb for whom I'd waited. She drilled me for details and finally conceded that our Gottliebs were two different men. I bought her a few drinks, and she began to trust me. I also loaned her my black negligee to wear on stage. She didn't have too many nice things. She relaxed, and we told our stories. I said my Gottlieb and I had split up a while back. I lived dreading the day he would call me back again. I would be tempted to go.

She said her Gottlieb had disappeared on her. She was certain that he was in trouble somewhere, waiting for her to find him. Then we discovered another "coincidence." Both of us were interested in going to Japan. Lola had an idea that was where Gottlieb had gone. The last time she saw him he had been talking about some plan to extort money out of Japanese businessmen through some kind of gambling scam.

"That's another detail to confirm that we aren't talking about the same Gottlieb," I said. "Mine was xenophobic. He'd have never given thought to going to Japan." But indeed he had. That much I knew.

I don't believe in any kind of providence, but it is incredible that Lola and I found each other at the Chez Doll Lounge. One might be led to think the coincidence was really indicative of Fate, but once the facts are analyzed, it is clear the odds not only made it possible but likely. The idea, though, that Destiny had cast me in the role of manipulator appealed to me from time to time, and so although I may have hinted to her, I never have confessed my identity. My secret would give me a certain advantage in controlling our situation. It's not that I purposely hid my name from her: it's simply that I had already assumed Charlie Dean for the purpose of working at the topless bar. She never asked either. She's either dumb or playing dumb. Perhaps, after all, she does know that I am *her* Gottlieb's wife and, like me, is waiting and watching. Maybe *she* is watching *me*, *her* other woman, one who has the initial and therefore most urgent claim on Gottlieb's integrity, his heart. Maybe she knows I am the one he would go back to, if he ever stopped running away. Yes, two Gottliebs does seem like too unlikely a coincidence to disregard.

8

Philippi

Gottlieb is narrating my dream again tonight. His voice is gruff and deep. Out of the corner of my eye I can see him standing downstage, with a smile that is crooked, precious and rare.

I dream I am unable to sleep in a tiny room which is stuffy because it has no windows, except one that overlooks the stairwell. My French door is open to let in air. I may have slept because I feel suddenly awake and aware that someone is watching me. The door is now closed. The room is completely black. I notice a faint smell of sulfur. Slowly my eyes adjust to the darkness, and I think I see the outline of a man in the room standing perfectly still.

I am not quite sure if I am really awake. I don't know if it is my imagination. No, I am awake. I feel adrenaline. I am naked: the summer heat made me kick off the sheet. Slowly, shaking, I pull up the cool sheet to cover myself.

The demon strikes a match. I try to get my voice to scream. The match ignites and fizzles. He holds it up to look at me. For a second in the hard darkness, I see his dark, drawn face and searching yellow eyes. The flame dies away. He strikes another match, and I do scream.

Jerkily, he shakes the match out, grabs me and says, "Sh, it's me, Gottlieb." He rocks me, saying, "Sh, sh," while I sob.

As my eyes adjust I examine Gottlieb's face for the millionth time. He has laugh lines and I wonder when he got them. His black, curly hair looks like my father's. He has his widow's peak too. He looks down at me frowning and the weight of his cheeks makes little wrinkles against his ears, and he pets my hair with his big, square, clumsy hands. He doesn't let us sleep. With morning, lightbeams of heat-phantomed dust come searching for us in the bed. Eyes aching, I, in his lap, look at him and wake up in my room on Thirteenth Alley.

The door is slightly ajar. Rocco makes a perfunctory tap and lets himself in. I lie in bed, curled up with a twisted rope of a sheet twined around my shoulders, my hips and my legs. With crossed feet, I kick once as I .turn. Not unlike a fish-tailed mermaid, thinks Rocco, who quietly closes the door.

After watching me awhile, he's ready to wake me. He softly says: "Good morning."

I wake to find Rocco sitting cross-legged at the foot of my bed with a sketch pad in his hands. "When you didn't answer the phone, I came straight over, and I found your door open."

"You're kidding. I must have forgotten to shut it." I begin to pry myself up off the pillow, using my elbow as a lever. Rocco motions for me to stay put.

"As you were. Close your eyes," he says.

I do so.

"You have the countenance of an angel, with your eyes closed."

"Do I?"

"Out late last night?" asks Rocco.

"Lola and I went out."

"I almost have this sketch done." He makes a final mark on the page. "There, that's done it." He lays the sketch pad on the bed and kisses my forehead. "I'll get our coffee."

"Thanks." When I first agreed to let Rocco sketch me nude and recite history, I imagined other implied arrangements. Rocco, the dear, sketched me and recited history. It's true he sometimes says things that aren't exactly true: for instance, he says "thank-you" to me when I should be thanking him; he says he is not inconvenienced when I'm late or when my phone is off the hook. These are the extent of Rocco's lies, When one is as kind and undemanding as Rocco, such lies are called politeness. When he makes a gift of dinner, money, chocolate or pastries, it is, remarkably, a gift indeed. So I know when he says, "There, that's done it," kisses me on the forehead and says, "I'll get our coffee," that is exactly what he'll do, and that is his only thought.

Rocco returns with a tray of pastries and chocolate and attaches it to the rim of my bed.

"Tell me a story, Rocco."

"May I?" he asks.

"Please."

"An old Roman tale? Would you mind?"

"I'd love to hear it."

"One about Brutus?"

"Yes, please."

"You know, Brutus of *Et tu, Brute?*"

"Yes, Rocco, I know Brutus."

"Yes, well of course you do. I'm sorry. May I?" He straightens his tie. "Yes, well, the *story* differs from the events portrayed in Shakespeare's *drama*."

When Rocco tells a story, he tends to emphasize, with brows raised, unnatural stresses in his sentences.

"I'm less familiar with that version; I confine myself to the ancients. Brutus, as you know, helped kill *Caesar*. He proceeded to lead campaigns, and all that." Pause. Eyebrows. "Well, Brutus, of course, was very successful, but success for ill-fated Brutus cannot last. Oh no. Brutus woke one night to find a ghostly, skinny *old* hag, long yellow-gray hair, with breasts like a pair of socks full of loose change, holding a crooked old broom made of a wispy bush. What should she be doing, but *furiously* sweeping out his room!" Here Rocco imitates the hag, making quick angry jabs with a pretend broom.

I shake my head.

"The old woman says," Rocco puts down his broom, "'See you at Philippi.'" Rocco whips off his glasses. "See you at Philippi." Quick nod. Replaces glasses. "Can you imagine? Waking up and finding this old hag! And she says, 'See *you*

55

at Philippi?'" Rocco drops his jaw and shrugs as Brutus must surely have.

"Where is Philippi?"

"Exactly! Some empty field. Certainly it meant nothing to Brutus."

"I guess he finds out, huh, Rocco?"

"Yes he does." Rocco's smile broadens, and he peers over the top of his glasses, raising one finger. "Brutus ignores the hag's warning." Rocco throws up his arms, replaces them on his thighs and leans back in a there-you-have-it motion.

"And then what happens, Rocco?"

"Oh! Do you mind? It's a short one. May I?"

"Please."

"Well, I would not want to bore you, dear." Rocco teases.

"Rocco!"

He chuckles. (After a while I find myself chuckling like him.)

"Well, finally his luck expires. Brutus and his men meet the enemy on a"—Rocco pauses, cocks an eyebrow—"*plain.*"

"Philippi?" I venture.

Rocco, lips pressed, shakes his head slowly. "See you at Philippi." Then he frowns.

"Whereupon Brutus took his own life because he believed no man can avoid his Fate," I say to provide the moral.

"Ah, so you know the story?"

"No, I was only guessing."

"But dear, I've monopolized the conversation. How *are* you holding up at the piano bar?" He pats my knee.

"Monday night," I say with a shrug.

Rocco waits.

"*Mondai nai* is Japanese for 'no problem.'"

"Oh, good." Chuckle. "I was only concerned about you. I have a friend—or rather an acquaintance, lovely man really—who was a pianist in a Japanese club for a short time. Once—by coincidence during polite conversation—he mentioned that some of the women went to Tokyo with customers *as* escorts."

Poor Rocco. He's tried to phrase this as delicately as possible. "So, you think piano bars are really fronts for prostitution?"

Rocco is politely quiet.

Indeed, the hostessing business does seem dubious. Questionable activities yes, but rhetorical questions, if you like. No answers required.

Gently, "Well, *I* certainly can't say," Rocco says, "Perhaps, dear, it's not arranged by the mama san *per se,* but hostess bars are definitely fronts. Mama san is in the business of serving. Her customers are kings, to use one of *her* phrases. She must accommodate clients' requests, even if her business doesn't offer what they want. She's a go-between. She provides a place where inquiries can be made and *questions* answered. From sushi to white slavery, I imagine she knows whom to ask."

As always, Rocco does not mean to tell me the way it is; he merely suggests one possible way of writing this script.

"You've seen too many movies, Rocco."

More chuckling.

It's not that I lied to Rocco about my desire to go to Tokyo as an escort of a Japanese business man if necessary. I simply don't know how to explain it. There was a time when I would have been disgusted by the thought of hustling, topless dancing, even hostessing. Now I'm caught somewhere between having a great time and feeling unethical.

Still chuckling, softly now, Rocco says, "I pretend to still believe in Romance," waving his hand. "It's fun for me that way." Now sadly, "To believe that in life, as in any mystery, clues," now happily, "will be discovered, riddles solved and in the final scene: the answer to the questionable existence of man."

There is something very endearing about Rocco's position: hope. He's a Darwinist who still says his prayers at night, who willingly suspends disbelief; he comes very close to appearing mad, but comes away very human in the end.

Rocco lays two twenties on the bed and apologizes (with an ironic smile) for not getting enough sketching done.

I phone up Lola and her voice sounds funny, a bit off. As if I walked in on a you-had-to-have-been-there joke. The voice tells me someone else is in the room. She says, "Oh? 'ello,

Charlie. What was that? Share a cab to work you say? Club Kiki, tonight? Tonight, tonight, let me think."

I ask if I'd interrupted anything. She continues to repeat everything I say, a sure sign that I have. "Did you interrupt anything? No. Certainly not!"

"Got a client with you, Lola?" I ask to see if this will be replayed for me.

This time I get a non sequitur. "Sure, darling, I know what you mean. All right, ah ha, bye." The line disconnects.

Privately, Lola and I have agreed we are too cool for any businessmen. Prostitution, of course, is out of the question, not only because we would find it extremely distasteful, but more importantly because (and we're wonderful altruists here) it would not be fair to the wife who would be home dutifully waiting. We women have to stick together.

But the voice at the other end of the phone said, "This me isn't your me." An alternate truth is an awkward area to trespass, Rocco says. We can judge such truths in one of two ways: with our egoism or with our insecurity; she loves me (she tells *me* the truth) or she does not love me (she is a liar). But really, Rocco says, it's a bit of both.

9

Waltzing with Hiro

At least three times during the night dogs howl, starting in the apartment above mine with a deep mournful shudder from the bass throat of a heavy Alsatian. Then a boxer on the other side of the airshaft returns, barking sharply. Chiquita yelps earnestly but without effect. Soon the chorus is spreading down the block, in chain-letter fashion. Someone evil nearby must have a high-pitched whistle, because it all starts suddenly, and we humans have no idea why. We merely lie still and listen to their agonized whimpering and wonder.

Captivated by the swirls on the insides of my eyelids, I cannot sleep. Lids flutter the more I concentrate on keeping them shut. I try to forget about my eyes and soon I'm trying to forget about trying to forget. My mind maps out thoughts, ridiculously connected, from pigeons to fruit pies, playing tether ball in an empty field, Lola, a ring I lost once while swimming. How did I start thinking about that? I wonder with irritation and retrace the logic back to the unlikely source. Somewhere along the way sleep overtakes me and deposits me in the Carlton Hotel, mid-morning, where I am still in bed.

I hear Gottlieb's boot buckles jangling as he climbs up the stairs. He coughs, a hacking cough. He opens the bedroom door, entering with sprightly flair, full of energy from being out all morning while I was a slug-a-bed. He gets into the

bed and pulls me by the leg, positioning me. He unfastens
his belt buckle, unzips his jeans—he never wore underwear—
and he moves my thong aside. When he finishes, he makes
an expression like a defecating dog, sad eyes looking up. He
stands and zips his jeans, which hadn't even been pushed
down further than his hips.

Back on Thirteenth Street, sunk in my futon, it is late afternoon, my skin is moist. My cheeks are feverish. That incubus
Gottlieb has gotten me in my sleep again. Sometimes I don't
mind. He needed me in the morning. Whom else could he
grope day or night without ceremony? He could make love
to me without permission or even waking me. He loved me
like he loved himself, without fear. He was never clumsy or
afraid with me. I thought.

After coffee, bath and dressing, I close my door. Since Lola
won't meet me to share a cab, I set out for uptown alone.
When I reach the landing, I check my mailbox. It's loaded
as always: magazines, catalogues, temptations, bills, more
bills. With junk mail in hand, I go scuttling up Fourteenth
Street on my way to work.

Bills, bills, bills, catalogues, bills. Past the Con Ed building,
I see my favorite bum, Bowery Man. He has a long yellow
beard, wears several overcoats, has a red clown nose, exposed
thigh flesh like mildewed tomato skin, and he lies, stretched
out, comfortably invisible, right in the center of the sidewalk,
splayed out like a discarded newspaper, tattered coat flapping
in the slow hot breeze. He could be a corpse, I think, as I
step over him. How could one tell in New York? An incongruously new hat partially covers his face. From beneath it he
smiles at everyone. Only I smile back, imagining that only I
can summon the sympathy he deserves.

But he haughtily laughs at me, thinking: *Fool, you have no
idea, no idea.*

I walk on and read my second letter, a note from the IRS:
Your balance is past due. Please remit promptly.

Clear and to the point, even polite, hardly subjective or
bitter. I am, however, disappointed that it's merely a form
letter; I was counting on something more specific to my situation. Apparently, they weren't moved by the request that I

enclosed with my return, instead of a check. I typed the note neatly and signed in crayon. I can recall it even now:
Dear IRS:
Any money I may have earned has been spent or rather re-invested. I honestly have no cash. Be a dear and commit the following information to the correct form. You see, I owe more rent than the amount of my taxable income, and although home itself is comfortable, my neighborhood is a slum.
I only make and spend money to appear sane. Remember all those insane years, those joint returns with "0" in line twenty-four? Those were even stranger times. We could only afford to eat eggs and wheat toast at the 24-hour Polish diner. We never ate anything but breakfast; we were always just getting up. The way we slept, we would wake up in the same position we'd fallen off in. I don't remember ever tossing or turning—or dreaming—I slept hard straight through the day, wrapped up together, stuck. I look forward to more uncomplicated times when I will never have to find, read, fill in, or mail one of your forms.

I figured it would be particularly effective in showing how my mind is unraveling. I reckoned if the letter was weird enough they would start a file on me, and I can use it to back up my insanity plea when they drag me to court.

As I'm waiting for the sign to say "walk," I notice a smiling Japanese businessman standing next to me. I hand my IRS bill to him. "Could you take care of this for me?" He looks at my impossible features, my electric blue gaze and takes it. The sign turns, and I run. Maybe he's a philanthropist like me, only richer.

More junk mail. I must be on one weird mailing list. Only last week I got both an invitation to join the United States Airforce and a brochure for cemetery space in the Bronx. This was disguised, of course, as a brochure for some kind of resort colony: "Quiet peaceful acres of rolling green hills. Time for reflection and strolling." Only when you turn to the last page do you realize it's the eternal vacation. By then you're already sold.

I look up from my mail to see how far I've gotten. Fourth Avenue, near the fruit stand with the "no dog allowed" sign in the window.

I also got a pamphlet asking me to join the Peace Corps.

Victoria N. Alexander

I must be on the list of people who are on the verge of something, able to roll one way or another at any moment. I guess those market research people know their targets. I would never get a flier from a cable television company. Sure, sometimes I find one in the box, but it's addressed to "t.v. viewer," and I assume that's a former tenant. But the cemetery one, that had my full name, middle initial and all. That one was definitely directed at me. I get things from life insurance companies. I bought term life insurance, pays quite a lot for sudden death. My father gave me the money to buy it, as long as I named him beneficiary. Wise move, smart gamble, my dear dad.

I cross the street. It's hot. The asphalt is spongy under my feet, reminding me of something in my childhood, the Moon Walk at the carnival. The body remembers longer than the mind does.

I open a letter from Kerr Steamship Company, a notice that I've been put on the waiting list. There's a good chance I might sail in three years.

Approaching Union Square, I realize no one has offered me a ride yet. I decide to call work to say I'll be late. I see a phone mounted on the wall outside the bodega across the street. Halfway through the crosswalk, I notice a sign on it that reads: "Out of work."

On another corner, I find derelict phones with ears missing or wires hanging out of their mouthpieces or that have been used as urinals. At another phone I pick up the handset but hear no dial tone, only an eerie sea noise or a whispering voice. On the left side of every phone is written, "Thank God," on the right side, "Love God." Every public phone that I have used in New York has this scratched on its face.

Finally, I go into the lobby of a new condo and ask the doorman for a phone. He very kindly directs me to one which he is sure works. I follow his directions down a stairwell, which leads to an elevator bank. The elevator takes me to the sub-basement. I cross a long narrow viaduct, use the key he'd given me, enter a storage room. Behind an old ping-pong table propped against a wall is a phone. On its face is scratched the words, Thank god, Love god. Who is this mad

62

writer? He is all over. Why telephones? Does anyone else wonder about him?

I use my calling card to dial Club Kiki. Mistakenly, I dial my old telephone number from seven years ago. Funny how memories never leave the body. No one home. Finally I get Club Kiki. Mama san answers with a fake giggle, "*Moshi Moshi.*"

I tell her I'm on my way, but late.

Back on the street I hear, "Need a ride?"

Another night of yawning, eye-twitching fun at Club Kiki, the small-talk sweatshop. Hostesses should form a union, demand mental health insurance and a five-minute break every hour for real conversation and primping.

While I am putting my bag away in the back, I pass Mama san's door as quietly as possible.

"Angel san?" she sings out.

I cautiously poke my head inside the door of her office.

"Could I have one of your cigarette, honey?"

Although I have seen the smoke curling out of her office, I'd never actually seen her smoke a cigarette, and I'm a bit surprised, oddly. What did I think the smoke was coming from? I step inside her cramped and pitiful office where she so often hides, brooding over unpaid bills in a haze of smoke, cursing, counting tabs, examining counterfeit hundreds. Her nest is surrounded by stacks of papers and undrunk whiskey. To see her there is like catching someone on the toilet. Her vulnerability is, to me, embarrassing. Mean Mama san, hatless, lips undone, smokes hatefully.

"How is it working out?" she asks.

I, nervous (is this a trick?), respond as tersely and politely as possible, "Yes, it's interesting work."

She snorts and smiles. "Yeah, you know I saw Mr. Tanaka dancing too close. You don't have to take it, you know."

"Oh, I take it in the best possible way. I'm really not bothered by such things."

"Well, you know sometimes customer tries to take advantage of you. Don't let him. Tell me, and I'll move you to another table."

"That's nice to know." It is one of her off-days, I can tell. She reaches for a cigarette.

"Customer can be real jerk sometime," she says bitterly, squinting one eye at the sulfur of the struck match. "They think I'm going to sleep with them, ha!"

She draws in long and hard. I smile uncomfortably. I don't want boss/employee relations to become this intimate.

"I make more money than most of those fools. Do they think they can buy *me*?"

I hope she doesn't really want an answer. Thank god, Love god, the phone rings. She holds up a finger of silence, and I take my cue to leave. Closing the door I hear her bitter voice gone sweet. "Ooh, Mr. Tanaka, how have you been? I miss you too," then employing a bit of a growl she adds, "You need to come in tonight to squeeze beautiful breasts!"

Mama can get awfully bawdy with the customers, more bawdy than any of her girls. Once when I was inquiring into some of the more basic laws of physics with a customer, who was in the aerospace department of his company, Mama san tactlessly interrupted to say, "She's sexy huh? You want to take her home?—just kidding."

It's a hurtful joke, her business. She sells hope a la carte.

As soon as I've made myself comfortable with the other unoccupied girls, Jun whispers that Hiro san is waiting for me at the back table, which means a ten dollar commission. (Jun didn't whisper the last bit. I extrapolated that myself.) I walk past Lola and, I think, Ohno. Yes, Ohno—engaged in conversation. Ohno looks up, leers at me and then at Lola, then at me again. He had probably requested "the blonde" and got Lola instead of me.

I sit with Hiro. "You've come to see me again, have you?" I ask in my adult-to-child voice which makes me ill the moment I hear it.

He nods his head shyly.

"I hope you're deducting our conversations as a business expense."

He smiles and takes a cigarette from his pack of Hopes. "No," he says with the gruffness of a samurai. He sniffs the length of his cigarette before putting it in his mouth. A sweet habit—I'd noticed it before. I make a move to light it, but he takes the match from my hand. "You don't have to do that," he says and lights it himself.

"Trying to take my job from me, hey?"

He smiles with the Hope clenched in his teeth. I hadn't noticed his pointed ears before. Have I gotten it right? Is this the same guy? Graying . . . no pretty much gray, not that short, rather tall for a Japanese. He is fairly attractive. I smile, a real smile.

"Would you like to dance?" he asks.

Why not? I'd seen him dance earlier with Lola. He seemed quite a good dancer. Most of these guys can't waltz to save their reputations.

He lifts himself, grunting. I walk to the area near the piano, swinging my butt, and pirouette to face him with my hands extended. He saunters up; his bulldog arms hang at his sides. Then he takes me into his arms, places his hand on the small of my back and gently draws me in. His right foot steps in between my feet. Either he or I has crossed a line. I've lost some control of the situation. He's leading. The tension of his knee on my taut skirt tells me to step back. Suddenly, the job doesn't seem so bad. My body feels content to sway in directions that are not my own. My breasts brush his chest. I remember when that unpopular boy in first grade kissed me. I hated him and was repulsed, but thrilled. That purely physical part survived the prejudice. My head wants to worry about my phone bill, but my body is beginning to respond to Hiro. He sighs, like a child after long hours of sobbing, and tightens his embrace.

Then a ghastly image hits me. What do I look like in this strange room, with my feet shuffling noisily on the carpet, while George san plays *Love Me Tender*? Charlie Dean dancing with a businessman! What would my East Village friends think? Impossible.

When the song ends, he thanks me as if I'd saved his life. After applauding politely, we take our seats. As long as I remain in the context of a Japanese Businessman, he appears fine, safe from my biases. But I am forever remembering my own ridiculousness.

"Hiro san," I ask tenderly, inoffensively, "why do Japanese men come to these kinds of places? I'm not being critical. I simply wonder what *I* am doing here. What is it that the customer expects?"

"To talk with pretty ladies," is his gentle reply.

"Just talk? I mean, excuse me Hiro san, but Kiki talk is a bit expensive."

"Well, we bring clients, so they can talk to girls. It's simply business."

"But do any of the men think that the girls really like them? Do they think that for one minute," gruffly, "that a girl would speak to them if she weren't getting paid for it?"

He looks surprised as if he's never considered this before. Immediately, I fear he thinks I group him with "men." I hope he realizes that my taking him into confidence excludes him from the others.

"I know most of the girl have boyfriend, and aren't really interested in Japanese businessman—but there's always a chance," he adds.

"That's pathetic. I mean, that's really sad. And 'the customer is king' thing. How can anyone have real power, or real hope for that matter, if they have to pay for it?"

"You'll see," he says.

Near closing time, Hiro offers Lola and me a ride home. I agree to meet him out front. When I ask Lola, she declines. Mr. Ohno will drive her home, she says. She also says she is quitting. I expected this more or less. I, too, have been at Kiki too long. I'm beginning to understand that indeed hostessing is not a front for prostitution. It is, though, a place where a man finds a mistress, whom the Japanese man tends to treat as a kind of best friend. I wouldn't mind being Ohno's "friend." He's cool-looking actually. Hiro, on the other hand, though somewhat attractive, is definitely a dork. While Lola hustles, lies, and gets money from men, they like it and so does she. My balancing honesty and politeness gets nothing but a Hiro's misguided infatuation. I remind Lola that Ohno had requested me before Hiro started monopolizing my time.

"Bad luck," she says.

We go into Mama's office to get our paychecks. Mama san is all smiles until Lola shyly hints that she's got some bad news. Mama's pen pauses on the amount and she says meanly, "What is it?"

She's heard this before. Every month she has to place a new ad in the *Voice*. She takes girls in, gives them a job and connections, geisha training, and then soon after the second paycheck—she's learned to withhold the first payment three weeks—the girl has "some bad news" for her.

"You're not quitting," she says. This isn't a question.

"Oh no," Lola cowers, "I have a temporary job in Japan for a month. It came up suddenly."

"A couple of week off?" she says irritably. "You only here a month. Already you want time off?" She completes the amount on the check, omitting the numbers that should have gone in the cents column. She's powerless to stop this conversation from occurring, yet pretends that she still has control. Her only means of keeping her employees is to make quitting as unpleasant as possible. Pathetically, she attempts to be stern: "I'm sorry. I've already put you on schedule this week. I'll see you Friday."

She rises, puts her arm around Lola and walks her to the door. "Jun san, call Ohno's car for Lola."

Jun is on the phone before she finishes speaking. She turns to Lola. "See, *I* make arrangement with Ohno. We'll talk Friday. Don't ever arrange thing with customer. Always through me."

On the way out, we pass Jun, who is furiously sweeping the steps like Rocco's hag. He says, "See you at Friday."

Parked in front of the club are two limos. First in line, Hiro, followed by Ohno.

"What was that about going to Japan?" I ask.

"Tell you later. Take care, love," she says getting into Ohno's car.

Hiro's driver opens the door for me. I climb inside the dark and roomy car, sit across from Hiro and put my hands on my knees.

"Ready?" asks Hiro and informs the driver of my address. The driver questions him, "East Village, you sure?" before proceeding.

"Angel, ever think going to Japan?" he asks.

"I'm starting to. I mean, being immersed in Japanese culture, the idea tends to seep in. I'm not watertight."

"Would you like to learn Japanese?"

"Well, going to Japan would be the best way to do that. You have to be motivated by necessity."

"Or you could get Japanese boyfriend."

Offering yourself up for that job, are you? "Perhaps, but the kinds of things I might learn from a boyfriend might not be useful in many situations."

He grins, and I realize he's taken my comment the wrong way. "I could teach you to say useful things." My hero judges this an apt moment to burp. "Pardon me."

"No, I mean the conversation between lovers is usually immediate: I want this. Let's do that. That's the sort of thing I'm bound to learn first. I'd rather learn a language by hearing stories, fables, or reading folk literature. The best way to study a culture is through its fables." I often says things like this to inspire conversation on something other than my breast size.

The two myths I've most often heard in reply are the Several-Headed Dragon Myth and The First Strip-Tease Myth. I say *several*-headed dragon because the number changes from customer to customer. Most often it's seven or nine. The several-headed dragon must be killed in several different ways. The hero kills the first head by chopping it off with his sword, easily enough. Frantic Confusion kills the next two. Heads two and three were so angered at having lost one of the heads, they start having spasms. They get tangled together and strangle one another in an effort to get free. An argument over who should take the blame for the deaths ensues, and one particularly nasty head barbecues another. How many is that? Then, the hero tricks a head into drinking a barrel of sake. This head drowns itself. Two heads left. One tells a funny joke, and the other laughs to death. Finally, the last dies of loneliness. Supply your own moral.

The First Strip-Tease occurred because, once upon a time, the sun would not come out for several months of night, and the people decide to throw an extravagant party, hoping she would want to come. To this party, strippers were invited.

When the sun heard the cheers and hallos from the men, her jealousy finally drew her out.

These are my favorite myths. I have heard many variations.

But Hiro san ignores my cue. "I don't usually like hostesses because they are after money. But I like you. You are intelligent."

"Oh, gee thanks."

"No I mean it seriously. I think we can talk very well together."

At Fourteenth Street the line that separates uptown from down, I feel a buck in the road, and a calm feeling comes over me. When we pulled up in front of my apartment, Hiro doesn't let me get out of the car without giving me his card, a hundred dollar bill, and a large box. I say grace for getting home alive. He doesn't seem impressed with the neighborhood, looking concerned as I close the door.

Upstairs I open the box: a set of tea cups, tea, a welcome curtain for the doorway, Japanese language tapes and, ironically, a book of Japanese myths. I put these things alongside the rest of the useless gifts from admirers. I get in bed, stuff a pillow between my thighs and stretch while the world outside howls, sighs and quivers. I bypass the insomnia and fall right into a nightmare that seems to have been playing without me. I am the passenger in a speeding car about to crash into one of the pillars under the Brooklyn/Queens Expressway. Gotty and I are in the middle of a screaming argument. I grab the wheel. We swerve. I jump out of the car and run toward a warehouse. Gottlieb doesn't come after me right away, because he knows I can't go far. I am wearing four-inch heels, a short flimsy dress, a platinum wig. I have left my purse in the car. I run a few blocks, find an alley and sink down against a brick wall, trying to melt into it. I hear the sound of an approaching car. I put my cheek to the damp clay and broken glass and close my eyes. Headlights come searching. I lie perfectly still, afraid to be found, afraid that no one is looking for me.

I dream I sleep. I dream I wake damp and shivering. The gate of a distant warehouse bangs in the wind. Everything else is silent. No more headlights. I wander the desert of dead-ends, locked doorways, and alleys of rushing night wind.

With my shoes hooked on my finger, I walk. Only one long red nail left. Stockings are torn. I am the only soul on the street. Silent cars pass occasionally, without slowing to look. A wolfish watchdog appears out of some dark recess and stands in my crooked path, tail down, growling. He forbids me to cross the parking lot. He lunges, and I go running backwards, back to nowhere. I hide in a doorway, listening to the frustrated bark. I lie down. Someone steps over me and goes on. The sun is coming up, but I still have the night on: no one seems to see me. I look so alien in whore's wig and torn dress people choose not to see me. Invisible, I walk to a bus stop and climb on a bus when it comes. No one asks me to pay.

At home, the Hotel Carlton, the rooms are empty. I change my clothes and get some money. In a trance, I go to work, riding the subway with that warehouse quiet still beating in my ears. Gottlieb is standing outside, waiting for me to arrive. He says hello. So good to hear his voice. The last sound I had heard was the watchdog barking.

I wake up for real this time to the bark of Caveman's Chiquita.

10

Gifts

Next morning I'm on the phone with the Con Ed man in the extortion department. He'd sent me a letter which asked for a ninety dollar deposit because my payments are often late. I've had conversations with him before.

"I thought we were friends," I tell him. "Last time you sent the same letter. I called. We talked, and you said everything would be okay. I paid my bill a couple of days ago. Can't you forgive me for being late?"

Most people aren't personable with "people in departments." They have their account number handy when they call. They only mention date, name, complaint, don't joke or include unnecessary information. I imagine life cramped in those tiny cubicles breathing used fluorescent air is nearly unbearable.

"We're sorry ma'am, on April 23 you called in to report that you had paid your balance, and we waived the deposit; however, we're only able to waive the deposit once. You'll have to pay it this time."

"But last time you were so nice. I thought you liked me. Do you mean to say you were only following policy guidelines?"

"Sorry, your service will be disrupted unless you pay the deposit."

He's no fun anymore.

"Well, when? I mean how much time do I have?"

"I'm authorized to turn it off right now."

Notice the use of the first person. What happened to the collective "we"? The passive voice? This guy's getting subjective and scary. "You mean there might be one of your men in my basement right now with his hand on the switch?"

"I can turn it off from the main office."

"Have *you* got your hand on the switch?"

Silence.

"Just tell me when. I can't live in fear."

"Anytime, Miss."

My call waiting beeps.

"Ed, could you hold on? I've got another call. Don't do anything drastic while I'm gone. Hold that hand steady; don't accidentally twitch or slip."

"Hello?"

"This is New York Telephone."

"Oh, hi! I've read your work, Thank god, Love god. Great stuff."

"Charles Dean?"

"Well, that's my pseudonym."

"I'm calling about the past-due balance on your account. Two hundred sixty-five dollars and twenty-three cents."

"But I don't even use the phone much. I don't have that many friends to call. It must be a mistake."

"Looking at your bill, Mr. Dean, I can see that you use your credit card to check your answering machine from pay phones several times a day. Why can't you use a quarter?"

"I'll see what I can do." I flash the hookswitch, but the Con Man has vanished. A knock at the door.

"Who is it?" I ask, peering through the peep hole at the enlarged blackheads on a nose.

"Your neighbor from across the hall. I got some of your mail."

I hesitate. He might be someone off the street, or worse he might actually be my neighbor/crack dealer, or even worse the mail might contain another bill. When I open the door, I do recognize a neighbor, or at least someone I had seen earlier coming out of an apartment carrying stereo equipment.

"Here's your mail. It was in my box. Say, could you loan me a dollar till my father gets back?"

Dad is probably dead or gone forever. "Sure." I give him his dollar, my dollar, our dollar.

As I close the door, the phone rings.

"Hello?"

"This is Apostolos Michalos Isadoros Anthanassakis."

The Landlord.

"Now it's been a few months, and you don't seem to be catching up. In fact, you're falling behind, Ms. Dean, and I was wondering what you were planning to do with the apartment."

"I could send a small check, but I assumed you'd rather have it all at once." It was I who preferred not to have to write out his name too often.

"I don't mind small checks."

He's certainly understanding. When he hangs up, he sounds satisfied, even thanks me. I wish I still had that kind of charm with the Con Ed man.

I have to start buying a cheaper brand of shampoo or something. The phone rings.

"Angel?"

Anxiousness. Only Japanese businessmen call me Angel.

"It's Hiro. I found your number."

I congratulate him.

"I'm calling regarding discussion we had on English lessons. What do you think is reasonable rate?"

Recently, I'd heard that the Japanese will pay as much as forty dollars an hour, but I know the standard rate at the universities is about ten or fifteen. I consider asking twenty.

He says, "I think eighty dollar per hour would be equitable considering your time and travel expenses. Could you meet me near my office in restaurant?"

I explode with laughter. "Hiro! What schemes you devise to get me to spend time with you!"

"No, really I meaning to learn English."

"Okay," I say, "but only because I want to go to dinner, and I mean to teach you English so be prepared."

When we meet for the lesson we are both stiff and nervous

in front of the maitre d'. "Would you like a cocktail?" I look to Hiro. He holds out a hand in approval. I order a vodka. The drinks come. We discuss the advantages of improving his business English, the special qualities of Memo English, the collective "we," and he questions the appropriate use of the passive voice.

He wonders at and is grateful for my explanations. Although I use no flirtatious language, my lashes have a way of flirting on their own. I am shocked when his first writing example turns out to be a love letter. It reads: *I sometimes feel that you are like bird. The bird looks so attractive and her voice is so beautiful that is now almost irresistible for me to chase after her. I would even walk across town bare foot though I didn't know way. I would fall into dream: I caught the bird in my hands and put her on my shoulder, feeling that she settles her warm soft breast against my skin. I make a cozy nest for her in cage. I enjoyed her singing beautifully. But after a happy night with her I found in next morning that door of the cage was open and she was gone. I fell into deep sorrow, missing her so much. Awaken from the dream, I looked into your face. The pupils of your eyes reflected me, but you saw a vast ocean to fly over.*

Please let me know if you are ready to fly. I would sail out a boat to the ocean to look after you, to have a moment to see you again. I wish by chance you might rest your exhausted wings after long flight on my boat.

I am embarrassed for him with his stupid sailing metaphors and do not know what to say. Although the letter is grossly inappropriate, it was bravely given.

I compliment one nicely turned phrase, hand it back to him and get ready to leave. When he asks about additional lessons, I feel his desire tighten on me like a vise. He gives me a box from Tiffany's. Inside is a gold bracelet with diamond-inlaid hearts. He says it symbolizes his feelings for me. He asks again about the next lesson.

"How many such bracelets have you given away?" I laugh.

"You're only woman I buy something for. Not even my wife. I like you a lot."

You mean you want me to like you, I want to say.

"I'm sorry if story offends you. It's nothing really. I wanted to try poetry. It's only creative writing, not real."

"Yes, it is make-believe. You don't know me. Okay," I say, "I'll meet you again, but no more gifts."

11

My Lola

Alone in the semi-crowded Chameleon bar, I'm conscious that I appear to be waiting and that everyone is watching me do it. In a state of hopeful expectancy, would I appear foolish? Is it possible, could they (the people at the bar) imagine that I'm not waiting for anything, that indeed this is it? Might they suppose that I have no particular vision of the future, no designs on the next thirty seconds? *This* second, this bottle, this glass, what I can see, touch, drink, are the only occupants of my thoughts.

While everyone is watching me not waiting, I recline with the most feminine of manners, despite my masculine name. These are my public manners, special East Village manners too volatile for the private Club Kiki. Watching me here, one would hardly guess that inside lurks the tender Charlie Dean that you and I know. In public, I'm always either batting my eyelashes, fingering my pouting lips, or twirling my blonde hair. And I should specify now that my voice is very soft and raspy, but that's easily guessed.

I have a special way of speaking here. For instance, when I say "good bye" I do so breathlessly, and my eyes are only open for the initial "g". From there, the head tilts back, slightly, as if I were to be kissed. Just past the final sound my eyes open sleepily, full of recognition. Closing my eyes at crucial points in the conversation is a tactic which makes me appear naive and vulnerable.

When I'm at the bar, I prefer standing to sitting. This position, though more difficult to sustain, promotes the appearance that I won't be here for long. Of course standing I'm more self-conscious of my leg and arm positions. Currently, my legs are crossed at the ankles, giving my posture greater instability and encouraging a subtle sway in the hips. Another stance I like is keeping one foot on the railing beneath the bar, the other foot cocked backwards and suspended behind me with my fashionably shod foot waving like a cat's tail. Chest forward, breasts and elbows on the bar, cheeks resting in hands. This position is used when I playfully signal the bartender. After that's done, I resume this current position of standing with crossed ankles.

As said before, my well-rounded bottom swings gently to the beat, and one arm, the right, is thrown over the back of a man's chair. I can use the left hand to twirl my hair, making soft flaxen ropes to tickle my neck. When I drink, I clasp my glass in a childlike fashion with both hands and tease the cocktail straw with my tongue. One or twice a night pretending to need a stretch, I arch my back and extend my arms and chest like a ballerina although *my* chest is nothing like a ballerina's.

The Chameleon is an ordinary neighborhood bar, and ordinary neighbors drink here. Supply your own cast of regulars to fill up the booths. Your own Bovie, the circus techniques instructor, balding, bearded, friendly and in the corner with a Coke. The scratching couple who arrive every day coincidentally ten minutes after the NA meeting up the block has let out, who would find no friends here at all if they didn't own a car. Wolfie, short and mustached, the man for whom we all wait (myself not included) is not here but his scouts are. Every minute or so the phone rings. "Wolfie in yet?"

At eight in the evening, two dozen people are here all told, nine in line for the bathroom, two behind the bar, Joe and Hilde. Joe's a regular English bloke, and Hilde's a buxom Danish barmaid.

But all eyes are on me the ominous queen bee, grown fat in religiosity. Which is why I find it curious that I've invited Lola here. A sure rival for my position she is, and yet I've invited her in, over the threshold.

On cue she enters. She is wearing a short white skirt and a man's v-neck tee shirt, probably nicked from last night's lover. Heads turn in her direction and then return to mine. They're anxious to see what I'll do.

"Lola, darling!" I sing out. A sense of relief fans over the crowd as now they will be able to approach her without offending me (detailed schemes of how to do this began to crystallize in several minds, before I had the chance to greet her).

"Who's your friend?" the bartender quickly asks, forgetting the shots he's set up for us.

"Joe this is . . ." I start to say, but Lola's already sidestepped my introduction and pronounced a "Hello my name is Lola" with that distinctive dropped "h."

Several weeks later, I will hear my friends remark while they watch her performing some spectacle, dancing on the table flashing a bit of "bum" with a wave of her skirt, "Crazy Girl, that Lola!" and I'll be jealous. Her performances are of a ruder variety than mine. I play a Marilyn Monroe to her Madonna. But after a few jealous tempers flare and a few male prides are harmed, the remark will change to, "Wild Chick." Then, after a few flung beer bottles—Lola's hot-tempered and drinks too much—the boys in the bar will whisper consolingly to me, "She's nuts!" And yet she'll still have their attention, for they will not be able to help themselves. She's a vacuum of need, not like me. I need an audience, but Lola needs to be loved. Not to love, but to be loved—exclusively.

You could say I am jealous. But jealousy can be turned to appreciation with a simple manipulation of words. When beauty makes me uneasy, I'm compelled to possess it. If it's a beautiful painting, I want to buy it, a beautiful landscape, photograph it, somehow make it mine. If I can establish that Lola is *my* friend, her beauty will be in a less threatening place. But there are so many things and people to be jealous about, so to be completely secure, since there is no aesthetic absolute, I find myself quite busy, if not schizophrenic and bi-sexual. Similarly, poets conquer the world through cataloguing. Name it; describe it, and it's yours forever. She's my Lola, crazy girl.

While we're waiting for the commotion to settle down (Lola's just climbed up on a stool to dance), I'll relate the week's events with Hiro to Joe. When I tell my story, the truth is slightly altered to increase the dramatic effect. Here it goes:

Angel arrived at the hotel restaurant wearing her navy spring jacket and matching pleated skirt, the one that makes her look like a truant school girl, but the outfit is businesslike enough to be confusing. Oh, and the blouse was unbuttoned too low to not be an accident. The choice for the meeting was hers. At noon in a public eating place, one can be pretty sure English will be the only thing instructed, but with the hotel suites stacked above their heads, there would be room for a nervous imagination.

Hiro concealed his confusion with an agitated smile when Angel came in carrying a briefcase. (She really is pranning to teaching me English!?)

"Now the first thing you have to do," she said, seating herself at the dining table and opening her case in a single move, "is perform this diagnostic."

Here Angel paused, allowing Hiro to endure the ambiguity of her statement.

"Your first assignment is to write a short letter. It doesn't matter what—whatever happens to be on your mind . . . right now." The "right now" was said with a whisper and an arched brow. Again she inflicted a painful pause, closed her eyes and inhaled.

Then plainly she said, "You have twenty minutes. Begin."

While he was writing, Angel ordered quite a lot. She was hungry. When he finished, as she was wiping her lips, he handed her a love letter, something like, "Angel reminding me of a bird, who might fly away. When I seeing her I want her to rest on me like ship on ocean. I wanting to make her comfortable nest, but I find cage door open, and she is gone."

Angel swallowed a gulp of wine, took out a red ink pen, corrected the grammar, chided him for his lack of articles and handed it back to him. She said nothing of the content.

When asked what would be the most convenient way to pay her, she said it would be best to mail a check, thinking of the connotations of cash changing hands, and knowing he'd be more likely to give her more once he had time to think about it.

The lunch came to fifty dollars, and the check that arrived three days later came to three hundred. He had paid in advance for three meetings and included reimbursement for carfare.

"Oh, you bastard!" laughed Lola. She came in at the part where I got out the red pen.

Anyway, the following Friday, which was yesterday, we had our second appointment. I stood him up. Actually I *was* there. But I was watching from above. From a window I surveyed the street where we were to meet. He arrived, and I saw him hope, stand, look around, adjust his tie, his watch. When he returned to his office he would find a phoned-in apology from Angel, and his dashed hopes would reconstitute themselves with even more vigor. Although there had been nothing there to lose, he'll have a sense that he's regained something lost, and thus it will be all the more precious to him.

This plan of mine, had it actually been a plan—I have to leave the Chameleon. Lola's assumed one of my positions at the bar. I can't bear to watch.

As I was saying, had this actually been planned it would confirm what you all think about the Manipulative Tease. I, admittedly, did fall into that role momentarily, but only by accident. My true part in this last scene had been that of Despotic God. I'd intended to meet with him as arranged. I'd even prepared a test on infinitives and gerunds. But due to happenstance and my insensitivity, Hiro fell victim.

The truth of the matter is—I'm getting my keys out here— the truth of the matter is I had a spot on my chin (I like Lola's word "spot" better; it's kinder than pimple). I'm actually not an evil omniscient narrator, playing with Hiro's life, I merely have a spot. I hate to flirt when I have a spot. I felt really ugly with a big red pimple on my chin, and I simply couldn't go. Instead of canceling the day before, I, wrongly, waited to the last minute, hoping the spot would clear up in time. But it didn't. By the time I called his office he'd already left. I often flub things up for stupid reasons. It's so stupid, in fact, that I can hardly admit to it. Instead, I pretended as if I had meant to stand him up, and I tried to make the dramatic most out of the situation. I sat in a lounge, a suspended glass structure which hangs over the street, my own kind of crow's nest, and I watched him stand in wait. He imagined me stuck in traffic, and invented all sorts of excuses for me. I know because I've been in his position before. I know what it feels like to want to believe the best in people. I realize that optimism is a quality that humans generally find admirable, but when I see a man like Hiro, optimistic beyond reason, I feel ill, saddened, and I begin to feel contempt for him, only because I was foolish like him once too. I've learned not to be hopeful to the point of making myself vulnerable to others' caprices. Sometimes my lack of trust sounds too much like distrust; that's something I have to work on.

After watching him awhile, I did relent. I took the elevator down, went out to the street. He was still standing there, thirty minutes past the scheduled time. I waved. He didn't see me. I went to cross the street, but the light changed. A cab pulled up. He got in it and drove away. I felt really creepy about what I did to him so I bragged about standing him up to Joe and Lola to make myself feel better.

When I was a little girl, I was mean to a boy called Quentin who liked me. He had made fun of the way I wasted entire recesses talking to a small willow tree. "Weirdo," he hissed, and I could not argue. I liked that willow, and it liked me. I was sane and precociously wise enough, however, to realize that Quentin liked me, and that was why he called me names. Every night I would form delicious plans of revenge. And it was fun to brag about it after I got my revenge, but the truth is that when I finally socked Quentin in the nose, I didn't like the way his face felt so soft under my fist. I felt ill watching his eyes water, and my stomach turned when he tried to speak, but couldn't. The moments between the punch and when he finally recaptured his bully persona, I saw the real Quentin. I saw that he only wanted to be liked, afraid of rejection.

Revenge was not satisfying at all. But everyone was so proud of me. My parents had me retell the story for friends. While it was fun making myself sound tough, *being* tough is not fun.

I drop my purse and slap the kitchen counter several times. The Formica is dotted with tiny dead roaches. I rinse my hands. They're everywhere. Got to smash them when I can, else they'll grow up to be fat and juicy.

Hiro reminds me of Quentin. If he wants to have sex, he should say so, instead of trying to outsmart me. Nonetheless, I regret what I did to him, all for a spot.

The kind of spots I get are even worse because I make them happen. When I'm alone and bored, I sit fish-eyed at the magno mirror and try to push out the little black specks on my chin. Two days later, Mt. Vesuvius erupts. I try to alter it cosmetically, caking it with coverstick and powder, creating a large white, fizzling lump, instead of a bright red one. But minutes later, a damp center begins to form. Make-up won't stick to the chafed spot that you've mercilessly squeezed. And days later, even after the swelling has gone down, a delicate ring of scaly skin marks the area. When I'm especially desperate, sometimes I make spots into false moles with a dot of eyeliner.

The only thing good about this pimple is it's not on the end of my nose, but it visits the left side of my chin so regularly that I've given it a name, Doris.

Luckily, there's a twenty-four-hour drugstore downstairs. I disguise myself in hat and sloppy clothes and try, as discreetly as possible, to purchase some spot medicine. But it's so embarrassing even to stand in that aisle.

Nonchalantly, I shop for other things in order to take the focus off my real purchase. I couldn't possibly buy only spot medicine at midnight; the clerk would scan my face for the thing that drove me out into the night. Other embarrassing items help: toilet paper, deodorant, household cleaners of any kind and roach spray. With enough to make the minimum, I get in the credit card line. I notice the guy in front of me is buying deodorant, soap, dental floss, Trojan condoms and personal lubricating gel. I wonder which is his "real" purchase.

On the way back I think about how much money I've just wasted. The roach spray, though, I needed anyway and would probably have gone over for that even without Doris. Last night, I was awakened by something tickling my shoulder.

When I shot up in bed and brushed it off, I distinctly heard a "tick" as a big New York cockroach hit the wall. Yesterday, I caught a roach sucking the moisture off my toothbrush with its straw-like tongue.

Months ago, I placed bait traps in strategic locations around the apartment because according to the commercials, bait traps are the most effective way of controlling roaches. But I've found I'm not satisfied with letting my roaches crawl away and die. I want to see them die. I want to kill them myself. Apparently, most people feel the same way. Sprays, as ineffective as they're said to be, are still number one in sales.

When I get home, I undress, tie up my hair, apply the spot medicine, push the furniture into the center of the room and spray the corners. I hear no screams.

Then I go into the bathroom and begin spraying the top of the door frame. Three roaches, big adults with filmy wings, scuttled forth. I target them directly, watch them shudder and spasm. The leader writhes as his nervous system is destroyed. He clings helplessly to the wall with one hairy foot and finally falls to the floor, comically.

On the top of the medicine chest is one of those baits motels. When I spray it, legions come scrambling out, children first, reeling like drunkards. Then slow, heavy pregnant females come out dragging their blocks of unborns between their legs.

I'd supplied them with their happy home. Roaches check in and order up room service. But now they're falling around me, nailing the floor like French fries.

Later, I get in bed and spend a few hours listening to Hiro's language tapes, *Japanese for Beginners,* learning a few useful phrases like, "It's very nice weather today. Do you know the name of a good dentist?" I'm on lesson ten of twenty-four. Some of the phrases annoy me because they simply don't translate. For instance, *gozaimasu,* a common polite word, has no English translation. I asked Hiro about this, and he pointed out that in English, we have phrases like: How the fuck should I know? "Fuck" is a common rude word that has no Japanese translation. He also told me, by the way, that learning Japanese increases left brain activity.

Still later, I apply more spot medicine and go to sleep.

Somewhere along sleep's rutted terrain, the phone rings, thirty-six times louder than it ever does in the open daylight. Startled, terrified and dumbfounded I grope for the receiver. The chill in the pit of the stomach, the senselessness to what is actually happening. Is it an alarm? A terrible scream? My arm, by instinct only, finds the phone. But after the two rings, the line is now unoccupied, only tone. I feel exposed, silly at my terror. The fogginess sifts away. Only the phone. Of course when I try to get back to sleep thoughts harass me and keep me awake: the hum of the refrigerator, the hum of thoughts, ticking and engaging and following the seam along the wall, "WBL kicking S FM," the roaches, Lola, Doris. The mind meanders with an armful of items, so much more than I need to buy. At last I call the Chameleon to see how Lola made out. Who but Lola should answer the phone. "'ello Chameleon!" Laughter in the background. I hang up the phone, green-eyed. Damned Doris.

12

Bon Voyage Lola

Days later, Rocco and I plan to meet Lola at the Chameleon. As I feared, she's become a regular, getting all the attention, drinking free. Lola's even throwing herself a party. Says she's finally got some definite news about Tokyo.

We walk the seven blocks because I want to get as much air time out of my new outfit as possible. I'm wearing a Lola-esque affair, black splat platform heels and hot pants, belted, that hang low on my wide hips and reveal my washboard stomach. My bra matches the pants. Rocco is a distinguished escort and completes the ensemble. As we pass the Thirteenth Street Boys we hear: "Whew, Blondie bust a nut!" At the deli: "A pack marbles? For you anything." Crossing Tenth: HONK! "Hey baby, need a ride?" As we walk up The Hall's crowded sidewalk, I make a point to twist the soles of my feet on the pavement with each step. My high heels click noisily; a blind man whistles.

As we walk up, the music from inside the bar can be heard in the form of a giant and repetitive dull thud. A woman in an apartment across the street hangs out of her window, putting her cupped hands to her mouth. A loose wedge of fat jiggles from her upper arm as she does so. She yells to us, "Hey, when you go in there tell them to turn it down." Rocco tips his hat to her. We push the door open, disturbing two dovetailed lovers who were pressed against it, sliding up

85

and down. I kiss the doorman. Inside people are cemented into a thick crowd holding cigarettes or drinks under their chins or over their heads, and dancing in the same pendular motion. The sex-commingled social irony of a rap song dangles with unnumbered cheerful ribbons hanging from the ceiling: "I'm gonna fuck you . . . up."

We move to the bar, finding it impossible not to dance while doing so. Rocco holds both arms in the air, and across his face flash expressions of surprise as if he were being tickled by an invisible sprite. I fall into step. The hips work in a semi-regular thrusting circular motion, while the hands, limp, are kept near the oblique and breast areas, touching myself lightly from time to time, especially when the beat or the words to the song correspond with the act. ("Touch my body, touch my body, all night yeah . . . ") Soon complications arise. Dancing a la music videos exposes one to risks in real life. People take you seriously, you see. Some homeboy, two in fact, slide in and make a sex sandwich of me. I dance with them for a while. I'm pretty much unable to move anyway. I can smell the salty sweat on the back of the dark neck just under my chin and feel the navel of the one behind me—we're that close. I squeeze from between them—one grabs my wrist, "Hey baby, where you going?"—and I push my way toward the back of the bar still looking for Lola.

My velvet hot pants and bra tend to distract me from my course. The day-to-day existence of Charlie Dean is punctuated with interruptions to the tune of: Your tits are nice. That this is a self-imposed "handicap" raises questions to be dealt with; the answer to this figures largely into the understanding of the heart of Charlie Dean. Why do I need to project my features well beyond the footlights?

As I make my way to the rear, I'm patted on the shoulder by the regulars who are in formation along the bar. I shout to Lola, finding her at the end (my spot). She's going on a trip to Japan! she announces. Can you believe it?

I try to get to her. We are still separated by the crowd. Someone pulls my wrist, that black dancer, and whispers, "Why do you dress like that if you don't want it?"

Why *do* I dress like a *fille de joie*? Actually, I'm making a fashion statement, poor me, not a sexual one. Why, this outfit describes the kind of music I listen to. Psychofunk and hi-phophouse. Sometimes, I even dream that out of a slavish dedication to some new fashion I'd seen in an advertisement, I go grocery shopping bare-breasted, or sometimes without pants. In the fresh vegetable section, I begin to get the feeling that some shoppers aren't aware of that particular style. I begin to suspect I've gone too far, and I feel really silly, but I conceal my shame, trying to act naturally.

Or it is shortsightedness? The optimum beauty is the traffic-stopping kind. As a topless dancer, I learned that if every customer didn't gasp and hand me a twenty the moment I walked on stage, I was not beautiful enough. Conspicuousness, that's beauty. If blonde is pretty, blonder must be prettier. If big breasts are nice, bigger breasts must be nicer. If a mini-skirt is sexy, a micro-mini is even sexier. But when does it stop being beautiful, become theatrical and then finally ridiculous? When you see that showy image of yourself alone, with no one watching, without an audience.

So there you have it. I'm caught, a child in her mother's make-up kit—red lips, perfectly round and garish circles of rouge on her cheeks, neon blue eye shadow. Naively, I believe I look beautiful, but Mother, who knows better, says I look like a little whore, and I squirm giggling as she wipes the mess from my face.

But I've learned that kind of girl gets all the attention, and wanting to be one is probably not merely a taste for the illicit. There must be some objective reason why we like whorish looks, some staid sound value, or chemical reaction, or something, but something undeniably true and real, something unworthy of contempt.

That kind of girl gets to sail to Japan to Gottlieb.

"He called," Lola tells me. "Gottlieb finally called. Said he'd been deep in trouble, and he was tortured that he couldn't get in touch with me. He was all worried that I'd be livid. But now he's ready."

"Ready?"

"Yeah, he was caught up with some people in a gambling business, like I thought. He didn't call because he didn't want to put me in danger. But now he's doing good. Charlie, he is finally doing well, running a prestigious gambling house."

"That's what you thought he was up to, wasn't it?"

"Yeah, I was right. And by coincidence the very night after Gottlieb called, Mr. Ohno offered to take me to Japan. He has a shipping company you know and he is bringing a boat to Japan. It's some weird antique ship, a lightship that was once sunk off the coast of North Carolina."

"Cape Fear. I know all about that ship."

"Really? Well, anyway, I told Gottlieb about it, and he had a great idea. In Japan, the new thing is private boating, and a lot of Chinese are running gambling houses offshore. Gottlieb had a brilliant thought—since the Japanese like American stuff so much—we could open the *Frying Pan*—that's her name—as a casino. We leave in two weeks."

Lola assumes I will be part of that we. "I'm not going."

"Not going? This is exactly what you wanted, almost."

"I wanted it to be my thing." I didn't want to go on a gambling boat as Lola's guest.

"I thought of it practically for you. Mr. Ohno even said you would be interested."

"Interested? It was my idea."

"Well, you should have been nicer to him. He used to like you, before he met me."

* * *

Since I was a child, I have had this irrational urge to decamp from this shore, inspired by old family chronicles, and fueled by an unreasonable hope and superstition that there is no such thing as coincidence, at least not as far as saltwater and I are concerned. I was meant to be at sea. Two of my ancestors happened to have been in shipping (the only transatlantic, transpacific transportation at the time, and they were Scots) and recited yarns to my father and these became my bedtime stories. Whenever I needed a part-time job, I found my index finger trailing down the shipping column. Yes, I've worked in docks and shipping houses, for custom agents and finally for the Maritime Association and as the New York marine operator. Still, never have I gone out beyond the twenty-mile mark, where the shore is no longer visible. Nevertheless, I have some kind of romantic notion about "returning" to sea.

Lately, I've altered my dream to include a destination, the port of Japan, Gottlieb loitering there on the horizon. But you know, all things considered (the fact that Gottlieb wants Lola back is certainly one of those things), what I really want is just to be at sea. Anchoring off the coast of Japan, after all, would be as bad as sinking in Cape Fear.

13

Thank god, Love god

After abandoning plans to go to Japan, I floundered for a time, wasting spacious hours in bed while Self watched over me in disgust. I reread the good parts of *Middlemarch*, snickering and muttering to myself or Eliot. The phone rang. I watched it suspiciously. It rang again. I picked it up. It was Hiro. Hiro intervened between me and madness.

We have a date for the weekend. Last night, I met with him at Club Kiki, and without prompting, he provided the scenario. While he designed the arrangements for our upcoming little weekend, he pointed with his cigarette. I was struck by his business language. He said he was willing to "subsidize" my work, "reimburse" me for my time, "cover" my "expenses." He confidently extinguished his Hope and folded his arms. I was almost convinced that he believed he was offering me a job, not a date.

My plan for night number one is to be not quite suitably attired for the occasion. An understated dark green cocktail dress with a tailored bodice and a slim skirt will look excellent, but with it I'll wear a disturbing accessory: a black hat, wide and shallow like a lampshade. Not that many women get away with wearing fancy hats these days. Hiro, sitting across from me at the candlelit table, will come under the influence of a beauty that has something amiss and therefore promotes an almost imperceptible sense of dissatisfaction, which will lead to desire. The delicate straps of this sexy green dress will rest on the edges of my white powdery shoulders, for the moment defying gravity, but soon one or both will slip down and reveal bare shoulders and arms. I'm to look like a gift partially unwrapped, a flower unfolding, Venus losing her draperies.

Now, as I undress for my bath, trancelike unknotting my silk robe, I imagine dinner at the yet unknown posh restaurant somewhere near the ocean. The dining room ceiling is low, and large clear windows offer a panoramic view of the surf. Everyone is quietly tucked away in private red leather booths using heavy tableware to load into their mouths butter-soaked morsels of the catch of the day. Water glasses glimmer. Napkins are patted on salty lips. Enter a five-foot-eight Japanese businessman in a gray suit and a tall, exotic blonde, hair loosely tied and tucked under a straw hat, wearing a green silk dress, the seams of which are dangerously stressed. Heads turned. A fork is dropped.

I sink into the tub, leering at my warped reflection in the chrome faucet. A dab of foam sits on my abbreviated nose. Pouting my lower lip, I blow it off. I am jealous of Lola. She has a port to sail to.

As I recline in my bath, I sponge my beauty-spotted neck and plan the next day. Hiro will arrive early tomorrow morning, about eleven-thirty. I'll hear him ring the buzzer, which, since it is cross-wired, will ring next door. I won't be able to answer, and I'll have to carry my four tobacco brown leather bags down myself. I will also bring a beach hat, boom box and an armful of books: Amis, Barth, Bellow, Gay, Meredith (is it insulting to my date to bring along an oversupply of reading material? I once took *Ulysses* along on a dinner engagement). Hiro will be wearing tight plaid shorts that hit at his knees. I'll be embarrassed at seeing his skinny legs for the first time. I'll wear my traveling suit, a pink dress with a white pillbox hat and short cotton gloves, the outfit Jacqueline Kennedy wore the day of the parade. (I am shaving now, sliding the razor forward and clicking it twice on the soap dish.) I'll load up the back seat of his convertible with my bags, topping the pile with my tobacco brown leather hatbox. Hiro will hop behind the wheel and fire up the cranky engine of his little red sportscar. I'll hold my hat as the car jerks into motion, slipping a psychofunk tape into the player and turning up the volume in order to drown out his comment on the "nice weather." He'll maneuver badly, with amateur shyness, into FDR traffic. "Sorry," he'll say with a raised hand to the snarling truck driver he cuts off.

Last night, the night of the "interview" when the "details" were "settled," Hiro sustained a reserved posture, concealing his hopes and fears with politeness and vagary. He said I would have my "own suite," and he would be "away at meetings" most of the time, and I should "not feel obliged." He sat opposite me, and I kept my hands together on my knees. I held my chin up and nodded whenever it seemed appropriate. His dark, liquid eyes dared not venture below my prominent clavicles. The delicate gold chain (which he'd recently presented to me and which I would lose by the next morning) dangled down my cleavage. Again we waltzed while I pretended to decide. His warm breath informed me of the scenic seascape beauty he was offering. I told him I enjoyed his company a great deal—loved the dancing—and would join him on his weekend business trip to the coast. He sighed and brushed his sparse beard against my cheek.

There was a degree of hypocrisy and cold assessment in the way I proceeded, but underlying this there was sincere feeling for Hiro. There was a multi-complex stratification of truth, vulgarity, egoism, manipulation, and then—thank god, love god—human need too. Hiro sensed he was manipulating a financially troubled, excitement-seeking East Village girl, but then again, he couldn't help but wish that Angel, whose swayed back he pressed with a slender hand, loved him.

What I may need is to remain at sea. Will it be better to simply drift, the way Gottlieb always could? To have no plans or goals. Let myself drift from man to man. To not discriminate, to accept anyone's offer for the sake of experience.

We arrive at Mystic Seaport late in the afternoon. As the fantastic sun glances off the windshield, we turn and park at the "Welcome Center." Hiro turns off the ignition and announces, "We're here." I stir from my slumber, straighten my hat and twist the rear view mirror to my direction. Hiro, dressed as I'd imagined, a tourist in his ill-fitting shorts of a pastel plaid pattern and shirt which boasts of some past excursion to St. Thomas, goes into the lobby for the keys. After I curl my eyelashes and click my compact shut, I begin to wonder what is keeping him. I get out of the car, crunch across the parking lot of crushed seashells, spike heels sinking and plunge into the revolving doors after him. I am ejected on the other side into a lobby of polished pink stone and distressed pine paneling. Behind the check-in desk, a wall glitters with brass keys hanging in an imperfect checkerboard pattern. Two young clerks with tawny faces and bright blue eyes are treating poor Hiro san like an "oriental." They don't even try to understand "Mr. Highro's" question about his arrangements. They simply repeat his reservation confirmation for him. Hiro seems to have no idea how unhelpful they are; he's apologizing, "sorry," smiling.

I say, placing my arm around his waist, "He says he'd like two suites, instead of one."

The condescending clerk turns friendly and makes the arrangements. The taller one spins the registration book around and offers it to Hiro for his signature and address. Hiro applies the pen, writes first in kanji, marks it out, then redraws his name and mine. The desk bell is sharply rung, and suddenly the bellhop appears, a pustuled boy with a long nose, watery eyes, and closely trimmed hair. He decorates himself with my bags, garment bag on his shoulder, suitcase in each hand, shoulder bag on his back, and hatbox roped around his neck. We ride the conspicuously silent elevator one flight to our rooms, which are indeed separate, thank god, love god.

My door is opened first and then Hiro's, which is right next door. The boy tells Hiro we can unlock the connecting door if we like. Hiro fumbles in his trousers for a dollar while the boy rocks with his hand in his pockets. Hiro gives B.B. a bill. Taking it with a narrowed green-grey eye, he leaves.

Hiro and I stand at my doorway for an awkward minute. Then Hiro says he must run off for an appointment and pushes his hand through his hair. Bowing, he closes my door, leaving me alone in my room.

Nice place. Cherry sleigh bed. Long crisp white curtains that puddle on the floor. French windows that open onto a terrace. Brass-handled doorknobs shaped like sea serpents. I hang up all my inappropriate-for-the-beach clothes: my new green silk dress, two simple cocktail dresses, one with sleeves, one without, my butter suede skirt and matching vest, high-heel shoes to match. I had hoped there might be a nightlife here. I'd hope to grace the bar and dance floor of cozy dockside clubs. Hiro would light my cigarette and set my sun-burnished cheeks aglow in the tender matchlight, compliment my dress. But alas, from the look of my fellow guests in the lobby—casual J. Crew shirts and shorts—I'm afraid evening wear may not be up to my standards.

I decide—as I'm wrapping a towel around my head and examining my complexion in the bathroom mirror—we'll skip the social scene, saying this aloud. People in the lobby were staring enough at the Japanese-Businessman and his Tall-Blonde-Mistress. Sighing, I flop onto the bed and inventory the contents of a complimentary fruit basket.

Hours later, Hiro knocks on my door. "Come in." Hiro finds me dressed in my kimono with my feet propped up on the table, dropping white grapes into my mouth, with a paperback, *The Egoist,* splayed across my stomach.

"Hungry?" he asks, and we agree on seafood.

We go to a place overlooking the beach, The Pampas Grass Grille. It has red clay tiles and the walls have a faux marble finish to match my blue eyes. As suspected, no one except the cute blonde hostess has the decency to wear evening clothes; men and women are clad in khaki shorts and cotton polo shirts. I am wearing my emerald green dress, and I'm the whitest thing in the restaurant, but my skin goes nicely with this soporific green (Rocco says). My outfit is the sort of thing that should be worn to the beach according to any major fashion magazine, so I can't understand why in real life I'm so overdressed. It is silk, yes, but raw silk, so unless you touch, it could be mistaken for brushed cotton, and the flouncy skirt hits a casual five inches above my slender knees. And my hat, well, this is a beach town, and it is a beach hat— there's a nice matching green scarf around the brim and the extra ribbon floats deliciously in the air behind me. My high heels aren't *that* high. I take Hiro's elbow while the hostess leads us to our table. A chain of elbowing sweeps down the bar as we pass the off-duty golfers. The hostess politely shows us to a "private" table in the back.

Hiro san orders everything on the menu and we eat quickly. Both he and I are anxious to clear out of there. We slurp and gulp down our crustaceans, clams, scrod and scram. When we arrive back at our room I start to say thank-you in an octave that means good bye.

"Ah, yes of course, good night," he says nodding and embarrassed. He puts his key in his door. He waves clumsily. In synchronization we open, enter and close our doors.

Immediately I unbutton and allow my dress to slip past my waist. I march out of it and over to the radio, tuning it to a rap station. Shaking out my long, wavy hair, which feels nice against my back, I open the French doors and stand naked with my hands on the brass knobs and breathe deeply. Out on the terrace, I hear the sea, see the shifting lights, watch the swaying masts of the anchored vessels and beyond that the *thumb-print moon.*

Next to mine is Hiro's balcony. Through his window, I hear him switch on his television. He's probably pouring himself a scotch, loosening his tie, slipping off his shoes with a sigh, undoing a couple of shirt buttons, lighting a Hope. Sitting in an armchair he lays an ankle across one knee. As he dozes, as his ice melts in his scotch, he regrets that I'm on the other side of a very expensive wall.

After a while Hiro hears a tap at the connecting door. At first he's mistaken and opens the front door to find the empty hall. He peers down the narrow hallway, inspecting the stillness of Angel's door. He hears the knock again, this time from inside the room.

Hiro opens the adjoining door, looking as I've described him, the glass of scotch and smoking cigarette on the table. The room is dark but for the gray light of the television. Probably porno cable because he backs in front of it and clicks it off.

"Hi," I say. "Watcha doin'?" I'm wearing a "friendly" outfit: shorts and a t-shirt, decidedly not my silk kimono.

"Oh, watching T.V."

A painful moment passes in which nothing is said.

"Would you like glass of scotch?" he finally asks once he's assessed the situation.

"Sure." I sit cross-legged on a Victorian sofa. He pours the drink and sets it in front of me, then sits down himself behind his scotch, several feet from mine.

"T.V.?" he asks.

"Okay."

He finds a sitcom and adjusts the volume. "This all right?"

"Yes, fine." We both take a drink. "I forgot to ask you, how did your meeting go?" I ask, sounding terribly much like a wife.

Husbandly he replies, "Oh, fine, fine. How was your afternoon?"

"Quiet—but nice."

We take another drink. He offers me a cigarette, and I decline. Then I laugh at a joke on the television, and we begin to watch. Several commercial breaks later, he refills the glasses and sits down more comfortably with his feet up on the coffee table. I relax a bit more too, even though everything about the room is alien to me. The wall-to-wall carpeting, the central air conditioning, the tidy bed, the show on television—even Hiro and I—epitomize decorous American domesticity. I feel as if I'm playing house. Husband looks lonely there by himself, so I scoot over beside him.

"Thank-you," he says and puts his arm around me. When he sighs I feel the depth of his disappointment about the weekend so far. Against my side, his warmth is tender and comforting. A half hour of quiet later, he brushes my hair over my shoulder and kisses my neck once, not long and not softly. Then with his hand on my other shoulder he squeezes me, as a father might do to his daughter.

Then it occurs to me, "Hiro san, are you married? Do you have any children?"

A wife. And a daughter—my age.

The scene turns taboo and ridiculous. From Married Couple we turn back to Japanese Businessman and Blonde Mistress. What would Rocco think? That I'm doing it for money? The question makes me look at my reflection in his eyes. I find the woman I sought there, an illicit woman, in a hotel room with a man who paid her to be there, and I kiss her greedily. He pulls back and looks at me. My tiny t-shirt has slipped up on its own accord revealing one excellent, full breast. With my assistance, the other bobs free. He looks and sighs, his breath shaking.

Crossing my arms I gather the hem of my shirt and pull it up over my face. The collar frames my face and then slips back over my hair. I toss the shirt on the bed next to him. He picks it up, holds its warm cotton folds to his face, closing his eyes. Then I jump up from the sofa and examine a room service menu on the table with pouting lip, lay it down, run my finger along the dresser top, tilting my head side to side, as if I'm thinking, check for dust on my fingertip, turn to him and ask, "Well?" He looks at his wallet on the dresser, gets up grunting, walks over to it while I watch. He opens it, looks at its contents, looks at me and my obscenely swollen lips. He takes out five hundred dollar bills, shows them to me in a fan. He is smiling. I laugh, and he lays the bills next to my drink.

That done, I rush at him, unbutton his few remaining buttons while he stares at the ceiling swaying. I notice a half dozen odd, wiry hairs springing from his brownish-red nipples. His breast muscles are flatly defined, very tight skin, and the muscles in his abdomen form six impressive squares. I slide his stiff shirt off his brown shoulders—Japanese have such plastic smooth skin—and lead him by his wedding-ringed hand to his bed. There he sits on the edge with hunched shoulders and boyish anticipation while I roll the elastic band of my shorts down a few inches, letting him enjoy my shallow navel, then I roll them down a little further and finally off. After looking long and hard for a full minute, he closes his eyes and swallows.

14

The Captain Said to Bill

Salty night finally comes to dampen the air in Hiro's hotel room. I wake. The room has become dark. In the corner of my eye, I see ghostlike curtains waving. The fan of money is on the table. Ice in the nearby glasses has melted, diluting the scotch. Hiro has shrunk into sleep, and I have expanded into the unused night. As Rocco says, my thoughts are more pure and unhindered when I'm alone. I swing my feet out of the bed. Hiro, with mouth open, drooling on the pillow, grunts. His wristwatched arm grabs my warm pillow, now abandoned. He smacks his lips and smiles. I tiptoe from the bed and into my room without closing our connecting door. Silently, I slide open a drawer, find a black, slinky slip and step into it.

I'm a terribly large secret, as I unlock the French door and punctuate the perfect silence with the "chock" of the turning knob.

The night air makes my skin goosepimply. I rub my arms while I look, neck stretched, over the balcony and down, low enough to provide escape onto the roof below and then to jump to the grass lawn. I have to squelch my giggles of sneakiness as I swing one leg over, straddle, swing the other over and hop to the roof with a surprising thud and onto the lawn, smarting my ankle.

Before me is the ocean, below the cliff. I cross the dark

parking area with a waltzing gait while behind me flickering television light spirals in the suite windows. Inside, people, content and unafraid, begin to doze. A night watchman's car prowls past with one bright, accusing eye atop. I walk across a weedy strip to the edge of the seacliff, where I loom in my fluttering night slip. The water before me gently crashes several yards away on a sand bar. The tide is out. I gingerly step down a rickety stair with blind bare feet finding cool, sandy, weathered wood.

The sky is not quite inky black. By a gibbous moon, I can see cumulus clouds behind the opaque black, like persistent memories, fat and expectant. As I go lower, I can't see the next steps below me. My toes touch cold, wet sand. Alarmed, I jump back. Silly me, I laugh at myself and again pursue the sound of the waves.

Frightening, the beach is at night. The horizon sky and ocean are exactly the same empty shade of gray, a thicksoft gray, like quicksand, I think, and it feels just as dangerous. The gray seems to pull me, and I think about drowning, about shipwrecks, washing up on shore. I think about my dad sitting on the end of my tiny bed, with that deep-voice-seriousness, saying, "The Captain said to Bill, 'Tell me a story Bill,' and Bill said, 'I will. A thousand mixed with sticks and bricks were killed in the battle of boiling water.'"

My desire to go to sea started then, I suppose. I was three or four. Since then I have often dreamt about swimming out till the land becomes a thread and disappears. A tiny, tiny swimmer surrounded by strange, warm, motherly water. I am buoyant at first but soon the water seems thinner than mist. It starts to suck me down. The surface gives way under my aching arms; my head goes under once, and bobs up again. Under again now twice, arms flailing. With bitter salt in my throat, I'm coughing and gasping, the honest sea bottom still miles beneath me, but hard and waiting. Is it too late to change my mind, say I didn't really mean it, didn't really want to go under a third time?

And suddenly I'm fighting and sick-at-heart that I could have been so curious and swum so far and been so anxious to see the ocean floor. I'm fighting, cursing, gurgling, but I've finally gone under. I'm curling up like a fetus, swimming, floating, grabbing my bud toes, sliding my hand along the curve of my legs for the last time. Gently sucking my thumb, sinking, surely down. I'm drifting, huge in a placenta pond. Then in a new watery consciousness, I realize I could grow gills and breathe new thick air, evolve, return or leave and live! Flapping armfins, taillegs swishing, spine whipping, seaweed hair flowing. Swimming deepbluedown where pearl bubbles seep from my grin and my dumb blinking eyes.

I've been able to walk out about a mile past the first sand bar and stand on the ocean floor. Suffocating, frightened fish flap helplessly. Shells, chunks of granite are exposed. I run around them, slapping soles on the saturated sand and listen to the gurgling of sea creatures left behind by the tide. Then I hear something plodding up from behind, a sniffling, snuffling animal sound. I try to judge, from the sound of his smacking chops, his size, and I am scared; my face grows hot and red. I can hear my heart pump blood to my ears; the jowls smack; the waves crash. I run.

I run madly to the shore and down the beach, stumbling in giant-sized footprints left earlier in the day. I feel mad. I feel sea-changed. Do I hear voices? I turn this way and that. Is that another figure on the beach? Or a shadow invented by my shortsightedness? I run toward it, tripping. Could I pretend I'm out jogging? in a night slip? I'll say I'm the ghost of a sailor's widow, still waiting for his return. And then, if it's a handsome man, I'll invite myself over to his place to watch television. But it's merely a shadow of a post, so I head back to my room. The mosquitoes are beginning to bite anyway. But looking back from the top of the stairs, hanging over the cliff, I wish I were back out there, standing on the extraterrestrial sea floor.

With sandy feet, I slip between my starched sheets.

15

Hope

I lie in my sleigh bed face down, under the down comforter, bright hair sprayed on the pillow, right hand hanging off the edge of the mattress. On the floor a letter addressed to Angel is opened and its contents scattered. Nearby is a red pen. Hiro slipped a love poem under my door this morning. It is overrun with far-fetched metaphors. If there were a "reckless steed" and a "maiden with spun-gold hair" in bed too, I didn't notice them. I corrected the grammar and threw it aside.

Hours later, as I lie in bed half-asleep, I'm aware of my love-letter writer knocking about his room, noisily dressing and grooming. A hair dryer screams for a minute and a half. Medicine cabinet is opened, closed, opened. Teeth are brushed. Nose is honked, then I hear him leave his room and trudge past my door, with a heavy step (hauling bags?). He pauses briefly, perhaps even raises his hand to knock and demand an answer to his confessions of love, but decides against it, and presses the elevator button which responds instantly to his touch. Ding, elevator doors close; Hiro is gone.

Four hours later at ten, after two hours of insomnia and same of fitful sheet-twisting sleep, I call room service for a pot of coffee. "Knock once and leave it outside." At ten fifteen, when I wheel in the tray (I also ordered fresh fruit and toast), I catch a glimpse of Hiro dragging a golf bag off the elevator, and I quickly close my door.

I ignore the ringing phone for an hour (who could that be?). At noon, on his way to his scheduled luncheon, he sees the ravaged cart standing outside my door, with half-eaten fruit and tossed coffee cups. As soon as I hear the elevator doors close, I, dressed in my minuscule bikini of thong bottoms and gold high-heel sandals, poke my head cautiously out the door, find the hallway clear and proceed to the beach for some sunbathing. At the elevator I experience a spasm of guilt, and I decide to slide a note under his door saying that I've gone sunbathing. I omit the location so he won't be able to find me.

In the elevator, I wrap my towel around my waist to serve as a kind of skirt to walk through the lobby, As planned, it accidentally unknots and falls to the polished stone floor. Several nervous bellhops and clerks run to pick it up but, no one is too quick to hand it back.

Now with an audience, I click out of the lobby and into the bright sun and walk across the parking area to the edge of the cliff, taking the same rickety stairs to what is now an abbreviated beach because the tide is in. The beach is sparsely populated with brown people who look as if they've done this kind of thing before. They have with them the necessary accoutrements: ice chests, beach towels, sunblock. I haven't been as good of a planner, no lotion or snacks, and my bath towel is rather small. Nevertheless, I decide to go ahead with the tanning mission. I haven't been under the sun naked in at least five years.

I walk as delicately as possible across the shifting sands, causing arguments between husbands and wives. When I find a clear spot, I spread my towel, lie down and squirm until my body makes an indention in the sand (a Charlie bas-relief). The sun stares at my fair skin furiously.

Exhausting, sunning. It's really a lot like work. From under my book I watch bathers stumble past; from my vantage point I can see them seeing me. Two teenage girls with more bikini material than I (I'm beginning to realize I have less bikini material than most) point and whisper, "So white." I frown and roll over a few times, wavering between hallucinations and sleep. Finally, I wake blinking, dazed and with wet cleavage and brow. The beach is now crowded. Energetic peo-

ple are sitting prettily nearby, basking and smiling. I feel not
very energetic at all. I feel stunned, sitting with bent knees
and limp arms, trying to gather some strength to leave. I
notice my skin seems a little pink. When I press my finger
to my hip, an ominous white mark lingers.

Too exhausted for vanity, I carry my shoes back to the
hotel, tuning in on the whispers of the brown people I pass:
empathetic oohs and ahs. By the time I reach the hotel parking lot, I've developed like Polaroid to a fabulous red.

Indeed, this is a bad one. I find it difficult to raise my legs.
The two steps to the front foyer door are almost insurmount-
able. I clutch the bannister and go up sidewise one leg at a
time. The desk clerk thank god, love god is busy with an
incoming guest, so I am able to sneak past and into the quick
elevator. By the time I make it to my room, it seems my skin
has shrunk three sizes, and my legs are stuck in a semi-bent
position. Hobbling around like Rocco's hag, I undress and
fill the huge shell-shaped tub. Carefully holding the handicap bars on the shower walls I lower myself into cold water.
Steam rises from my skin. I could run small appliances on
the energy I'm putting out. My calves are tongue red, and
my thighs, my tender thighs are a purplish red. My ashen
pubic hair sits in a triangle of pasty white. My bottom throbs.
My shoulders ache. I paddle cool water onto my tummy,
creased in white. I stay in the tub till I've thoroughly warmed
the water. When I try to get out I find a throbbing pain wells
up in my thighs and sends me splashing back down. Limp I
lie, Charlie on the half-shell.

I hear a knock on the door. "Who is it?"

"Hiro."

"I'm in the tub."

I hear him try the door.

"It locks."

"Yes, I know. I can't get up."

A few minutes later the phone rings. Fortunately, I've managed to stand by that time and reach the phone on the ninth
ring. I tell him I scorched myself. He asks if he can do anything for my burn. I tell him not to worry, that I'm simply
playing things up as usual. He asks if he can get me anything.
I say painkillers and an emerald ring. "What size?" he asks.

"I was kidding, Hiro."

When I look in the mirror, a pink, wrinkled newborn looks back. I soak a washcloth with ice water and press it against my face. It warms instantly. As I hobble to the closet, my knees begin to unbend a little. Clothes would chafe my skin so I sit naked, very carefully on the bed. Even the quilt feels like sand paper. Hiro knocks on the door. "Open," I yell. He enters bearing a gift for his Indian princess. "Ooh for me?" I ask with unchecked greed and tear away the wrapping of the small box which contains a green stone set in platinum. Hiro, delighted, sits beside me. Forgetting my burn, he places his grainy skinned hand on my back.

I react as if I'd been shocked. "Watch it!" I say a little too rudely.

"Huh? Oh, *hai* you looking red."

I look like a boiled and peeled tomato.

A bottle of aloe vera later, and after Hiro cautiously slipped my white seamless sundress over my head, we walk into the restaurant. No folks, don't adjust your sets. This is my actual color. After we're seated, the evenly tanned hostess, hugging a stack of menus, looks at me tenderly and asks, "Something from the bar?"

"Hot cidered rum," I say queerly, staring at the white linen tablecloth. I seem to be thinking I'm on a ski holiday because I'm awfully cold and my head feels light. I feel consciousness is steaming out of me like a fresh road kill in December. Hiro orders a lobster and when it comes we stare at each other with weak recognition.

Hiro looks at me with screwed-up brows, a bib hung boyishly around his neck. Clearing his throat he begins an obviously rehearsed speech, did it in the mirror shaving I'd bet. "About last night . . . I really enjoyed spend time with you. I like you very much, and I hope that—because you left—I hope that you don't regret . . . I hope that you like me too—I . . . "

"I never liked that word *hope*. Do you know the story of Pandora's jar?"

Of course he doesn't. He nods.

"Well it's a myth. She had a jar that should never have been opened, but when it was, disease and misery and death escaped into the world. In that same jar was Hope—personified—represented in human form, female (not coincidentally)," I clarify, as he looks a bit confused. I go on, "Hope stayed behind. The meaning of this," I point at Hiro with my fork, "I've always found to be rather ambiguous."

Hiro looks at the ambiguous fork.

I continue, "Does this mean Hope wasn't released to the world? Or Hope was kept safe for human use? In either case, Hope seems rather like a practical joke. Don't you think? The punchline is: humans will suffer some and die completely; this is inevitable, but they foolishly hope against it."

"You're saying hope is not positive thing?"

"Faith in something that doesn't exist?"

He sees me there in the chair in front of him.

"I am here with you tonight, but you paid me to be here." The emerald flashed brightly on my red hand as I split open the lobster tail. "If truth be told, I prefer paid sex to lovemaking, Hiro."

He is flattered that I used his name.

"Why hope for something else? We waste what we do have."

Have I been cruel? I feel a bit queasy. My head whirls as the last lick of warmth leaves my body, and I feel myself sliding in my leather seat.

My face lands nicely in my chowder bowl—Hiro in confused alarm asks, "Angel, is there something wrong?"

They were really nice at the clinic. The doctors said they get a case like mine every few years, second degree sunburn, but never so evenly, over the entire body. The chilly fingered nurses antisepticized my skin. Then Hiro bundled me out to the car and carried me to bed. He ordered fresh, extra soft bed linen. Now he is cooling my skin with wet cloths, speaking gently to me, sometimes in Japanese. Perhaps I wasn't as mean to him as I seemed to me. He pretends as if I weren't. He talks about his work. Perhaps I asked him to. I don't remember. I'm still a bit fuzzy.

"*Enno*," he pauses, "it is done by so-called tramper. They are called dry bulk cargoes and since those cargoes are literally bulky, the freighting is made by tramp vessels. The shipping is opposite. Namery, it has to be cheap, low freight rate needed. It doesn't necessarily have to be fast. The owners try to save their cost of carriages."

Did he say "ship"?

"That makes tramper shipping business interesting since we ought to fight against owner's tricks, tactics and negligence to minimize their operation cost. Examples are tramp crew are usually from developing countries Philippines, Bangladesh. Low wage! They go on strike occasionally then file suit at Maritime Authority at wherever port ship calls."

"Hiro did you say you have something to do with ocean shipping?"

"Yes. I thought I told you. My department ships potassium."

"That's very interesting," I say, sitting up and lighting a Hope cigarette for each of us.

16

Angel's Different

The week after returning from Mystic, Hiro turned on Thirteenth Street and thought, God, what nice street. No, it was not tree-lined like uptown, but that was what make it so open and honest. There were grand institutions anchored here. Back of Post Office overlooked one side and back of Catholic parochial school the other. What honor, what stability. Angel lives on this street. She calls it "Thirteenth Alley." Broken windows and piles of scorched debris, greasy stoves and broken tabletop heaped up on the sidewalk only made her face in the doorway more beautiful. Angel was really starting to like him.

It was difficult to find a parking place. Hiro could not read the faded signs. Hiro thought parking was okay for Friday. Backing in, he heard a scrape of metal against the curb. He opened door little and bumped into traffic blockade that was in the gutter. He turned off the car and lit up another cigarette. He removed his overnight bag from the trunk and remembered to take Angel's bouquet from the back seat. Still fresh, black orchids.

A Spanish man got up from the stoop outside Angel's building and picked up blockade. The super, what did she call him, Caveman? "Is it okay park here?"

"'Scuse me?" said Caveman taking a cigarillo from his mouth.

107

"Can I park here?" Hiro said with a smile for the super's scowl.

"It's your car," said Caveman.

"Thank-you."

Hiro entered foyer where he saw a note: "Buzzer's probably broken. Get in by any means possible—Angel." What does Angel want him to do? Is the note for him? Maybe Hiro should call Angel from the street first, to make sure she was home. He was so worry when Angel was not home. She had told him not to worry about her because to do so would be a full-time job. Hiro pressed number twenty-two buzzer.

"Hello?"

"Angel?"

"Who?"

"I looking for apartment twenty-four. Could you buzz me in?"

"Sorry wrong apartment."

He tried twenty-four.

"Hello?" a man's voice.

"I'm sorry. I'm looking for an Angel."

Another voice came on. "Papa san? I'll be right down."

Was that man in her apartment?

Angel met him in the foyer with purse in hand. Hiro guessed she didn't want him to come up. He felt awkward that he'd brought his overnight bag and flowers. "Angel, shouldn't you put flowers in water?"

"They'll keep."

They drove to the restaurant, a few blocks away. Angel said she did not want to walk, something about her stockings. He hoped she was not embarrassed to be seen with him on the street.

The restaurant was dark and crowded with people wearing black. The hostess knew her. They smiled and glanced at Hiro. When they sat down, Angel ordered "the usual." Waitress brought vodka martini and Hiro's scotch. Angel ordered tuna steak, rare, with tomato and mango relish. Hiro ordered angel hair pasta.

A bald man, bulky, fragrant, leaned across table, touching Angel. "Can I borrow your ashtray?" he said, taking it.

Angel smiled. Hiro wondered if the bald man was friend of hers. "Do you know him?"

Angel shrugged her shoulders, smiling at the man as he walked away. Hiro wanted to look around. Finally, she looked at him. Her sunburn had peeled and her face was pale again. For the last three days, he had helped her peel the dried skin from the inside of her thighs. He had piece in his wallet, for good luck.

Angel looked down, played with her fork. Her lids and eyebrows were lined in black like a silent-film star. When her eyes met his, he took few quick drinks of his scotch and ordered another. He felt his face getting hot.

"You *are* beautiful."

Angel looked at him and frowned, "Who says I'm not?"

He never said that. "What?"

"I'm sorry darling. I'm just teasing you."

Hiro wished he spoke better English. "Oh, Sorry."

"Now, you're supposed to teach me about Japanese culture. Remember our deal? What's the Japanese notion of fate?"

"Was that, 'note chun'?"

"Idea."

"*Hai,* in Japan, on grave markings, we have saying." What was it now? He had memorized it as a boy. "It's actually written in Sansklit, yeah."

"Sanskrit. Don't touch the roof of your mouth with your tongue when you pronounce the are. Position your lips as if you were saying double you."

"Yeah, Sansklit." He thought he said it right that time.

"It's not an authentic Japanese notion?"

"Part of Buddhism," Hiro said. Angel didn't know much about Buddhism. "Japanese believe that fate . . . "

Angel interrupted, "Fate is like fiction, a belief that life is contrived by some kind of author." Angel sighed, looking through him. "It's ridiculous, of course, but I am still human, unable to resist the temptation to—not hope but—*worry* that I will regain my faith in plot, in providence . . . "

"In love?" Hiro offered hopefully.

"Well, I don't know about *that.*"

Hiro didn't understand Angel. Although she seemed happy—she was smiling—she said she was sad.

"I'm sad. I'm so sad. But I appear bitter." Angel took a final sip of her martini.

He tried to clear his throat, smoking a lot of Hopes lately—nerves. When he coughed, spit flew out of his mouth and landed on Angel's sleeve. He felt his face grow hot, and he reached for napkin to remove yellow glob before Angel noticed.

"I want to tell you that Charlie Dean is not a monster, not a monster."

There. Just in time, got it. He sat, hands at his sides. "Sorry."

"What?" Angel asked.

He guessed she hadn't notice. "Would you like drink?"

"Maybe one more," she said.

Did Hiro bring his gold card? Maybe Angel liked him for his money, but all women need a man helping, especially her. He wanted to tell Angel he worried. He wanted to tell her how foolish he was for worrying. The scotch was making his sight slow and fuzzy. Hiro said shyly, "You like me, don't you? *Enno,* sometimes, the money, I wonder . . . "

Angel stared at her vodka and said nothing. Did she hear him? He waited. Finally she said, "Money is only important because the lack of it can be distracting. It's nice that you've eliminated that problem for me so that I can concentrate on going to sea. Hiro I . . . "

She looked so helpless. She asked him if she were bad. He told her no. He told her it was all right. He would help.

When they got back to her apartment she jumped out of car, walked past her own door. Hiro figured Angel had too many martinis. Good, he thought, she couldn't handle liquor. "Isn't that your door?" He asked pointing, and she buried her face in hands and came back.

"Oops," Angel said and laughed with him. Hiro was little drunk too.

Hiro, with wilted flowers and overnight bag, followed Angel up her stairs. She climbed slowly, and he steadied her back in case she slipped. At the right landing, she handed him her keys. "Big silver one," she said. Angel needed Hiro. Inside, she immediately started undressing, kicking off shoes first. Rest came off on her way up to bed. He better get condoms out of bag. He undressed and folded his suit pants over back of chair and climbed up ladder that bumped against wall. Angel didn't move.

"Angel? You sleeping?"

Angel *was* sleeping, or was she sleeping? She didn't respond. But so soon? When she slept, she was remote. He listened for sound of sleep breathing, like he used to do with his daughter. He didn't want Angel asleep. He felt cheated. "Angel?" He felt claustrophobic. He couldn't move. He couldn't breathe for fear of waking her.

He sat motionless for a while, till finally, mustering courage, he decided to move close to her, carefully, and, maybe, hold her like a baby.

But Angel didn't sleep innocently. She was strong, even sleeping, stifling his movements. Maybe Angel thought Hiro couldn't do it, for too much drink. He'd show Angel he could. "Angel?"

She rolled over and turned her back on him. It was like a wall he couldn't see over. He leaned over her face, felt her cool breath. He opened wide his mouth and covered hers.

"Ugh!" Angel stammered. She shuddered, convulsed.

"I'm sorry, Angel. Did I waking you?"

"I'm really tired," she said face down in the pillow.

He wondered if Angel had been having nightmare, the way she jumped. His poor darling. He stroked her arm.

She twitched.

"I'm sorry. Does that bother you?"

"I don't mind if you . . . kind of . . . hold me, but the fondling really keeps me awake. I've got to, or rather, you've got to get up early tomorrow. You need your rest," Angel swallowed, "dear."

He smiled (she called him dear!).

"Go to sleep!"

"Oh," he said and laughed about it. Angel laughed little too and rolled over to face wall. But after a while, her breathing deepened. Again, he was disappointed. She was going back to sleep, where she had no time for him. And Hiro was scared. He was afraid of waking her. He was scared of her, her sleeping.

* * *

I manage to sleep through Hiro's early morning departure, mumbling "no" against his offer for coffee. I get up after I hear him tiptoe down the stairs. Afraid of waking me, he probably tiptoed all the way uptown. On the kitchen counter, I find a roll of twenties, and a reservation card for Club Kiki, along with a memo about moving into his condominium uptown. In Japanese he signed, "*ai shite imasu,*" or "I love you" with the formal, indirect address.

* * *

Angel was different, thought Hiro as he drove to the office. She was sleeping with him, but not for money. He didn't really pay her for the trip, simply made it convenient for her to go. She was beginning to see him not as customer, but as a good friend she can relying on.

Later that night at Club Kiki he asked her to live with him in his Manhattan condominium. Angel looked beautiful in a loose black gown, pearls around her bare, powdered neck. Hiro wanted to take care of Angel, make sure she was safe. Her neighborhood was very dangerous.

But truthfully, when he was at her apartment he felt uncomfortable. He didn't feel in control. He felt clumsy getting in and out of her loftbed. In the shower he kept forgetting which knob was hot or cold. They seemed to be reversed. On street the boys called him "gook." When Hiro ringing doorbell, the super looked at him rudely. *He* didn't feel safe or strong in her neighborhood, and Hiro didn't want Angel see him that way.

While they danced at Kiki Hiro asked her. Angel thought about it for long while—that's how Hiro knew it is not the money. Angel didn't rush in. But once she made her decision, she agreed to move right away—next morning. When Hiro went to pick her up, she was waiting outside. The boys on street surrounded car, tried to get money from his driver. He was so glad getting her out of there.

They went to Japanese restaurant. Japanese are very curious. Everyone was surprised to see Hiro there with Angel. She's so blonde and tall. The chef, the Master, winked at him.

Occasionally, he did feel guilty about his wife, his daughter. That's hard part. But he married young, arranged marriage. By the time they had their second tea together, their parents were pretty much committed to marriage. That is way custom is. Arranged marriage is a practical custom, Hiro still believed.

He was pleased that Angel liked Japanese food. What an appetite! She ate everything but sea urchin. He liked having American girl, but he also want her to learn Japanese way. He also planned to take Angel to Japanese performances and send her to a Japanese language tutor, a female tutor.

After sushi, they went home. When she walked in, Hiro saw in her face that she felt at home. In their bedroom, he stretched on the futon, wagging his socked foot while Angel put her thing away. Angel look like child in a new dollhouse, putting lingerie in one drawer, then changing mind and putting in another. She arranged her shoes neatly in row. Hiro watched her do that. Then he showed her the cubbyholes for shoes. She giggled with excitement.

"Everything is just so!" Angel said when she finished.

Hiro was in kitchen pouring their drinks when Angel came out of bedroom in new kimono. He wanted to show Angel a secret button that operates the sliding panel to liquor cabinet. He pushed it, and Angel, without surprise, said, "So that's where you keep it." She walked toward balcony, and wind blew her kimono open as she stepped outside. Hiro walked behind Angel and held her folded arms, slipping drink into her hand. The East Side sparkled over the park. She tilted head back, and they kissed.

In morning, Angel woke up early and made them both tea and brought to him in bed. They sipped it there together. Angel blew into the cup making tiny ripples on the surface of the tea.

Hiro would call his wife around midnight to say he would be home soon—though he knew he would not. This would keep Noriko from coming to city to look for him. Wife is always complaining when he doesn't come home. Angel never does that. Angel cares and understands him.

17

Angel's Recap

Although I live on an island, and lately I've been mingling with another group of transplanted islanders, and their island is a great distance from mine, and it would not be unlikely that boats would be used to cart goods back and forth, and perhaps these other islanders are on this island because they are involved in importing or exporting cars, chemicals or computers—all that notwithstanding—I am beginning to think Hiro and I were "destined" to meet. The sheer number—I'm leaning toward numerology here—of common maritime interests increases my superstition, having a synergistic effect—the sum is greater than the parts—so that I cannot but foresee an ineluctable end.

I'm going to sea.

Hiro will help me do it.

When I first approached him, he refused, alleging women were bad luck on ships. He countered his refusal with an offer to take me on a QE-II cruise. Now why would I want to do that? On a floating hotel there would be no seasickness, no chance of developing scurvy. There would not be thirty salty sailors to every lonely girl. It wouldn't be like being isolated in the nearest *mise-en-scene* to nothingness. I want to go on a small dreary cargo ship, where all these things might be possible, his company's cargo ship.

"I want to read all day in a tiny room and never set foot on land again, so long as I live."

"But I won't ever see you," he complained.

"Oh, I'll be in port every now and again," I explained. "You can visit." After much debate, he agreed to try to make the arrangements.

The deal is, while he figures out a way to get me a cabin on a busy ship, I will live in his uptown condominium, a high security penthouse, with signed artwork, a whirlpool, a sliding paper-panel wall to the balcony which overlooks Central Park West. He'll spend every Monday, Wednesday and Friday night with me. Of course, I'll have to quit Club Kiki. I have a new place of employment, Club Hiro.

We negotiated for three days after the trip to Mystic. Now all things are settled. With my bags packed, I wait on my front stoop for Hiro to come and take me to my new home. I sit with my neighbor's daughter, Jasmine. Lying nearby is her discarded Barbie. I'll miss stepping over her or her toys every afternoon. Jaz has long dirty hair with a cowlick on her forehead which keeps the hair out of her eyes. She has a way of crossing her twiggy legs and bouncing her ankleted foot back and forth that will be a very sexy gesture when she's older. I ask her how she likes school and what books she reads. I realize these are the kinds of questions adults always ask, and she probably thinks we're all out of touch with reality. She drops her chin and rolls her eyes up at me. "I don't have any books." I explain to her that she should be able to have all the books she wants. She names a few titles she's read in school. Our conversation is cut into segments because she keeps running to the curb where she wets a dirty rag with water from the gutter. Then she runs to the window of her mother's apartment and wipes the glass with quick erratic circles. As this goes on, the window becomes dirtier and dirtier. Zoo animals, too, perform bizarre rituals or rock catatonicly to pass the time.

The boys are out, making shy deals, hand signals and signs. Hiro pulls up in his limousine. His frightened driver parks the car, bumping the curb, afraid to take up much space on this intimidating block. Immediately, the homeboys flock to the car and ask, "'S up?"

"He's with me," I warn. The homeys snicker and slump away.

Hiro's driver loads my things into the trunk. I'm not taking much of my funky stuff. I'm even leaving Self behind, and Lola to look after him. I trust she'll be able to deal with the landlord.

Hiro and I stop off for sushi on the way to my new home. At his favorite restaurant the host greets Hiro by name. Hiro follows him to the bar, leaving me behind. Then Hiro remembers the American custom, retraces his steps and ushers me ahead of him, placing his hand lightly on the small of my back.

The ceilings are low; the tables are low; the waitresses go around shoeless, on bent knee. The atmosphere is clean, scrubbed and apologetic, everyone bowing, nodding, agreeing, "*Hai, hai, hai.*" We're seated at the sushi bar, facing the "master," or the chef. Again, the two seem to know one another. Hiro is even more friendly with the master than the host. They laugh. Hiro smiles at me nodding. Both grunt. I blush. They discuss the sushi order with deal-making seriousness.

Hiro orders in Japanese. When using his own language, ostensibly he's lucid and eloquent. It seems here Hiro is king. He does have an appealing reserved manner, like a court judge. His coal eyes are without opinion. Animal eyes are like his, dark and inarticulate. He smiles and flashes a gold cap on his upper canine, and, with embarrassment that has become habit, frowns to cover it. At least his eyes smiling seem human. I'm ashamed of the way I scoffed at his hope. What made me think I was inaccessible to him? Was it that he is Japanese and I'm a white American? Surely I'm not that small-minded. It must have been that I lived off The Hall on Thirteenth Alley and he was a businessman. Yes, it was on that matter that my prejudice had been constructed. It was, too, the desire to disprove my prejudice that made me knock on his hotel room door.

An older woman wearing a kimono hobbles out and pours our cold sake. She punctuates every other word with a soft mono-syllabic verification. Hiro explains that he's ordered in the traditional way, sampling several dishes. First comes a tiny plate of raw red snapper. Some vegetable cakes with soy sauce. Fish face. Sea grass. Raw beef (Hiro explains what I'm eating). I find it awkward to maneuver with my chopsticks, or *o-hashi*, but I insist on trying. I want to impress Hiro with my dedication to his culture. We pause for cigarettes which he lights. I've counted ten separate dishes so far.

I could grow fat on this life. If I enjoy what he offers he will be happy too. It's the parsimonious execution of two objectives. He's grateful that I'm willing to spend time with him without having to pay me for it. And I'll enjoy the challenge of getting myself on one of his ships. He gets to show his friends that a beautiful woman loves him, probably a wonderful thing for him.

I can't resist the tendency to justify myself by numerating the advantages that Hiro gains from our relationship. But that doesn't mean I'm in denial about my own selfishness. Can any act of human goodness be dissected from the selfishness? When we finally get at the core of goodwill, it is mean and ephemeral, sloppy, finite and blunt.

In one sense of the truth, I am starting to love Hiro; it's not just the illicit sex. I like his company. I'm interested in what he does—the shipping. I think I'm even beginning to lose my Anglo-Saxon prejudices, but then I overhear a thought at once ugly and familiar. Too close to home, as it were. Next door to our table sits a group of rude Americans. They order tempura, hardly the most interesting of Japanese foods, but the closest to American fast food. While Hiro talks about the shipping business (I asked him to educate me) I overhear one particularly ugly American say to his date, "Ever hear about those Japanese piano bars?" Then he, this man in a tight-fitting dress shirt, gives a detailed third-hand description of the kind of girls that work there, of the men who drain bottles of Chivas at insane prices then continue in staggering packs to the two a.m. Metro North train to Westchester known as the Orient Express.

The bimbos that work there (his description) are sold by the Mama san to the customer and taken to Japan.

The man believes this because he is afraid. (The Japanese steal *our* women; their genes will find their way into *our* culture and take over!) True, Hiro and I do fit his myopic scheme; Hiro probably did pay Mama well to show his appreciation for her having facilitated our meeting and also to compensate her for the loss of Angel's clientele. This is a residual custom from the geisha days. It has nothing whatsoever to do with me personally. Our situation defies the simplistic pattern laid out by our American friend. After demystifying the lump sum, the remainder becomes raw material for our friendship. After dividing out the formulas of our roles, that which couldn't be divided equally—our individualities, our humanness—is left over.

Oh, and what an untidy batch of stuff our humanness is. Simultaneously, I deny and participate in the rude American's story of Hostess and Papa san. I listen to our neighbor who laughs about the Japanese businessmen boring young American women with their inane conversation. Meanwhile Hiro is saying, "I was talking about bulky chemical trade; however other sophisticated chemicals categorized as fine chemicals including pharmaceutical products, plastic chemical . . . "

"The women don't really listen," says our neighbor.

Hiro continues, "should be going out and coming in to main ports in US are certainly such port in East and Los Angeles, Stockton are in West Coast . . . "

"Those jokers ramble on and on," says our neighbor, "while the bimbos dream about yen and real estate."

Hiro continues, "Also exported from Kenai, Alaska. Interesting thing may be that U.S. is importing because it consumes a tremendous amount. The biggest consumption are in Midwest, where Canadian potash can be delivered at lower cost transportation."

"That's very interesting, Hiro," I say just to prove our neighbor wrong.

But the bigoted American is right. I know he's right, but he doesn't know he's wrong too. In a way, I really am enjoying our time together, loving Hiro, too. I am. Honesty often contradicts itself. Sometimes I'm cruel and bigoted in the way I imagine his point of view. With a host of terms at my disposal, I nevertheless reduce him to a simple dork. And then sometimes I admire him quite a lot. During these moments I try to convince myself that I have real love for him, but ultimately such visions of an altruistic Charlie are scattered by reflexes of aggravation and comic disgust.

On the way home we stopped at a supermarket in order

to buy groceries for the condo. There we assumed the role of Inter-racial Couple, scrutinized. In Foodtown Hiro lost some of his charm. He had a way of being abused by store clerks which produced in me a mental shiver: "What did you say you were looking for? The lice? Oh, the rice. It's right in front of you, man." Hiro regained some of his charisma when he asked the same boy to box and deliver our things.

The threshold was before us. We crossed and were home. I put away my clothes in a closet that was larger than my bedroom had been. The walls of the closet had hundreds of thin drawers to accommodate one or two items each, so I'll need a reference index just to dress. My cosmetics hardly made their presence felt in the marbled bathroom where a large tub pretended to be a wading pool. A shower room had heads that attacked from several angles. There was a bidet, and a toilet bowl whose water tank was hidden in the wall. These extravagances fascinated me, and Hiro had to bodily urge me out of the bathroom to see the kitchen. There were several islands in the kitchen, one for cooking, one for slicing, one for cleaning. Shelved above the kitchen desk and near a tiny television, he had a cookbook collection that dwarfed my literature collection.

Despite the unlimited cooking facilities, later we ordered out and over tea, while we were sitting on pillows by the front window, I noticed he had a vein that slithered across his forehead and pulsed at me when he talked. I hadn't noticed it before.

The first few days were like playing house. I even cooked a dinner once. God help me, I did the laundry. But this situation became dishonest quickly. I make a rather unauthentic wife. The next week the place became more like my home. I rearranged the furniture; bought a desk and table to be put near the window; got my scent thoroughly soaked into the fabric of the curtains and upholstery; put white silk sheets on the bed; left my hairbrush on the dressing table; reprogrammed the preselection buttons on the stereo to WBLS; had Rocco over; spent entire nights downtown; left the phone off the hook; used Hiro's credit card and had a Great Books Collection sent to Jasmine on Thirteenth. In short, I was having a great time without him, and on Hiro nights I began to see him as an inconvenient guest, or worse a nagging spouse. Once or twice when an opening-night party downtown conflicted with a Hiro night I pretended it was my duty not to go, stayed home and drank sake with him and was miserable (many a husband choke down an otherwise delicious dinner prepared by the wife because he cannot bring himself to tell her he'd rather be out with the guys at Chez Doll). I began to feel bad—not about not wanting to go out without him, that's completely natural—but for pretending as if I did love his company. My sin is not infidelity but the initial promise to be faithful.

Regardless, three times weekly a certain duty is performed. But I have found it impossible to do so in the role of wife: eat dinner, watch television, dress for bed, "good-night, honey," switch out the light and "make love." Making false love is undeniably more distasteful and unethical than paid, frank sex.

But with this idea there is also the phenomenon of Hiro the man who loves. On Hiro nights he lies beside me on our firm mattress like a grotesque thought, heavy and awkward. He wants to—not just touch my body—but touch my mind. Every tenderly laid hand on my shoulder has another meaning. This gesture, my dear, is love. When Hiro kisses my neck I conceal a cringe which inverts like a thwarted sneeze. What is this new sensation I've discovered? Wifely frigidity? Ah, a ghastly thought. I shiver, not so much at his touch as at the tinny taste of my own deceit. As I lie face down in the pillow, Hiro is one more affectionate nuzzle away from being struck and spat at.

Then, with certain terror, Charlie finds a furious tingle, a sexual thoroughfare. Illicit? Maybe so, but it works. I throw off the sheets, uncovering my provocative butter-colored lace nightie—and I submit my warm body to his anticipated approval, lowering my head and eyes. Later, per his request, we run into the brilliant bathroom. While I hang around his neck he turns on the water with his free arm and dumps me in the tub. He climbs in too. Water splashes all over the floor.

I enjoy this especially because it's so Japanese, bathing together. I take special care to soap him all over. He closes his eyes and rolls his head around while I do his back. Then he turns around and lathers his hands together to do me. I enjoy it—but this, this is complicated with a sense of repulsion which still struggles to survive.

Six weeks later I'm bored. I sit on my balcony overlooking Central Park West and pick my toenails. "It's better than Club Kiki" was the thought for three mornings running while I was engaged in the contemplative act of my pedicure. I've just finished reading a "short story" from Hiro. I'd asked him to write about sailing, and he wanted to practice English.

Dear Angel,
 The following is a small writing my experience of seasick. Don't read it before you finish eating. I may be disgusting.
 Sticking up your middle finger to driver who nearly hit your car, you shout, "Fuck, you! Watch yourself, asshole!" The same hand sign, however, has a different meaning when you ride on a boat. If you get seasick, it means "Stick it in your throat, and vomit by yourself." Put it deep inside your mouth, pushing firmly the root of your tongue. This induces reverse flow of what you have digested. While it rushes out from your mouth and nostrils, you may retrieve momentarily smells of sweet chocolate mousse or banana shake or the bitter gin and tonic you took with dinner. It is like a fast reverse run of video scenes. But for the second and third times only bitter juice comes out of stomach.
 Sweet spittle gathering in your mouth signals start of vomit process. Grab paper or vinyl package at hand or make a pose in a bathroom. If you can't wait, I advise you to screw off bolts of a round window of your cabin and to stick your head out of window. A gusty wind would hit your face. Then blow out chunk of yucky liquid that is killing you. Weather permitting, go to deck to breathe in fresh air. Sea breeze may ease your instinct to gulp. If not, bend down yourself against handrail and stick out your longest finger. As soon as your stomach gets empty, dramatic sense of relief would overcome. Come back to your bed take a fetal position. Great comfort penetrates your body. You see homeostasis has worked.
        Hiro

It's true that when he said he didn't really know what to write about I told him to describe his most vivid memories, but what does he think he is doing? His startling use of "Fuck you" and "asshole" seems rather unnecessary, so too do the awkward details. What bothers me most about this letter is not how disgusting Hiro seems to me now, but how disgusting his misjudgment of me is. Did he think I would enjoy reading about this experience? At least his article usage is improving. But that hardly compensates.

Meanwhile bothersome details like papers, union regulations, procedures, and company policy eat at my hopes of Hiro helping me to go to sea.

18

Hotel, Echo, Lima, Papa

From here, the penthouse heights, weak traces of street noises are as urgent as a coarse whisper in silence. I strain to hear sirens, radios, or neighbors' arguments but cannot. I only hear the ice melting in the glass beside me, the numbers on the electronic clock changing and Hiro thinking. He lies beside me reverberating with need, need to express, connect, define, identify, establish something like love.

In order to sleep I recite the nautical alphabet, backwards this time, in my head. I want, I want sleep so badly—Papa, Oscar, November.

Hiro rolls over and lays a monkey arm around my shoulders.

Lima, Kilo, Juliette.

His warm breath tingles with acidity on the crown of my head. He kisses my nape, presses long and firmly and leaves a moist trace which itches to be wiped away. He loves me, he thinks.

India, Hotel, Golf.

Now a solid hip thrust against my butt. Darling, I love you, he thinks.

I want to sleep, Foxtrot, Echo, Delta. I shoot up in bed with exasperation, scratch my scalp noisily and take a drink of ice water from the night stand. When I try to set the empty glass back I miss, and it rolls onto the carpet. Hiro says,

"Oops," empathetically. Charlie, Bravo, Alfa. His legs wrap around mine. He tries to play lovers' footsy. Zulu, Yankee, Xray. It's no use. If I don't give in now, he'll keep at it all night. I turn over, pushing the sheet down and expose my breasts to him. I raise my arms over my head as if I were tied. My breasts feel so vulnerable, and, god, while he kisses them with what he thinks is tenderness, I writhe at first in disgust and then, I must admit, in pleasure.

Ah, that done, don't go on dear and try to impress me with your stamina. Endurance is for demonstrative sex, not the illicit sort. I finish him off by pressing his prostate and hop out of bed for a shower, but before I go I give him one falsely reassuring hug.

Is my feeble amicability a mere invention to rationalize my schemes? The bathroom is startlingly bright. Before the accusing mirror I rub my dark-circled eyes.

"Darling, are you all right?" Hiro taps lightly on the door.

"Yes, I'll be back in a bit. Go to sleep," I answer in sweet sing-song. I hear his feet shuffle away and the bed squeak. After rinsing my tummy and thighs in a gust of hot water with pressure that was so strong I felt massaged, I shut the tap and dry off with a towel that has been warmed on a special rod. I'll be going back in there soon, and what kind of bed will I lie in?

When I slip into bed he reaches for me and hugs me around the waist. After a while, I hear that his breathing, thank god, love god, has gone deep. He is sleeping. I untangle myself carefully, and lie face up, arms crossed over my breasts, eyes blinking. To lull myself to sleep this time I begin a memorandum in my head: *To All Japanese Businessmen Who Have Allowed Themselves To Be Conned cc. Hiro:*

Dear Sirs:

Let this stand as a reminder that hostesses are cynics and skeptics. Love may be met with rejection, even laughter. Keep this in mind when you negotiate agreements. Hostesses quite often feign naivete and thus receive moneys under false pretenses. Conditions of said arrangements may be as follows:

Literacy Dominatrix, i.e., Hostess agrees to correct the client's grammar and chastise him for mispronunciation. Under these circumstances client offers up to one hundred dollars for a one-hour lesson. If you have recently made such an offer, beware; hostess may actually take your money and only teach you English.

A second arrangement is Three-Day Mistress, i.e., Hostess lives in a condominium provided by the client and is expected to be available for three specified days per week. Under these circumstances client may find that hostess will be available for the outlined three days, but may tend to do as she pleases other days of the week. Be particularly wary of hostess who may agree to such an arrangement and then refuse to make adjustments such as to fall in love. In short, hostesses know what you really mean, but make you stick to what you actually say.

Post Script Personal Note: Ah, Hiro. I never meant to take advantage of you—in the cliché sense of the phrase. I vacillate between admitting my wrongs and defending my motives, and damn me, I can't see that it matters. As a whole, our relationship is an ethical perversity, but certain moments are principled. I enjoyed waltzing with you. I like sushi. We have, don't you think, healthy, candid conversations. Why, just the other night we spoke quite frankly about love. You had your scotch on ice. I had mine with water. I said real love can be finite, i.e., I can love a moment, a glance or a well-turned phrase, in spite of other surrounding distasteful characteristics. You agreed, wisely remarking that love isn't necessarily all-encompassing. We were eating, so jokingly we said (I don't remember whether it was you or I) love can be served a la carte. I even made a comment about how I was really only after illicit sex and your shipping connections. You countered with an admission that your powerful position at your firm was part of your attractiveness and said something equally blunt yet true about my firm breasts and infantine blondness. Yes, we laughed, love has no proper shape or color and, however sloppy, still merits the name love. Then, not a day or so later, prospectively you order soup to nuts. Perhaps it's inequitable to govern the administration of your love for me, but you are wrong—the world is wrong—for wanting it all for yourself. Did you forget that conversation? In our maturity we admitted monogamous love is imperfect if not impossible, adding that, of course, polygamy is an equal evil. And we laughed at the previous generation who, when they discovered that the line between good and evil is impossible to draw, decided nothing is wrong or right. We clinked our glasses; said, "kompai." I thought we had reached an understanding. But now you lie on one side of the bed hoping for moral love, absolute and faithful.

125

Thus, my kind of limited affection is pushed to the opposite side of the bed and made to seem base and immoral. Is it me? Have I gotten it wrong? Alfa, Bravo, Charlie, Hotel, Echo, Lima, Papa, sleep . . .

In my nightmare, I pay my last bit of money for a bus ticket home. It's been too long since I've seen my parents. It's a gentle ride, like rocking in a cradle, and for blurred miles I'm not cognizant that the passing landscape is not how I remember it. The corner stores, the odeum and the drive-thru don't match the yellowed photographs in my memory, but this simply hasn't dawned on me. I don't recognize the place, but I don't recognize that I've gone the wrong way.

Then all at once it's obvious. My face and ears grow warm. Trying to think where I put my ticket to check the destination, I touch my forehead, the center of my chest, then each breast pocket. I haven't even gotten over the chill of embarrassment when the bus driver, in a blue cap with a triangle of sweat on his chest, suddenly tells me to get off the bus. I have no money, no plan, no clue. I can't even find grounds to argue with the greasy-faced driver because I feel sure it's my mistake. Then, as I'm leaving the bus, he turns and says gently: It doesn't matter anyway. They weren't your real parents.

What to do? I continue, via inertia, off the bus onto the pavement. The bus goes on. On a deserted road I stand, a hermit crab's vacated shell. In fact, the original tenant had long since ceased to live there. And now that I was empty again I remembered the first thought I ever had. I was two or three staring out of my bedroom window on a crescent moon night. I realized *I* was the universe. I had made the whole thing up, but I'd quickly put that thought away, and my mother put God in its place. I needed something to console me. Nights I sat wide-eyed and quixotic in my bed, with safety bars up, wondering about *space, that big imagination in the darkness* which goes on and on and never stops (how could it?), and my feeble human mind hurt.

The bus lumbers painfully down the flat, endless, heat-rippled road. I stand, with my suitcase, hatbox, and wrapped gifts intended for my parents, gifts that are grossly obsolete now. Nausea gives way to humiliation. Infinite meaning means empty meaning, confusion. Oh, wouldn't it be better to be mad. This seems frightening; it's not. It, in itself, seems like a thing to embrace, give a big friendly bear hug. I'm mad. That's all. Madness, my friend, like an old dusty blackbird with frayed long-flights and tailfeathers, to remind me, cawing, "It's okay. You're just mad."

I wake late the next afternoon. When Hiro comes in that evening, I present Self, whom I had delivered from Thirteenth.

"Yeah, I am interesting in birds."

"I am interes*ted*," I correct.

"Yah, I am in-ter-est*ed* in birds too," says Hiro. The cockatoo bobs his head and extends his wings like an Egyptian.

"I hoped you wouldn't mind."

As I speak Self beats up a breeze which sends feathers and dust into the living room.

"It's nice having him here," says Hiro. "I have always been interesting in birds. In Japan I had a bird which lived in tree outside my home. It was big black bird, or crow. It was scavenger and stole food from our garden. It was vagabond bird. Every day on the way to school I would see him there singing, but when I tried to catch him he flying away. I called to him, and he mocked me. 'Caw, caw!'" Hiro imitates. "Then one day—it was winter—the Brutus—that was his name— was hungry, and there was no food to steal, so when I tried catching him, he did not fly away."

"You don't need 'the' before a proper noun. You're hyper-correcting your tendency to drop articles, poor dear."

"No," he says, "his name was The Brutus."

Hiro tells me that he had just broken off with his first love that same day. The girl, Hiro explained, who had been a hostess (just like me!), refused to marry him. He was sad and wanted a pet to cheer him up.

"I took tramp bird in and trained it," says Hiro. "The Brutus becomes very obedient—when rewarded with food. He learns many tricks."

"Uhum," I reply knowingly.

"But one day I gave The Brutus a command to sing. He did, but I did not reward him." The bird, quite naturally, responded with confusion. "I repeatedly gave commands, which the bird obeyed, but I still did not reward him." The bird, quite naturally, responded with confusion. "The Brutus looked at me with question on his face, for which I broke its neck."

"Ahem," I respond, trying not to look confused.

"In throes of death The Brutus bit me. I said, *Et tu Brute?*"

I suggested that he punished the bird for being obedient. Hiro said he did not like obedience.

"But then why did you train her, him?" I stammer.

His answer: "That's what you do with birds."

Should I be alarmed with this story? Should I suppose it is a parable of sorts? Hiro exhales in the French manner, bottom lip stuck out, smoke curls into his nostrils. Is strangulation his solution to unrequited love?

Then the doorbell rings. This has never happened before while we were both home. Could it be his wife?

"I hope that's not wife," he says. "I hope she hasn't decided to come into city for shopping," he says, waving his hand as a signal for me to retire to the back room.

I go to the guest room, leaving its door ajar. The front door chain is undone, and the door is opened. What do I hear but my Lola's "'ello! Charlie 'round?"

I find Lola pirouetting about the living room. "What a palace," she says, seating herself and flinging her leather motorcycle jacket onto a chair. "What a dream to live here." She's wearing, I notice, a black brassiere and jeans, no shirt. The bra I recognize as the one she "nicked" while she and I were shopping. As I was busy signing the credit slip for my panties and stockings—you know, filling in my name and address—she was in the back stuffing a seventy dollar demi-bra into her enormous bag.

I notice her jeans are the same dirty pair she wore weeks ago. As always she has that big bag with her that holds a black dress, her high-heel shoes and an opened bottle of vodka. Hiro offers her a drink. "Some ice and a glass's all," she says, pulling her bottle out and setting it on the table. "And I'm starved. 'ow about ordering some sushi, love?" This is addressed to Hiro. Without showing surprise he goes to the kitchen to place an order.

"So 'ow've you been?" she asks, fully reclined on the brown leather sofa. Waving her hand, she repeats the question. I shrug and indicate my surroundings as an answer.

Hiro, after making the phone call to the sushi place (speaking in energetic Japanese), returns with three glasses. "I had surprise for my Angel here. I wish I knew we were to have guest," Hiro says, pausing. "I would have bought three ticket." He sets the glasses on ceramic coasters which I've laid out.

"Tickets to what?" asks Lola.

"Japanese production of *Waiting for Godot*," says Hiro, looking at me for approval, sniffing and straightening his tie.

"I'll just stay home if you don't mind," says Lola.

Without flinching, Hiro says she's certainly welcome to stay. "Sorry about surprise," he says, turning to me. "I thought you might be interesting." He hands me the playbill from his breast pocket.

I sigh, "interest*ed*," opening the bill. The performance is downtown, my old neighborhood. Thank god (I am rather homesick).

Lola leans over my shoulder to read it, and I catch the scent of her lipstick. "*Waiting for Godot*. What kind of name is that?" she asks.

"Kinda like Gottlieb," I say facetiously. "Want to go in my place?"

Lola makes a satisfied grin. "That's very kind, but you really should go with Hiro."

Hiro offers me a cigarette as he puts one to his lips, but before he can light it Lola reaches around with her lighter already cocked and burning.

"Thank-you," he grunts. Hiro shakes his head silently. "If you excuse me I dress." He leaves the room tossing a folded fifty on the table. "Sushi man," he says.

When the delivery boy, prickly haired and smelling of oil, arrives, Lola jumps up and opens the door wide, waving him in, then she skips behind him and indicates where to put the bags with pretty, self-conscious gestures. Lola uses her highest voice to ask if he has change. He, bashful, searches through his deep pockets for a roll of bills.

Per her request, he opens the packages of food while averting his eyes from her breasts which hover just above the coffee table, and he sets the works of food art on our plates with that certain sense of ceremony that I continually note in the Japanese. Then he leaves (he wasn't hungry; she had asked) red-faced, with a nice big tip. "It's great having money to throw around, huh?" says Lola. "You must love it here."

"I'm leaving."

"Oh?" mouth full, chewing. "You're going to break his heart. He's trusted you," says Lola.

"He trusts me. He also believes in a god and plays the lottery." We turn suddenly. Hiro has been standing in the foyer with my coat.

"I won't need it tonight. It's warm."

"You *will* need it," says Hiro, pushing it toward me. "That skirt is a little short for the theater."

"I won't change." I take the coat and throw it on the sofa.

At my remark Hiro closes his eyes and leaves the apartment, saying, "I'll be waiting in the car."

"Have a heart, Charlie," says Lola.

I pause, "Okay, fair enough. A cynic's rights do end where a fool's trust begins."

"That's right."

"But he should take responsibility for the Mephistophelean effect of his yen."

"No," she says, "you do." She pauses. "So you can come on the trip. We're leaving soon, you know."

"No, I won't go. I won't go." I think I do protest too much.

19

Hope Deferred

While Hiro checks his coat, I wait in the foyer of the theater. A couple of homeboys outside watch me through the glass doors. The biggest one clutches his testicles with a quick discreet motion. I nod back and adjust a breast. I've got a scheme cooking in my head. I'm obviously a paid companion of this dorky businessman, and if I could just let the homeboys know (or lie to them) that I'm here against my will, perhaps then they would help me orchestrate some dramatic scene wherein I'm whisked away in a speeding taxi, leaving Hiro helpless and frightened. If I could manage that, then I could leave Hiro without assuming the responsibility of hurting him.

I smile at the boys when Hiro comes to my side and hands me my ticket. I take his arm without taking my eyes off the one leaning on the car, a good-looking man, tall, square-faced, heavy, big hands. He could throw me over his shoulder. I might even lose one of my shoes. Hiro could pick it up . . .

Hiro shows me into the lobby, red carpet, gilded chandelier with six of the ten flame-shaped bulbs out, ashtray standing in the corner. Behind the ticket booth window a girl idles in ultimate boredom, takes my ticket and rips it in a way that seems to insult me personally, and then, with politeness automatic to the words, tells us please to go right in; show's almost starting; please pick up a program from the vestibule and enjoy the show. We part the curtain and go in.

A black room, simple black wooden platform as a stage in the center, folding chairs in semicircle rows, no curtain. The lights dim. Several in the audience cough their last coughs, including Hiro. I adjust my shoulders and cross my legs. A samurai dressed in peasant clothes sits on the stage. His clownish white make-up could be happy could be sad, depending on your perspective. Even in Japanese I understand it. A couple of men struggle with ordinary things, boots that pinch, a hat that doesn't fit. They wonder what their chances are of Godot actually coming that day. I glance at Hiro's calm profile absorbed in thought.

In this production, the actors grunt like samurai, but everything else is much the same as Beckett's, a country road, a tree, evening, two men waiting. One man holds up three fingers. He is counting on something. Their chances are perhaps three to one. They discuss an old story, religion or myth in order to clarify by analogy, but only find more confusion. Oddly, confusion increases their odds. One man reportedly said he didn't know, that he hadn't heard anything about it. This creates doubt—doubt that he isn't not coming, or in other words: Hope. Isn't the human mind creative? After Act I, I realize much of the same will happen, more waiting, more deferment. It's all too familiar. The act of waiting makes present existence meaningless. Why would a discovery that Godot is not coming be bleak? When you realize there is no one to enforce morality or goodness and you proceed nonetheless, with all the more vigor, with mean but real hope and love—that is what makes the human the darling, the inexplicable pet of the universe.

I'd be glad to know Godot's not coming. I wouldn't wait for his call to say, "I'll be home for dinner, keep it warm for me." If he didn't exist he wouldn't tell me, "I'll pick you up. Wait on the corner." He wouldn't call collect from prison at four a.m. to see if I'm still waiting.

I begin to fidget. Hiro pats my knee to quiet me. "Don't you like it?" he asks.

"No, it's boring."

"It's supposed to be," he whispers.

I resign myself to sitting through the rest of the act, but the play has hit a sore spot with me. *Hope deferred maketh the heart sick.* I start to feel a bit dizzy, not with despair, but with old grief over the time spent foolishly waiting, hoping. The memory of my superstitious behavior—like a Skinner pigeon!—maketh me ill. The theater lights go up for intermission, and Hiro notices how I shake. He helps me up and escorts me to the restroom. It's occupied, and I have to wait, like Vladimir and Estragon sans. Finally, a woman exits, and I go in, turning on the light, closing the door. As I connect the hook-and-eye latch, all but one bulb extinguishes slowly. I begin to worry that this is the way my world is wired: my Sylvanias won't pop but will fizzle out with a dying light that will whimper and slowly fade. In the handicapped stall I sit heavily down with my miniskirt around my ankles, knees knocking. "Angel?" coos Hiro at the door. "You all right?" I don't answer.

When I finally come out of the bathroom, Hiro is not to be found in the hall. Off to the side of the lobby I notice a door, just a plain door, and there's nothing to suggest that I should go through it, except that I'd like to get away. I hear Hiro's cough around the corner. I go through the door to a dark small passageway. I begin to plot a dramatic escape, when someone takes hold of my arm.

"This way," whispers an usher, handing me a program. I'm led through another door down a ramp into a smaller basement theater, empty but for half a dozen dozing men. The air in the stuffy room is thick and sweet, like the odor emitted by squashed stink bugs. Those bugs crawl along the cantaloupe vines of the memories that I have of being a little girl. I used to smash them and imagine what I would be like if my only means of defense were to stink up the room if killed. (I sit down.)

I find it difficult to breathe, afraid I won't be able to inhale the next breath. My chest convulses and is flooded with more fetid but gracious air. The curtain parts to reveal what will surely be an amateur performance. On stage a man leans against a door with his pants unzipped and a prostitute—dramatically painted, showy, gin-breathed, a satire of the female—kneels with her head between his knees. Although the plot is more interesting than the *Godot* play, the actors act too boldly and speak too loudly. NEA funding, no doubt.

Nevertheless, I should suffer through the performance. Hiro will be looking for me everywhere, except here.

When my eyes adjust to the dim light, I read the back of the program with fascinated glee—because it's so obnoxiously trite and yet so oracular, sound and staid. *Bad Girls Go Everywhere* is the name of the play, intellectualized pornography. The ambitious playwright, who does not realize theories are deadly to art, contends that a preference for wanton women is quite natural. I myself had spent a great deal of time wondering about the undefinable connection between sexual desire and the forbidden, the lewd and shameful— the almost certain physical link between the gonads and the funky cerebral wrinkles in the naughty side streets of Greymatter, USA. With the mirth of a child who has just "discovered" some elemental law of nature and rushed in among grown-ups mad with her wisdom, I'm overjoyed, as if the same thought, the same revelation were spontaneously germinating everywhere.

Too bad the revelation should be found among such untalented players. While the play continues I think of superfluous matters: the lighting, the smell. I move uncomfortably in my seat and once or twice thwart a tickly cough. But as the characters became more and more recognizable—clearly the woman is meant to represent a Lola-type and the man is unmistakably some kind of Gottlieb—I am at once calmed and disturbed by what I realize is yet missing from the script. What's missing is the happy ending. Cynicism is just a Golden Calf after all.

Then someone takes hold of my arm.

"Rocco!" He is beautiful to see.

He chuckles unfolding his arms. "Shh," he says, puckering his lips and kissing me gently. "Come with me. Lola told me you'd be here."

"You and Lola?" I ask without surprise but with much jealousy.

"Shh!" warns someone in the front row. Rocco tips his hat to him and escorts me into the passageway.

"Of course Lola and I. When I went over to your apartment I found her there in your place. I needed a model so I . . ."

"Oh, don't tell me," I groan. "Can't she live her own life?" In the foyer, Rocco shakes a finger at me for criticizing Lola. "Listen, you have a friend in Lola. She knew that you'd gotten yourself in too deep. She's cleaned all your things out of the condo and sent them back to your old place. Let's leave before Hiro returns."

"No!" I remember my earlier plan. "No, let's wait and do something dramatic. Throw me over your shoulder, Rocco. Make it look like kidnapping—so Hiro doesn't think I simply left him, poor thing."

Rocco chuckles, still determined not to make a scene. "That's ridiculous. I could be arrested."

"Oh, Rocco please," I beg.

"Oh, all right," Rocco agrees chuckling. As we turn we spot Hiro walking toward us with a questioning, insecure expression. I scream. It sounds a bit faked unfortunately. Rocco chuckles and says, theatrically, "You're coming with me!" He flourishes a finger. Neither of us are very good at this. He bends and hugs me around the waist. I say, "Oof," as he throws me over his shoulder like a laundry bag. He misses, and I flop to the floor. Everyone in the foyer, excluding Hiro, watches with quiet amusement. Rocco extends his hands to help me up.

"Don't help me up, Rocco. Grab me!" I say with clenched teeth.

"Oh, yes right." Half our audience is laughing. The other half has become concerned. We exit.

"Some outfit!" Rocco says and puts me in a cab with a twenty. "I'll take another cab to throw him off!"

As my cab slips into traffic, Hiro comes out, sees Rocco getting into his cab, and watches with bitter frustration as the yellow car disappears into a pack of others just like it. Here he has the opportunity to jump into a taxi himself and demand, "Follow that cab!" but he doesn't. Instead, he searches for his keys in his pocket, and on the short walk to his own car, he wonders where to look for me first.

As we approach the apartment, the driver and I realize that the flashing red lights and the fire engine are indeed parked in front of my address (what a nuisance, I hope I'll still be

allowed in!). Then after this thought is a feeling of importance that comes with being "in" on a tragedy ("Yeah, I was
there when it happened . . ."). I get out a few doors down.
The driver has to back out. The ambulance has blocked the
way. To my horror—what a cliché, but in a television-like
drama, I revert to the phrases that go with it. "To my horror,"
as I approach, I begin to discern the shape of a small bundle
lying across the steps, being guarded, it seems, but not looked
after, by the "officials on the scene." The police stand arms
akimbo, facing out from the bundle, which is a body—I can
see that now—which is the body of Jasmine. Her sister—I'm
putting the scene together now and understanding—is in the
rear seat of the police car. The sister's boyfriend is being
handcuffed. The sister's an older, used-up version of Jasmine. One can almost thank her for putting a stop to it. And
to my horror, I am not stopped from passing the body or
hindered from stepping over it—to get to my home, and to
my horror I do.

I walk up my stairs "as if nothing had happened" and
think that I'm acting as if nothing had happened, and I con-
sciously try to change my thinking—to dwell on the scene
and make my emotions accordant with the circumstance. Jasmine! The pretense of my living in this neighborhood! Jasmine couldn't prevent her death. She just had no control. I'm
here, a temporary participant, a cold observer, pretending
to be poor and desperate but not suffering like my gorgeous
ink-eyed Peaseblossom, my Jasmine.

What do I do? I go on, throwing off Jasmine with a shudder. What's to be done anyway? I mumble, but in doing so
realize that this too is just playing the part of indifference
which doesn't seem to fit any better than pretentious
empathy.

My apartment is pretty much as I'd left it. Self is there as
well as a few of Lola's things scattered about, and an eviction notice.

I lie down, just for a minute, and suddenly it's around
midnight, and I'm at the Hotel Carlton, and I'm on the
phone with the coroner's office. I've been referred by police,
hospital, etc., till I arrive at this point. The coroner has just
asked a question so very demented that I cannot answer. He

wants to know if Gottlieb has any distinguishing marks, scars or dental work. I've answered, with automatic pride, about the five-inch scar on his left shoulder that had been crudely sewn. But I can't bring myself to tell him about the false front teeth that he wore on a retainer. The receiver dangles in my hand. He says, "Miss? Miss?" I picture the teeth in a drawer in a laboratory somewhere. I realize that Gottlieb dead is as useful as those teeth would be.

I peel through a second layer of sleep and find myself back on Thirteenth Street. Then the phone rings. The Tokyo operator says collect call from Gottlieb, will I accept the charges? I do without hesitation.

"Hello Gottlieb."

Gottlieb says this isn't Lola.

"No, Gotty. It's me," my voice falters. Gotty is quiet on the other end. "I wanted to see what the big attraction was Gotty so I've been studying her," I say, trying to sound breezy. "I love the girl. I get mad at her for being so naive sometimes, but I am charmed by her, really charmed."

He says he's glad he found me. He says with her it's not like it was with us. When they fought he just left her. They didn't keep trying and trying like we had.

I think of all the trashed hotel rooms, the broken windshields and police reports during that year we had tried so hard. "Are we going to try again?" I ask, letting out something between a sob and a shriek, feeling nauseated because I'm going back. "You really taught me, Gotty. I didn't want to know it, I didn't want to know, Gotty."

He tells me not be get hysterical, calm down, it's all right.

"I didn't want to . . ." I lose control of my breathing like an inconsolable infant.

Annoyed, he says he misses those early days when we didn't talk. When we never had anything to say because everything seemed to be out in the open.

"Yeah, I know," I say, with a sigh. That is impossible now: it's like a house that has burned. Even so, I want to forget what I've learned.

He wants me to come.

I was coming.

The line disconnects.

I flash the hookswitch, and with Lola's address book in hand, I get Mr. Ohno on the line, arrange to see him and Lola at Kiki later that week. Laughing, Ohno says he had expected my call. I certainly waited till the last minute.

When we meet at Kiki, they will beg me to join them on their cruise. This time, I will agree to go. You see, the tide has turned. Now I will be Gottlieb's mistress and Lola will be the fool.

I go to bed and sleep immediately. I have no trouble with insomnia nor with dreams. I lie in bed for an entire day not thinking anymore. I watch public television all day. I learn that shrimp fishermen in the Gulf of Mexico are killing hundreds of innocent fish. I learn how to translate *Frère Jacques,* and how to install a bathtub. I absorb knowledge for twelve hours without thinking once. Meanwhile, the landlord has started renovation work on the apartment next door. A team of Greek dwarfs is tearing down the plaster walls in order to put up new drywall. They are working on the other side of my bedroom, banging with sledgehammers. The plaster must be very strong. A little of my own wall gives way. Crash. Plaster dust settles on my face. Crash. They work on and on until they get to the part of the wall that is just behind my head. (I am sitting in the bed, leaning against the wall.) Crash. They probably won't break through. They only mean to knock out the plaster on the other side—but then again they might swing too hard. Crash. The impact of the sledgehammer shakes the wall and my skull together.

When Gottlieb and I lived in the Hotel Carlton, every now and again I would stand by the intercom and press the button, just to listen to the sounds in the foyer. Sometimes I wanted to call out to whoever might be there. Sometimes I swore that I would forgive Gottlieb in exchange for the sound of his footstep in the hall. I thought I was over those first couple of days without Gottlieb, but as we get closer they come back. The feeling comes from my center, where the fear is, and spreads out to my fingertips.

20

Noriko

I turn over and sigh horribly.

Since our final performance, I have been screening calls. I sipped my wonton soup while Hiro begged into the machine. I heard him lurk outside my door, and I heard Caveman chase him away. He told Hiro that there was no one named Angel living in apartment twenty-four. He left message after message.

* * *

The machine picks up again. "Hi, it's me. I went shopping. Leave a message, and I'll call you back when I get home at six." Somehow Hiro knew Angel's old number would still be working. Why didn't he realizing this before?

"Angel what happened? Are you all right? I went to police but they laugh at me. Angel, call me please."

Hiro looks at his wristwatch and spills little scotch on slacks. Already six-thirty. Where could Angel be, wonders Hiro.

He calls her machine again. "Hi, it's me. I went shopping. Please leave me a message, and I'll return the call when I get home at six."

Hiro begs machine, "Angel, just a call, to letting me know you are okay. I know you wouldn't do this to me, Angel, so I know you must be ... you must be in terrible trouble, Angel?" Beep.

Hiro resets carphone and glances at watch. He puts his Pinch bottle in glove box. Half an hour he will call again. He feels like he must have lost mind; he's been driving down Avenue A or calling her ever since the theater. So many people wearing black clothes under Fourteenth Street. But that's changing; the nineties are changing. The East Village has been dressed for funeral for a decade, sniveling, waiting, but now they don't want to dying anymore, Angel said to Hiro once.

Hiro goes to her old apartment. She hadn't told him she'd kept it. He guesses he has been paying rent on it too. When he presses her buzzer nothing happening. Hiro presses a different buzzer, and someone lets him in. Up the steep stairs. He listens to door twenty-four before knocking. He fears the man in old-fashioned white suit might be there. He could be a kidnapper or her friend.

"Hey buddy, you can't be hanging out in the hall."

Hiro finds Caveman standing behind him. He is startled. His nerves are on edge. He doesn't know how Caveman managed to sneak up like that. Anyone could smell him from probably good ten feet off.

"I'm not *hanging out*. I'm knocking on Miss Angel's door." To prove it Hiro knocks. "Angel?" He calls to door.

Caveman smiles, waiting.

"She's probably just putting something on. Be a minute. She is always running late."

"Look, Mister Ginzu, there's ain't no one named Angel living in that apartment. Why don't you just run along?"

Hiro's face colors. Oh yes, Angel isn't her real name, he remembers. Funny, it did not matter then. It matters now. How stupid he has been. He retreats downstairs, Caveman close behind him. "Thanks," says Hiro to Caveman as he slips out the door.

He gets into his car. Since Hiro can't stop thinking of what to do about "Angel," he has to keep driving. Hiro has to keep *doing* something, otherwise he starts thinking.

Isn't that Lola? He sees Lola coming out of sushi bar, laughing, handing cigarettes to group around her. "Lola? Lola?" Hiro gets out of car and waves, but a bus passes between them and she's gone. Hiro feels stupid now, waving, no one waves back. He feels stupid about whole thing. Is he ridiculous? He must keep driving.

No, they spent too much time talking together . . . but in unfamiliar language, in unfamiliar neighborhood. He hasn't been himself . . . but Angel knows the real Hiro. They were friend. They never had argument either. It was easy. Hiro doesn't know how else to describe. He didn't have to trying all the time. Angel never complained. Angel was content to read book when he wasn't around. She didn't mind being alone, not like Hiro's wife.

Oh, Noriko. He forgot to call. He puts his forehead in his palms and sighs, horrible. He lights another cigarette. What's to be done? Should he try to save Angel? Or did she run away from him? If he just *knew*, then he could act. He won't be hurt too bad—at least he can go on living. The worst part is not knowing, and without correct information behaving foolishly.

Angel *said* she loved Hiro once. She said it in Japanese even . . . or maybe in Japanese it meant nothing to her, only funny sound. But why did Angel saying it if she knows how it sounds to him?

In two hour, Hiro must be on plane to Chicago, but he feels paralyzed. If he only knew what was most important he could make decision. Is his work or Angel more important now? He didn't know.

The Van Wyck Expressway is pretty much free of traffic. Hiro can drive along to airport with those hypnotic yellow line cutting by on either side of car.

Angel. He resets phone. Still not home yet. He has to go on to Chicago not knowing. He's so tired. Sometimes maybe he hates her, if she really did this to him. She always says, "Hiro *san*" and "Mama *san*" in third person, stupid, only for direct address. She would be laughed at in Japan. Muscles in his neck feel like stiff steel chord. He needs some sleep, but couldn't possibly. And wife. He never called his wife. Of course, by now she thinks he had some kind of emergency. Longer he put off calling, the harder it is to call.

Suddenly the car begins to struggle. He looks at dashboard. Oh, he hasn't been thinking straight. Out of gas. Hiro

141

feels the engine pretty much die, and he coasts along quietly, under a bridge. The mile markers pass more and more slowly. A man in taxi passes Hiro and looks at him angrily. "Damn him! I'm in trouble. Doesn't man seeing?" Finally, Hiro pulls up on road shoulder. So slowly now. He knows couple of yards won't make difference one way or other, but he wants to keep going, going as long as he possibly can anyway.

Car stops. Half hour till his flight. He's almost amazed at himself way he keeps going. He picks up phone and calls auto club. Without any vexation he describes clearly where car is located, and he tells them to bill his account and send car to take him to airport. "Ten minutes," the dispatcher says. Hiro says, "Make it five." When you have money your problem quickly become someone else's. But still, even though he's acting, disposing of problem, it seem that inside he's stopped. He's stopped thinking and body is just going on via inertia. At some point, this too will stop. And when? This frightens him.

Before the five minute is up the car service driver arrives. Driver is friendly; he wants big tip. Normally, Hiro likes friendliness of any kind—in business we often have to be insincere—but tonight—he's so tired—tonight the idea of someone being friendly for money's sake makes Hiro ill.

"Yeah, I've pick up lots of your people on airport runs. You're real polite, y'know. Yeah, I don't care what them other people say I think you Chinese are all right."

"Is that so?" Hiro replies, taking out a cigarette.

"Oh, yeah sure, you can smoke. Say, can I have one of them? Not menthol is it?"

"No, they're Japanese, called short Hopes."

"They any good?"

"Somewhat strong."

"Hey, great, thanks. You Japanese, not Chinese?"

"That's correct."

"Hey, sorry man. You Japanese are pretty cool, too. Once I picked up these tourist, see and I. . . . "

"This story has nothing to do with me, sir. If you don't mind, I'm tired. Save it for someone who doesn't know what you're trying to do." The driver is "real sorry man" and gets him to airport in time. Hiro gives him good tip.

"Hi, it's me. I'm out doing a bit of shopping. If you like, leave a message; I shall return your call."

"Angel, darling," Hiro's voice cracks. He hates machines. You can't take back word you say. "Angel, call me please. Let me know you're all right. I'm in airport in Cleveland. I'm on my way to Chicago. There was storm, and we were rerouted. I'm so tired, Angel. I'll be in Chicago by midnight. Won't you call me there? Angel?"

He gets everything in before beep except room number. This trip has been disaster. Everything has fallen apart, but is sewn up again and again. In a way, he wishes everything would just completely end, plane crash or something. Then he wouldn't have to go on. At gate in JFK, agent had tried to inform him that door had already closed. But Hiro was flying first class, and the door was opened. Money can't stop storms, though. Planes were stacked, circling for hours.

"Hi, it's me. I'm out shopping, but if you leave me a message I'll be sure to return the call."

"Angel, if I just had some way of knowing you were still alive, I would quit call. Just leave message at desk." Hiro gives a new number. The hotel in Chicago had a small fire in middle of night. He, along with everyone else on his floor, had been evacuated. Thank god no one was hurt. The manager was nice enough to send Hiro to other hotel, after he tipped him well.

* * *

Hiro called moaning from three states. It became so brutal, after a while I had to turn down the volume. After I dumped him, his luck seems to have continued in the same awful direction. I attempted to put his mind at ease by changing my outgoing message—to let him know I am still alive and functioning. But he didn't take the clue. Then I do something inhuman, or very human, I give him one last flicker of hope—he sounded so tired. I leave a message for him at the hotel desk. The message is "I love you" in Japanese. I spell it out phonetically. I don't leave a name.

He's been looking for me, I heard, driving up and down The Hall. He spotted Lola, but she managed to avoid him.

* * *

"Aisheterrmuss," the message says simply, although misspelled. She loved him. Hiro knew Angel loved him. Why had he worrying so much?

Several days later, when Hiro disembarks at JFK, the air is beautifully light and the morning calm. His driver arriving on time, waits for him with small sign with his name on it. Traffic not bad all way to Westchester. Hiro tries call Angel a few times on way, but still machine is on. But at least he knows she loves him, and she's alive. That is all and nothing else.

It's all funny, when he thinking back. What awful trip! Of course, he didn't have time to pick up his suits before leaving so he had to buy new one there. The new suit was not a good fit. At the meeting his American counterparts treated him with disdain. Hiro often met this attitude from people who mistook him for a fool. Hiro didn't work out deal with Americans who bought the same shipload of potassium from a bankrupt company. Now Hiro's company will have to go to court. But Angel, nothing else matter.

Hiro's driver parks in front of the house he has not seen in days. He suddenly realizes that it has been days since he spoke to his wife. Noriko's Volvo is in driveway. Hiro didn't expect her home. She's been taking classes in Woman Study and Essay Composition, said she "needed something in her life." When she confessed this, Hiro thought her phrase sounded like something she had heard on television. Either you have a vocation in life or you don't. You don't go looking for something.

The driver carries his bag to the doorway and gives Hiro a nod of confidence. He finds his key still fits—she can't be too mad, and he goes in.

"Noriko?" he yells, but gets no answer. He slips off shoes and places them inside hall closet. "Noriko?" Still no answer. He sits on lounge chair and pulls off his socks. His bare feet on the carpet feels so good, and it's nice to be home.

All lights are burning. She must have been up late and hasn't waked yet. Some student she makes. Never was able to make good use of her time. No matter. "Noriko?"

Hiro opens the bedroom door. Windows are open, and peach silk curtain are drawn into screen and blown out again with the breeze. There she is in bed. Like child she is huddled, sitting with feet twisted behind her and her arm bent awkwardly at her side with the wrist turned up. She doesn't moving. "Noriko," he whispers. He is afraid. Noriko. She's too pale to be Noriko. He walks around the bed and looks in her face. Her head is back; her lips half open, red with lipstick but dry and cracked. Her eyes are half closed, just the whites showing under her lashes. There, on night stand, a note.

The note read strangely like his own thoughts. Noriko believed that if she had waited she would have eventually been okay. But the thought of not being in love made her "sick." She used the English word. She mentioned Angel, or rather his "heartless whore," again in English. But she reverted to Japanese to express the very thing he wanted to say to Angel, only Noriko did it much better than he could have (I want you to come home and make love to me and promise me you won't ever leave me again). But she didn't wait for him. She didn't wait.

21

In the Sauce

I lick the skewered *yakitori*. A bead of Teriyaki sauce clings, swells, then splashes back in the dish where I roll the barbecued meat, like everything, carelessly. I bring it to my lips, testing it first with my tongue, then my lips, kissing more than eating, then take it gently with bared teeth, tugging it free. As grease slips between my fingers and crawls down the back of my hand, I think each new bite is best. Sea grass is tart and incredibly unfoodlike. I am learning I can eat, and indeed enjoy, virtually anything. The sea grass is like fibrous phlegm in consistency but in taste remarkable, and, like all good appetizers, makes me even hungrier.

The table at Club Kiki is cluttered with small plates and bowls. I use my chopsticks like an extension of my long nails to reach across and pinch a glob of fermented soybeans. The others do the same. I close my lips around my chopsticks to clean them of gluey substance. A bowl of violet muscular material I should try next, says Mr. Ohno only he calls it something else. Each of us seize a slimy lump of beautiful purple, like a purple heart. I look at him as if I have serious misgivings, but pop it in my mouth. Surprise, the mushy appearing substance is gristly. I wonder if my teeth will be able to work through it, but I chew, and it feels good—as if I am sharpening my teeth on it. Finally, it dissolves enough to slide down my throat. "That was sea cucumber," says Ohno.

A bowl of potato things, for lack of a better word, stands untouched on the table. They are plain, lacking the beauty of most Japanese foods, of various dull shapes, round, egg-like, but one in particular is intriguing if not appetizing. It is cylindrical, hollow like a tube, or actually much more like a very thick artery. It also bears interesting blisters, baked a darker shade of tan. I taste it, with a little sauce, and say, "Mm, not bad," and swallow. The waiters bring in more hors d'oeuvres on silver trays, and behind them is Jun with fresh hot towels to clean our dirty faces after each dish.

Something in the table conversation dislodges my attention from the food, mention of my long absence. I look up in naive surprise and sauce. With the moist meaty smell of raw steak on my lips I ask, "Hiro been around?" That produces a lively chortle around the table, to which I innocently protest, "What?" Everyone laughs, even the waiters.

More lids are magically removed, fantastic foods appear. A small hot dish undulates with life. Sprinkled on top, Ohno explains, are fish skins which wave and crinkle from the heat of the cabbage pancake which has just come from the oven. Mr. Ohno grins and gives it a name in Japanese which I am able to repeat once, but forget immediately thereafter.

I am first to pick up a bite of *sake kama* or salmon neck, a fish head with garnish. The so-called squid-as-it-is, like the sea cucumber, requires elaborate chewing.

Looking around, I think how pretty the table is, even in its wrecked state: the colorful steamed spinach served cold and decorated with freeze-dried red snapper shavings, eggplant with sweet miso sauce, tiger's eye—roasted squid stuffed with salmon and seaweed rings. Oh, and the full cloves of roasted garlic—I pull them free with my teeth, like roasted chestnuts, one after the other. I smack a hard candy square of barbecue beef. Jun san and the waiters stand by at attention, watching the silly group. It is so nice to serve our every whim, when one could see how much we—the clients *and* the beautiful hostesses—enjoyed ourselves. The talk continues for some time about how juicy the meat is.

We are still eating and licking when the doorbell chimes and Jun silently disappears. He is back again, after a brief moment, bowing behind Mr. Tanaka. Tanaka sits down amid

147

ejaculated greetings. Our group returns its thoughts and conversation to the smoked eel.

The group is made up of Mr. Ohno, me and Lola who have come as customers. Lola convinced Mr. Ohno that he should order out. Food was brought in, and is still being brought in, by white-smocked delivery men from a restaurant across the street.

Our table has been provided with two hostesses—new girls—Velvet and Gloria. Mama San is shorthanded tonight, so our girls have to rotate to the other table to join the customers who have just walked in. They leave reluctantly. Since I've been gone, the belabored gender-specific roles have continued without me. They are still rehashing the same antique drama—in the same way religious pageants are reenacted every holiday to an audience of nonbelievers. Indeed, Kiki's celebration has an indigestible secular flavor, like Christmas. Velvet and Gloria, poor dears, still have the superfluous emotions of obligation and shame. They'll soon be over it. They're in the back now having their first Japanese dance lesson. They're wondering, "Can this be fun for the men?" and they're cringing at the thought of any of their friends ever catching them in—not so much a compromising position—but just a very dorky one. Their stumbling silhouettes remind me of the night Hiro and I danced. Velvet and Gloria face each other over the shoulders of their men. They mark each other's false smile with painful shame and quickly cover it with goofy gargoyle grins and dance on.

The hokey dance. Partners sway without rhythm, or at least, with two distinct ones. The customer's forehead is in line with the hostess's chin, and their height relationship is reminiscent of the prepubescent boy and taller teenaged girl at a high school dance, but has none of the charm.

Going around and around the truth.

One baby step left, cross right over his left, avoiding his right, turning slightly, stepping back left and to the right. Bump the couple to your left, turn left, back, and forward, hesitate, and step left. Got it? Let's try it one more time. Right forward, giant step right, around, step sidewise, back now around again. Don't forget to stumble! That's right now, step on her toe and apologize, left, back with the right, now round again and apologize.

At the end of the song they clap lightly, bow and make a few embarrassed gestures: You first, no you first. They bump, and then walk back to the table. In my absence, dance steps have not improved.

Mr. Ohno relaxes in a red leather sofa, fingering his breast pocket. We both watch the dancers and smile at each other. I can hear strength in the breath that swirls out of his nostrils. His head is shaved clean, and his skin fits snugly around his skull. Cheekbones are prominent, lips thin and ironic. I start to speak, but he looks at me disapprovingly. So I accept a cup of cold sake in silence. The waiter brings in a silver tray with two rolled hot towels. Mr. Ohno rubs his hands and face vigorously, then smiles and says, "Do you want to tell me what happened to the other gentleman who was taking care of you?"

"Hiro?" My face reddens; he knows.

"Hiro."

"If I tell the truth you'll think it's the tip of the iceberg."

"You're a strange girl."

I shrug. "I like you. I wish we could have talked that time. You know it was Hiro who called me away from your table."

"I thought it was a missed opportunity too. Thanks for the tip about the ship auction."

"Did you get a good deal?"

"Great deal. Like to see her?"

With my chopsticks I smartly pick up the remaining minute bit of *hijiki* and place it on my tongue.

Suddenly, we notice something funny is going on at the next table. Almost perceptible phrases are whispered in Japanese; I see a few heads being shaken. Tanaka whispers to Shiga. Shiga exclaims, "*Honto, ne?*" (Really, is it true?) and jumps up to leave. Soon Shiga has his coat on and is bowing good-bye.

Mama tries to head Mr. Shiga off at the door. Some low-volume Japanese grunting goes on.

"*Su'masen!*" Mama says in alarm. She bows and uses her sweetest voice. "Some mistake," she says, switching to English. "We no call wives! Mr. Shiga, please!"

I had never heard Mama san beg before, at least not seriously. Then she regains herself and pretends to go along with his joke—which really isn't a joke at all. "Mr. Shiga!" (giggle) "You have jealous wife at home, huh?" (giggle) "You're master of house" (very earnest giggle). If she can just keep everything "lite," fun and games, "just teasing," then she can avoid the horrible consequence of reality.

The door slams.

"*Angelchan*," Mama sings out. She motions to me, giggling—as if she didn't wish to reprimand me, but tell me a funny joke. I am relocated to an empty table in the back. A drink is sent to me, a cigarette, and I am told to wait.

What, I imagine, has just happened is that I have been accused of calling Noriko. She must have found out somehow. Perhaps Hiro, in his misery, confessed. That's fine. She *should* know. Wives ought to know what goes on in the real world. It serves the husbands right for all their cheating. We women have to stick together, Lola once said.

Despite Mama's attempts to put her clients at ease, one by one they make polite excuses while bowing and head for the door.

The dragon lady sits down beside me, saying in a friendly tone, "So I understand you and Hiro had an arrangement?"

"Did you?" I respond noncommittally.

"Did you," she mimics me with more cleverness than I had credited to her, "know his wife?" Mama has used the past tense.

"He never mentioned a wife—well perhaps once. No, I never really knew her." I assume this ends the conversation.

But Mama San informs me that Noriko, Hiro's wife, is dead, a suicide, and that I am ostensibly to blame. The discovery of this information produced in me a shameful self-pity at having been blamed for a situation that could not be my fault, but my own self-pity is too grotesque, and I'll omit it here for Noriko's sake.

I realize that if Hiro's wife is dead, clearly, I should get out of Club Kiki, Hiro's old haunt, his confidants all around. How close was Hiro to Mama san? In an imperturbable state, I remember what a Marlene Dietrich would do in such a situation. With a madwoman's precision I say one thing: "If anything happens to me I'll leave clues that will set the police onto you . . . "

But she has already risen, and I only say this to her back. "Stupid girl," says the voice of Jun, who is lingering somewhere behind me.

"Jun san, call a car for Angel."

Jun is on the phone before she finishes speaking. Mama turns to me, "A car will be downstairs waiting for you," and gestures toward the door. I get up and walk out. Ohno looks calm. He winks at me and mouths the words: "Wait for me."

On the street stands a limo with windows of smoked glass. The man standing next to the car is wearing a traditional chauffeur's costume and hat. A Filipino. This driver I think I recognize. Hiro's. He remains perfectly still until I approach and then, with machine-like rapidity, he jerks into motion and opens the door. Stupidly, I jump. He laughs.

A horrible turn—tonight is filled with prickly-eyed confusion and salty regret, fried dumpling nausea. "Thank-you, I don't need the car," I say, turning to walk a few paces up the street. The driver remains motionless.

It's late. It's dark. I begin pacing in my inconveniently high heels. Click. Click. Where is Ohno? The rotting garbage piled on the street is ripe with acidity, waterbugs and probably rats. Click. Click. I feel a tingle in my wrists and in the taut, pounding arteries in my neck. Some man quite harmlessly passes by, and I duck as if my throat were about to be slashed. A horrible fantasy of blood splashes across my imagination. Where did that thought come from? The man laughs in embarrassment and walks on. My dramatics. Jun is right: I am a stupid girl.

Finally Lola and Ohno come down. I say at once, "Hiro's wife is dead. They blame me. That's his driver waiting for me there."

Lola holds me and tells me it will be okay. "You need to get away for a while," she says. "Why don't you come with us to Tokyo?"

Mr. Ohno adds, "It's what you want. Will you come, tonight? We are leaving."

"Yes," I answer.

"I knew you would," says Lola.

151

"Now we leave," Ohno says.

"I should pack a bag," I protest.

"You'll get new things. Let's go."

So that's it. I'm going to sea. I'm going to see Gottlieb. We turn toward a second car parked behind Hiro's. Oh, yes, another limo was waiting, idling, shuddering as when a tuning fork hits the same chord of nervous vibration in the air. The car hummed a note lower in its sleep, in its dream of long open avenues, reflections of lit buildings wiped into streaks on its windows, in its dreams of red lights turning green in timely succession.

Ohno and Lola get in the car. I stand, unable to move. Ohno's driver asks, "Are you ready to go, Miss?"

I make a quick desultory check over the most recent events. He waits for my nod, before he opens the door with the pomp of a parading soldier.

I sleepwalk into the car, as if against my conscious intention (parapraxis). What have I forgotten? I seem to have unlearned something that would have kept me from going. Sitting inside the chilly car, however, is reassuring. The door is deftly shut. I feel on the verge of déjà vu. I try to remember, feeling a pre-orgasmic shiver, painfully protracted, and sweetly nauseating.

"Sixty-third Street Pier," Lola orders. The launch is scheduled at one a.m. She checks her watch (if it's right); the final preparations for the launch should be completed by now.

The car makes a wide turn onto the avenue. Heading south. I stare out the window, holding my aching wrists to my throbbing neck. Madness. This feels like madness. Here it comes.

22

The Launch

The car lumbers over the speed-bumped entrance to Pier 63 at Twenty-third Street where Worldly Yacht has its awful ships. "Elegant Dining Afloat," reads the billboard as we pass it and make our careful way down the narrow pier. Japanese tourists, with the need to say "I've been there," "I've seen that," thread their way out of the docked stillborn giant, a ship that never leaves the river, having come back from "nowhere," which is how its destination is written in the official schedule. The two-hundred-dollar-a-plate dinner was not fun, no matter how many smiling photographs will try to prove otherwise.

On we go past pier 62, passing the *Empress Queen,* the *Princess Royale,* the *Imperial Queen,* the *Royal Queen,* the *Majestic Princess Queen* and so on and so forth. All are very flash, very Fiberglass bores.

As we round the corner, the *Frying Pan* comes into view. "As you know," says Ohno, "the ship's name was taken from Frying Pan shoals of North Carolina where she was anchored some thirty miles off Smith Island, where the *Frying Pan,* the grittering and remote guardian of Cape Fear, bucked and reared at her moorings sixty years ago." He quotes the newspaper article I had referred him to.

The *Frying Pan* measures one hundred and thirty feet, approximately, pointed on both ends like a banana split. She sits high in the water and, unlike her neighbors, whose large-windowed hulls make them appear more like fish tanks than ships, she has only small portholes dotting her side. Her two crow's nests once housed beacons when she served as a light-ship in dangerous waters. The Filipino crew are scurrying about on deck, with ropes slung over arms, caps askew, packages in hand, all dressed in spiffy white, as sailors so often are.

Lola runs ahead of us saying that she'll have to get a bunk ready for me. She asks Ohno, "Under the helm?"

He affirms, "Under the helm."

Ohno takes my hand and helps me aboard. "Here she is," he says, slicing his arm through a meter of the sky. The deck is fitted with all sorts of hoists and hanging cables.

She is untied, the gangplank is taken away.

"Lola's friend, Gottlieb, will manage the casino once we arrive at Japan."

"What can you tell me about Gottlieb?"

"I've heard good things about him."

"You've never met?"

"No. We'll meet him in Tokyo."

"You don't seem to be a very practical businessman."

"With this? This is simply for excitement. It was your idea, remember?"

"Yes, but I had other things in mind for the *Frying Pan*. What do you know about casinos?"

Ohno looks at me. "I understand Gottlieb has a lot of experience in gambling houses. He will make good manager."

"I don't like gamblers."

"Is that so?" asks Ohno. "I gambled with this ship that you would tire of Hiro and come with me."

"You won."

Suppressing a smile, Ohno takes me down the hatch.

I'm taken aback when I see the ship's interior. The *Frying Pan* still shows the signs of having been underwater for a long time. Ohno laughs as he reads the surprise on my face. Although clean, the walls are textured with peeling paint of so many colors—red, white, cream, orange, a tinge of verdigris. It's impossible to read which layer of paint is the most recent. Barnacles, carefully preserved in a polyurethane seal, serve as decoupage along the seams of the ceiling. The plumbing, wiring and ventilation pipes run unashamed along the walls. Did I notice the large "elephant ears" on deck? asks Ohno. Assuming he means the huge scope-looking pipes prominent on the deck like Easter Island statues, I say yes. "Those are part of ventilation system which feeds into the vents. Here." Ohno points to some flat duct work on the ceiling, and several frog-eye like openings are scattered here and there.

"And this is the Ward Room," says Ohno, opening a polished wooden door. I follow him into a small lounge furnished in mahogany antiques. A display case contains artifacts found inside the ship when it was raised: emergency drinking water cans, coins, compasses, watches, a flare gun. Below a low ceiling are portholes. In the back is a semicircular seat conforming to the curve of the back of the boat.

Impaled on the walls are maidenheads, and in the center of the room is a roulette wheel. More green cloth-covered tables are scattered around. Four rooms connect onto this room, two on either side near the door, each with the luxury of a sink, Ohno indicates with pride. This, I take it, means my bunk won't have a sink.

Ohno then guides me out into the center of the ship, where we look through the galley portholes into a large high-ceiling room that occupies the center of the ship. The roof sweeps up, and at the apex are three open hatches. Through the hatches, glowing light showers a rusted altar-like watertank below. The room looks like a monstrous combination of cathedral and garage.

While Ohno talks about expected arrival times, whereabouts of life preservers and things, I know I'll either answer his question as to whether I've ever sailed before or vomit. I knew the moment I stepped on deck I would become seasick—I never could enjoy amusement park rides—but this feeling is not queasy, but uneasy. I expected some vile retching and nausea, but what I feel is simply confused, disoriented.

"No, actually this is my first voyage," I lie, as I have been on that *Worldly Yacht* cruise with one of the Club Kiki clients (those guys were always coming up with the expensive and corny dates—helicopter rides, dinner at Windows of the World, on the top of the World Trade Center). "But I've always wanted to sail—all my life."

Ohno grins, "So I understand."

Not seasickness, but sea weirdness makes me focus my attention on the workings of my body—my eyes where they're looking, my mouth if it's dry, my stomach if it's growling, my head if it's light. Step with the right foot, then with the left. Repeat.

"Bathroom is through here," says Ohno, pointing, "but only one shower. There won't be need for you to stay so clean and pretty, Miss," he adds, brushing the back of his hand on my cheek. He quickly looks away, clucks his tongue and says, "Well, I'll show you to your quarters."

My "quarters" are more like "eighths," just big enough to swing a dead cat in—if you hold it at the base of its tail, as the sailors say. He tells me I'll want a moment to rest, then I should go up on deck as we sail under the Verrazano Bridge and out of New York Harbor. He closes the door.

My quarters are well-lit and clean. I sit on the bunk, sturdy and hard. The only furniture in the room is a small reading table. The walls, covered with the dizzying textured finish, are decorated with rivets. One caged bulb burns in the center of the ceiling. There are two metal towel racks with bulbous joints, a slitted metal door with a bulbous doorknob, a pipe in the "stern" corner with vicious appearing hooks; one curious one-inch metal triangular ring dangles from a ten-inch chain for no obvious purpose; there is again that exposed air vent running into my room from the communal quarters and through the wall to the next bunk, and a flat vent with two frog-eyed openings, two portholes with a view of the Statue of Liberty waving as we pass, and also a rope hanging just outside my window, swinging slowly from the dead weight of something heavy, judging from the slow strained sway.

I hear everyone clamor up on deck to witness the bridge. I recognize Mr. Ohno's voice in response to the address: "Captain." I do not wish to join the others, preferring to take the opportunity to saunter along the corridors on my own.

Several of the original machines and engines, iron ogres, are on display in the hall. A huge, robot-looking antique radio looks important out of sheer size, like Hal the computer, a technological idol in its day. Next to it, another machine of unimaginable function squats, ugly with wires, stark gray. I follow an unfamiliar staircase down. What I find downstairs in a huge open room is disconcerting, like a horror movie set. Although the room is square, there is no sense of manmade order. The barnacles and corrosion are so extensive, the peeling paint and rust produce such a state of utter decay, that it seems as if vegetable matter has taken over a long abandoned building. A spaghetti of pipes and wires run up and down the ceiling, dotted with dials and gauges. An electrical board is the rear wall, with thirty or so giant-sized switches, caution high voltage signs, and wires. Corrupted metal or insulation fragments look like cabbage leaves hanging from the ceiling, and a touch reveals that it has been sealed under an icy polyglaze.

Looking up I find that I am inside the room with the high-pitched roof that Ohno had shown me through the galley portholes, a Cathedral of Weirdness.

Suddenly, Lola is with me.

"I'm sorry. I didn't mean to startle you. I wanted to see how you were doing."

"I'm just looking around. This is fabulous." Then I add, "Gottlieb will be impressed."

"Charlie, you want to talk about it?"

The blood runs to my cheeks because I think "it" is my failed marriage to Gottlieb. I say nothing.

"It wasn't your fault," she says.

I start to say that it was, but then I realize she's talking about Noriko. She still hasn't figured out who I am.

She adds consolingly, "Hiro had his problems before he met you."

"Lola, I know all that. I think it's terrible, but I'm just glad to be out of it."

Lola seems disappointed that there is no need to comfort me. "So you like the ship," she says, leaving.

"I got a phone call," I say. "It was night, but his sun must have been rising. I could hear the deafening chatter of sparrows on the other end of the line, of the world. Birds are so loud at sunrise, aren't they? He'd probably been up all night and was calling from some pay phone outside of a bar." Just like old times. "I accepted the charges." Just like old times.

"It was Gottlieb?"

"It was."

"My Gottlieb?" asks Lola.

"Yes," I answer, truthfully enough.

"What did you say to him?"

"I told him I was coming."

Lola smiles wryly. "Oh, then you introduced yourself? I mean, you told him you're a friend of mine?"

"Yes, we had a chat. He sounds just like you described. I can't wait to see him in the flesh." The ship pitches. We're suddenly aware of the endless rhythmic thud of the bow against the waves that would be with us for the entire voyage.

23

Lightship Frying Pan LV115, mean draft 630 tons: 133'33"OA: 108'9". Beam at midships: 30' draft: 13'.

Charlie's Log:I folded up my silk gown and packed it in my locker. It was nearly impossible to climb up and down the ladders in a long, narrow skirt. Someone, a steward or purser (*Nota bene:* must learn correct terms) brought me ship clothes, two pairs of men's trousers, worn rolled above my ankles and gathered at the waist with a thin leather belt; half a dozen men's buttondowns with grease stains and interesting rips in the breast pocket or elbow, worn tied above my pretty navel with the sleeves rolled and collar upturned. These days, I tie my hair back with a loose kerchief, and I've stopped wearing make-up, except a little mascara.

I've become a real salty dog—except that I'm still unaccustomed to the rocking and perpetual dizziness which makes much of what I say sound askew. The pitching seas have made an idiot of me: I feel dull-witted, childish.

I was strolling the deck barefoot and stopped to watch Juan, the first mate, a Filipino with sharp eyeteeth and green irises. He was welding a small metal plate to the deck. Juan said he hoped I wouldn't be bored on the trip. I told him I loved the idea of being locked in a small room for months on end with nothing to do but read. I squatted to get a closer look at his work. He glanced at me sidewise and relit his torch without replying. I'd spoken with, mayhap, excessive zeal. Watch your feet, he finally said. When he finished he headed toward the wheelhouse. I followed because I had nothing better to do. Along the way, I commented on the various devices, hoists, chains and things that I found so very fascinating and new. My comments were adolescent, excited and uncensored, punctuated with exclamations like "wow," "cool," and "neat." He didn't share my excitement, and when I said I thought the ten or so cranes hanging over the ship's sides made her look like an Alaskan King Crab, didn't he think? he screwed up his brows, had a second look, and respectfully said, "Nope." I asked if it was really cool to be a sailor. He thought for a minute, scratched his chest and said, "Cool? No. Being the captain would be."

"Well, wasn't it just kind of neat to get all dirty and sing sea shanties around the mess table?" He looked at me mutely.

"Watch yer head," he said as we entered the wheelhouse. Inside was an instrument, a binnacle, about three feet high, greenish brass, with a compass and two marvelous iron balls on either side. I was attracted to it immediately and pressed my palms on the cool metal orbs, peering into the dial. "What are these for?"

"Offset the magnetism of the ship," replied Juan tersely.

"Oh," I said. Behind the binnacle was a four-foot wheel of dark wood and worn handles. The five-foot, big-armed sailor who held it steady stepped aside and offered to let me steer. I gripped the handles and steered the ship, looking ahead through a row of portholes. I asked the sailor why there were portholes instead of a windshield. Without answering he continued to grin at me. "He doesn't speak English," explained Juan. The quiet sailor nodded at the wheel which was beginning to turn on its own. I tried to wrestle it back, but couldn't keep the ship from dragging in the direction of the current. "You better take it," I said to the grinning sailor, and he retook his post.

Juan was busy at the chart table. "What's that for?" I asked, standing tiptoe, looking up at a blinking instrument, a small black box that was fastened above the portholes. This time Juan didn't even turn from the curling chart that he was holding flat with his elbows. I backed out the little oblong door in search of another playmate.

I looked in on Lola, whose cabin was behind the wheelhouse. She had a large bunk, a foam mattress on a wooden chest with captain's drawers. She lay in her bunk with the back of her hand pressed to her forehead, eyes closed, complaining of dizziness. I went back up on deck and leaned on the railing to watch fishing boats pass. The common fisherman was usually a big guy with a bloated stomach and inflated arms. He wore jeans, dark blue and very dirty, hanging below his gut. Most of the boats were pulling in lobster pots. "What kind of ship is that?" one man called when his boat circled near.

"It's a lightship!" I answered.

"Oh," he said rubbing his beard. "What's it for?"

"It's an antique," I explained. "They were run by the Coast Guard and used to guard the shoals."

He said, "Oh," and paused. His fellow fisherman dropped his line. "Weirdlooking," one said to the other, and they waved and turned away.

We were sailing along the Atlantic coast, in heavy fishing traffic. I could still see land. It wasn't really like we'd gone to sea yet, and I was anxious to become a real sailor, and that I couldn't be until land was out of sight. I put my chin at the rail and squinted at the horizon. Juan came up from behind, put his hand on my shoulder and asked me if I would like to be in charge of keeping the log. I said I'd love to.

I'd have to record various weather conditions—he would help me with that—and report any usual occurrences. He gave me a leather-bound folder that was quite worn and wrote, "Charlie's Log" on the front page.

We made Cape May by evening and anchored for minor engine repairs. Winds were at four to six knots. There was a gentle breeze, small wavelets with glassy crests, but not breaking. I had a quiet dinner with Lola, Juan, and Ohno in the officers' mess. Lola had come in to dinner after the three of us had already been seated for half an hour eating smoked oysters and talking. Wearing a prepared smile, she sat down across from Ohno and beside Juan. During chowder, Juan and Ohno quarreled over the engine problems and only occasionally brought Lola and me into the conversation. We were collectively referred to as "the girls," and it was said of us that we were anxious to be underway. "I know the girls are eager to get to Japan, Captain. The wiring will be fixed by morning."

"Can I help with anything?" I asked.

Ohno said, "Charlie's passionate about shipping," at which Lola laughed and declared that it was good that Charlie Dean was passionate about something. I was not at all offended, but our group fell silent.

Lola pressed her spoon into her soup until it filled up around the edges. The others scooped it away. Lola's method was thoughtful, a meditating child. I looked at her, her borrowed shirt, her sleepy eyes, her silver rings, all the details of Lola, as though by sizing up the surface I could know the person within.

As if Ohno had been conscious that I was thinking about Lola's appearance, he interrupted the quiet and offered to buy us several new dresses once we got to Tokyo.

"What's wrong with the ones I have?" asked Lola.

Ohno kindly said that he liked her dresses, but the Japanese expected hostesses to dress more conservatively.

"How silly," was my response.

"That's the way it is," said Ohno, and when we got to Japan, his wife, who had been a Mama san for years, would help us choose new clothes.

Lola said what I was thinking. "You know, you never mentioned your wife before."

Ohno appeared to regret that he had mentioned his wife. He seemed terribly typical to me that evening, an unhappily married man. I sighed.

Lola offered to piece together the bliss of the Mr. and Mrs. Ohnos that lay broken on the table. "Your marriage must be very romantic: since you're always separated, you must really miss each other." I told Lola I thought she was keen, and asked her if the remark had been influenced by whatever paperback she was reading. At this Lola snapped, "How come you never talk about things you *do* feel?"

She had me there, and I realized, as the grilled shark dish was brought in and set on the table, that among my friends I had a reputation for being rather cold. Nevertheless, the tomato relish was making my mouth water, so I let the remark go and ladled the juicy chunks of fish into my tray, putting a spoonful of shark in each of the three sections. Ohno said he hoped we liked shark steak, because they'd caught a three-footer.

"And you didn't call me?" I complained, dropping my fork.

Ohno smiled into his napkin, "No, but we will be sure to wake you next time we reel something in." Lola asked about our schedule, and Ohno said we'd be reaching the Panama Canal in three to four days, depending on that wiring. He glanced at Juan, who bobbed his head after putting a forkful of shark in his mouth and mumbled, "Free days" (gulp) "tops." Lola, the anxious lover, sighed.

I had managed to put our destination out of my mind. Since I'd come aboard, Gottlieb hadn't bothered me in my dreams. I was glad, but I knew that eventually the dread and hope of seeing Gottlieb again would creep back and spoil my sleep. If only I could remain at sea, enjoying the sailor's life indefinitely. Or, alternatively, a sailor's end. This why I favored the dubious *Frying Pan*.

After dinner I went to my bunk to read *Moby Dick* in order to learn how to imitate boat speech. I identify with Ishmael. I admire his generous sensitivity. When I switched off me light, the reflection of the glass from the open portholes left a string of lights along the wall like a pearl necklace of inconsistent quality. I also noticed spider's webs on each of the "four dogged" portholes (referring to the four screw and bolt fasteners). Then the spider shadows moved across my walls growing bigger and then smaller as the light of a passing ship moved on.

In the morning, we weighed anchor and went to sea, finally. It was, however, a cheerless, anticlimactic departure. I simply noticed a change in the measured swell of the waves. I went up on deck to cheer, but my crewmates were all busy, and I didn't want to bother them with my naive happiness.

After we were steadily underway, the crew sat down for a late breakfast. The deckhands, a noisy gaggle of Filipinos with long sinewy arms that reached across the table, grabbing roll-away oranges and sliding plates, occupied a stainless steel picnic table near the galley. The officers, Lola, and I had our meal in the stateroom, and between coffee and toast, I took the opportunity to scrutinize my fellow passengers. I've been trying, without success, to make a head count. Never are we all in one place at the same time. Naturally, I considered the absent members of the crew who were at their posts, the navigator and the one steering the ship, the lookout, who is usually making a quick dash around the ship, stopping to pose with binoculars here and there. I also counted the "wick," who is in charge of keeping the lights lit (he often mutters to himself: "red, right, returning"). He also dons a chef's hat. I noticed him energetically whipping our eggs in a metal bowl. Counting myself, Juan, Ohno, Lola and all known deckhands, I consistently arrived at the number thirteen. Then I realized I'd left someone out or counted someone twice. I could be more methodical and write the count down on paper, but I'm afraid our number just might be thirteen indeed.

After the captain and first mate left us alone in the stateroom, Lola and I finished our coffee together. She said her seasickness was ending. I thought she'd just had too much to drink the night of the launch. Now Ohno kept the liquor cabinet locked. Anyway, she looked quite pretty and rested as she dipped her head to take another sip. Her shoulder-length blonde hair, brown at the roots, was tousled and sexy. She wore athletic socks and a cotton terry cloth robe, collar all bunched up around her throat. Tightening the belt and shifting on the sofa she said, "Well, we're off."

"Yep," I agreed.

Lola was a charming creature in her simple way, and I understood the attraction that Gottlieb must have had for her. In her quiet little oblivion on the Queen Anne sofa she sipped her coffee, scratched the corner of her eye with her pinky nail and made her plans with Gottlieb. She set down her cup and yawned, cocking her jaw left and right. Then she poured out the last of the pot into her cup without offering to fill mine, not that I cared—I would have the wick make more. In fact, I admired her selfishness. She was very attractive when she wanted something and took it without worrying.

We spent most of the afternoon at the ship's stern watching the white V drag out behind us. Juan had been able to coax the ship to a terrific speed, and since the experience of sailing was still novel, Lola and I couldn't tear ourselves away from the railing. Every new wave might show us a new aquatic animal and every passing ship might be returning from some exotic shore. We small-talked between sightings, and again she checked in with me on my feelings about Hiro. "He was just a dork, forget it. I can't believe I was with him." I told her the one I really liked was Ohno, always had.

"Yeah, and he's married too." We hesitated as the name Noriko was recalled.

"Well," I shrugged it off, "I don't have much sympathy for her: she was such a victim." Lola, looking out across the water, slowly turned her big wide eyes toward me, frowned and slightly shook her head.

"Wasn't Gottlieb married before?" I asked.

Her mouth dropped open, but no words came out.

"Never mind," I said, and I left her shivering on the deck as the sun was going down on Virginia Beach.

I went to my bunk early and read a few more chapters of *Moby Dick*. As the ship is moving now, with every roll my cabin door swings open, but I don't mind because I seem to sleep more peacefully with the door open. I can verify, by the shouts and the familiar voices, that the crew is still with me, that they haven't jumped ship or anything. The helmsman's shouted commands (my bunk is just under the wheelhouse) reminds my sleepy, vague and innocent mind that someone is still at the wheel after all. At least that is the assumption given the shouts, which I think I hear and take to understand.

By morning, we had finally sailed beyond the twenty-mile mark and can no longer see land. Now, the weather is the greatest feature in the landscape. The view is suggestive of the those artists' renderings of the surface of Venus. Extraterrestrial. Doubleplusearthy. Nothing but water and air. My ego seems to inflate in the low-pressure, empty world, but my phobias are also magnified. When I'm on the flat, broadfaced deck, exposed to the greasy sea spray that whips hair into my eyes and distorts my features, I worry I'll be tossed over the side. Yet I remain at watch.

One afternoon a protuberance emerged under a cloud and swelled downwards. Lola and I watched as the sea was stirred up and whirled like an inverse drain. The waterspout spouted fifteen minutes; the spidery finger crooked and then broke off. "Ooh, creepy," said Lola shuddering.

In the stateroom, I watched a big swinging device that is connected to the wheel and steers the ship. When it moved, I knew the captain was turning the boat along our course. I was soothed by this knowledge. As I thought of him he ducked his head through the doorway. "Hello there," he said. I put down the book I was reading, Freud's *The Future of an Illusion,* and unfolded my legs. He sat down on the circular lounge next to me—the foam cushion let out a breath of air. He examined the title of my book and said that Freud sometimes went too far. I assured him we all do. He agreed. He was wearing white pants and white shirt, the only man on board who managed to stay clean. I happened to be wearing a pair of navy pants with rust smears on the knees because I'd been scrubbing the galley floor that afternoon. I sniffed and swallowed.

"Are you enjoying yourself?" he asked. I nodded with wide eyes. "Good," he said. The conversation found its way to sexual fetishes, because of Freud.

I told him I had some pretty strange obsessions.

He thought awhile, wagging his foot, and concluded, "Obsessions give one character."

I agreed. He leaned back on the lounge and put his feet (white canvas shoes) on the table and said, "Yeah," reflectively, then, jerking his head up from the cushion, he smiled. "I like you."

I feel unashamed with the captain, exposed, but not afraid. Talking with him is like praying: he understands. "I like you," I said warmly, then feeling embarrassed, returned to Freud. "In order to have a monogamy you'd have to cultivate a fetish for your spouse." I was looking at his wide shoulders and his big hands that were folded under his chin.

He looked at the carpet. I saw his eyes describe the Persian pattern. Then they looked at me and traveled down the buttons of my shirt, paused at my navel and came up to meet my eyes. "Make certain this person is good at heart before you 'cultivate' that obsession," he said and changed the subject. "Didn't Juan find shoes for you?"

Juan had, but I'd rather go barefoot than wear flats. Ohno smiled and shook his head. He stood up. I lifted my face to him. "Goin'?" I asked with one crooked brow.

"Going, gone," he joked.

I jumped up to walk him back to the wheelhouse. On the way, I told him how I was developing a sailor's walk. I demonstrated, feet spread apart, knees slightly bent, toes gripping the floor. "Very effective," he said, "but don't forget to unlearn it when we get to land."

"Well," he said at the wheelhouse, "I have papers to get in order; we're approaching the canal." I told him I hoped to see him at dinner. He touched my cheek and said he was glad I was having a good time. If I wanted, I could explore the ship; there were storage areas behind the engine room that hadn't been investigated since the ship had sunk. They still contained original food supplies.

I went exploring. Everything was rusty, dusty, and fallen into unrecognizable shapes. Four inches of silt covered the shelves, and I, armed with a flashlight and a dust mask, conducted the first investigation of the stores. I couldn't help but be touched by the willingness of the sailors to remain isolated at sea for such long stretches. In addition to the storage areas the size of bodegas, they also had their own water distillation system, two walk-in freezers and huge tanks for fuel.

Ohno also told me to check a book on lightships which I found in the library. I learned the lightship was built to withstand one-hundred-foot waves, and could be immersed in water and come bobbing up again. Nonetheless, several lightships did sink. Ships often honed their radar in on them as points of reference on the channels. In a fog a liner made straight at the *Frying Pan* and sent her to the bottom of the shoals at Cape Fear.

At dinner I asked Ohno about the accident. He said I could have a look at the repaired hull if I wanted. Later, I went down a hatch to a hellish level near the front of the ship. The room had a much lower ceiling than the one above. These were the cells that would be used to count and store the money. Further down below was another even shallower room. I had to crouch physically and mentally lest I be overwhelmed. Two small doors opened on either side to chambers of two feet in width and the length followed the curve of the ship, a wedge-shaped room. The decayed or missing floor planks only partially covered a watery floor. Its only use could be crew incarceration.

Just under the four or five inches of bilge watⁱr, the ship came to a point, and I could see the rivets where she had been repaired. The *Frying Pan* did not rock at this level, the fulcrum of her swing. In this most dangerous section of the ship, I sat thinking. If we snagged on a reef, the metal hull under my feet would be torn like an egg carton. The salty water would gush in, knocking me down, making me lose my sense of direction. My only escape would be back through the maze of hatches and staircases. Would I remember the way? Or would I take a wrong turn, past the staircase, forward instead of up, struggling in the rising Jacuzzi waters, and find myself in the small storage compartment in the bow of the ship, just under the anchor hoist, as the ship began to point her stern at the bottom of the sea?

The next morning Juan lured me from my bunk with the invitation to show me "rooms I bet you haven't seen yet." With my insatiable desire to find all hidden passages, I followed. He led me to the very cell that I thought was a prison cell, and guess what: he locked me up. I was saying to Juan, "Oh, I know this place; it's no big deal. I come here all the time to think," but as I spoke Juan was closing the door. With a stupid smile I said, "Hey, Juan, Whatcha doing?" Then I heard the bolt slide. He said he had orders from Ohno to keep me locked up while we went through the Panama Canal because I don't have papers. I slept for probably two days in the ship's bottom, locked in that cagey cell where the officials would probably not inspect. Lola whispered to me through the ducts, the darling. She said I sounded tired and advised sleep. I suppose I was tired. I fell asleep on the floor. I dreamt I was in my bunk, but it was very dirty, and I heard clamoring outside the door. I said "not again" to myself, but I didn't know what again. A man pushed the door open. His smell was terrible, sour, dead, and he pulled at my sheets. I woke yelling, "Oh!"

Slowly I began to recognize the pie-shaped cell, the orangy walls, but the uncomfortable dream did not go away at once. Though I didn't sleep again I heard the man's stuffy breath, and thought I saw, when I closed my eyes, his smug smile. I heard dry-bone whispers filtering in through the vent.

To distract myself I sang every sea shanty I knew, rocking catatonically.

me. "You're not a prisoner. You're hiding," he said. I therefore assumed the active role of stowaway rather than captive. In this way, I more or less entertained myself until I could leave.

Once safely out of the canal, I emerged and resumed my log-writing activities. Ohno said that several officials had come on board and wouldn't leave without a bribe. Obviously, someone had tipped them off. Perhaps my old lover?

"Hiro?" I asked in a high-pitched voice.

Ohno said he thought it might be Hiro's doing. Anyway, Ohno apologized for locking me up and said he was afraid I might not have agreed. I shrugged and said I would have played along. I wasn't that difficult to deal with. He took a deep breath and said, "Oh, yes you are," twice.

We were in the Pacific now, on our way to Japan. The weather was warmer this side of the continent. On the third morning, we got quite a storm. Although forewarned, the sudden fog that quickly replaced a harmless cloud on the horizon reminded the crew to more diligently mark the signs of a forerunning spray of a white squall. When the squall struck the crew were sent clamoring leeward. Our competent helmsman was able to keep the *Frying Pan* away, but she was so tossed that the rudder only spent half the time in the water.

The tempest drenched the deck. Topside promenading on

the slippery metal was impossible. If anyone went topside, it was in a yellow slicker. I passed Lola, so attired, coming from the wheelhouse. We yelled our hellos and went on. The spray coated the pilot house and elephant ears with a thick salty bark. When I retreated to my bunk the view out my porthole alternated between sky, water, sky, water for six hours straight. Most of the crew watched the first big storm on deck, in person. I was content to cower in my bunk listening to the shrill howling through the cordage.

We rallied for dinner despite the storm, but we couldn't ignore the fact that the floor rose beneath our feet. Lola's face whitened as she tried to pick up a breadstick that was rolling back and forth. Ohno, naturally, praised the *Frying Pan* for her sturdiness and buoyancy, and he reminded us that others before had withstood one-hundred-foot waves safe in her bunks. But finally, the creamed spinach got the better of us, and we ran from the table.

Sometime in the night, the storm was canceled, and on calm seas, I slept well. When the wind and water settled, so did our minds, which, unanchored by the storm, had been flying after some of the Old Beliefs. Now, calm water, miles traveled, miles to go. Nothing but to wait and see. Wait and see nothing, nothing but sea. Old age must feel like this: no longer any irons in the fire, no decisions to make. Waiting contently for oblivion.

I went off to find my friend Ohno. He was seated at a compact writing desk applying a red marker to a tattered chart that kept rolling up at the ends while he tried to read it. Papers and ancient instruments lay at his elbows, and on the wall there was swaying a framed caricature of a woman's head on a tiny body. It was one of those drawings you have done at the fair for twenty bucks. While the artist drew her profile, his pen had caught her glance as she looked over to see how he was doing. There were both insecurity and shiftiness in the expression that made her seem absurd. Ohno, noticing I was looking at it, admitted it was his wife.

"Not very flattering," he said.

Nevertheless, it characterized a unique woman, who would

certainly have turned upon her husband at that moment with her rebuking stare.

"Is she excited about the new club?" I asked.

"Satsuki?" he said, jerking his head at the drawing. "She gets excited about money." I looked at Satsuki grinning in her absurd human way. "I should be more appreciative of her." He was looking back and forth at papers side by side on the desk, comparing columns. "It's her money and her family that put me in the shipping business."

Now I think I understand Ohno a little better.

This morning, as the sun was just rising and the air in my cabin was still damp, I heard an unfamiliar sound, a squeak, but not mechanical or human, the sound of birds. I stuck my head out the porthole and saw the same wave repeatedly crash against the ship. We were anchored. Then I went up on dock to see several of the crew in the motor-driven boats, bashing into the waves than were headed toward some foreign shore. Ahoy! Land ahoy!

It's been twelve hours since the entire crew jumped ship and left us, Juan and me, lifeboatless. It's one thing to be idle while the ship is moving. It's another altogether to be idle and waiting for someone to return. The horrible part is I have no information. While I know the land out there is the Philippines, I don't know why don't we dock. Why did they go ashore? To these questions I get a frustrated shrug from Juan. I believe he, too, is in the dark. He stays glued to the radio, waiting to be hailed, but no voice calls for us.

Lonely and confused, Juan and I watched the sun set. When you take the time to witness such an event in an environment of nothingness, you can understand why religion was invented. Someone seems responsible. A singular event this sunset was, an impressive event. Juan and I ate all day. We also pretended to make sacrifices to the sun god (my idea—I'm not sure he understood the joke, but went along with it anyway). We entertained ourselves with a makeshift barbecue on deck. We fished, fended for ourselves. Recited sailing stories. (I've since developed some of my own.) We went a little nutty—the effects of being so long at sea and so near to land. We started to wonder what would happen if they never came back, and in a giddy state we talked about becoming a new Adam and Eve, wondering what kind of demented race we would spawn.

Another day and still no word or sign. Juan, at least, hinted that we did have some instructions, that is to wait and keep watch, mind the ship. That gives me a tiresome bit of hope that we haven't been abandoned. (We have a task to do: wait!) I passed some time today straightening up the galley. As I was washing the sink with Ajax, scratching my nose with the back of my arm, I imagined Ohno coming home at any moment and catching me in such a state: hair kerchiefed, wearing rolled-up trousers and plaid button-down. I imagined the captain as the omniscient narrator of all my activities as I vacuumed and swept. If He came home just now He would see me: moving the chair, lifting the garbage bag, carrying a tray. But He never came. With a curious combination of pleasure and irritation, I discovered my happiness hung on someone else.

I began to imagine disasters and plot ways out of them. What if Ohno had been killed by pirates? What if they attacked Juan and me too? The imagination is a terrible thing when used to worry. One can easily go mad, waiting, with little, or worse, incorrect information. I could go mad not knowing.

Juan and I were becoming good friends. He was catching the fish and making the dinners. I was providing the conversational topics. Then he tried to have sex with me. He was furious when I said no, after all he'd done. I retired to my bunk.

Around midday the boats came back. I heard the motors, which at first I thought were mosquitoes. I looked out my porthole and saw the boats were loaded with supplies. Lola and Ohno acted as if it were no big deal to have been gone so long without calling. I felt very wifey when I demanded of Captain Ohno, "Where have you been? I've been worried sick." Then I added to show concern rather than self-interest, "I thought maybe something had happened to you." Even more wifey was I—feeling jealous and forgotten—when I discovered the reason for their little outing. Later, a Filipino ship came, apparently with fuel, and most importantly an addition to the crew. Out of that boat filed a swarm of swarthy, noisy, gum-smacking, cigarette-smoking Filipino "ladies" with gold jewelry and brass hearts.

24

Sexy Death

I watch the wick ascend the crow's nest to install red lights in the beacon. We've weighed anchor again and are now making for Japan. Since the "ladies" have come on board the ship has been topsy-turvy. The crew members are all fornicating in their bunks. Sailors and ladies alike are stumbling about, half-clad, or not at all, bottles in hand, crooning and swaying. The little tarts are snappy, yelping chiquitas—not that I'm jealous. You wouldn't catch me bunking with the crew—fantasizing about bunking the crew, yes; however, the actual act involves distracting realities such as sailor breath which would ruin the fantasy. It's just that I thought *I* was the favorite, the darling. How could they? with them? Ohno himself has been locked in his cabin with the loudest one with the largest butt. The deck rings with the din of their dancing spiked heels.

I knock on Lola's door, and without waiting for an answer, go in. Dim room, one yellow light burning. Reclining on pale yellow sheets is a dear and flushed Lola, pulling the coverlet over her breasts while a smile curls on her lips. Her sleepy eyes are half open, a look of idiocy or drunkenness on anyone else, but on her of irreproachable beauty.

"Charlie darling, come lie down," she says patting the bed.

I do. "Did you see those women?" I say with annoyance, "Ohno has such bad taste. Did you see those women?"

174

"They're not so bad." Lola never misses a beat. She has a way of dismissing the need for tiresome analysis. "Ohno's wife will buy them good clothes and teach them how to talk, don't worry," she says with an ironic smile and reaches up, opening her porthole to look at the thin line that was the Philippines. On a table, her mascara and lipstick tubes roll around. One drops to the floor.

As if thinking about something else, Lola sits, mouth open, jaw cocked. "Now c'mon," she says with a tinge of peevishness, lifting the coverlet.

Obediently, I crawl under it, settle against her pillow and slip off my shirt and trousers, too dirty for the bed. She helps me with my socks. Lola scoots next to me, clutching me with all four baby-strong, dewy moist limbs. "You smell the same as I do," she says, dragging my nose along her neck, "nutmeg and oil."

"Almond," I correct hoarsely.

"Yes, almond, of course," she says, stopping at my ear.

Soon she is asleep, her round Cupid lips open, a gentle distance from my own. I return her embrace, holding her tiny waist and pressing my abdomen to hers. When my arm under her neck starts to go prickly, I try to pull away, but she tightens her hold on me the way a sleeping bird's feet automatically constrict on a moving branch. Her skin is unfamiliar, soft and white. Compared to my cold, full, aqueous breasts, hers are surprisingly warm and squashy. The hair between her legs is coarser than mine, and I think it has probably been shorn. These were the breasts Gottlieb had kissed after mine. What did he think of them? Did he make the inevitable comparisons even as I have done? How would he compare us now that I have been altered so? I release my Lola, and she goes on sleeping noisily beside me.

From the perspective of the bunk where I now contemplate the past, the celluloid frames seem hairy and fuzzy around the edges. But real, real like a movie in my head. Overacted perhaps.

That night, someone, Joe from the bar, had spotted Gottlieb's car, wrecked, on the West Side Highway. I should go over and see if it's bad. It looked bad he said.

It was one of the few times that Gottlieb's friends called

me with any information as to his whereabouts. I was at the scene of the accident before the police. Our car was crumpled head-on into a Jersey barrier. Gottlieb was standing by the car, looking queerly dazed and neutered, surprised that I should appear out of the back of a taxi cab, but then not surprised because I always did seem to show just when he needed me most. I now know what a burden that must have been for him. He fidgeted awkwardly with my shoulders, which he meant as a kind of hug. He was very, very drunk.

At first I didn't notice the girl.

"Were there any other passengers in the car?" asked the police officer who had arrived behind my cab. Red lights whirled. Gottlieb's drunken eyes widened, trying to focus, like a madman looking deeply into his worst idea. Lola was in the car.

The policeman struggled with the door handle. Locked. He leaned through the window, shouting the name which he had managed to get out of Gottlieb. The door was pried open.

I saw Lola's little chubby hand, index finger flexed and her thumb twitching. She was stuffed under the seat. The police were getting the door open and trying to push me back. I wanted to see. She stiffened with convulsions, little shoeless toes pointed, belly out. The eyes went back. Her head lopped over like a loosely connected sack with a ball inside. Closely-cropped hair, boy's cut, a gracefully long neck.

Lola's mouth was open and would be warm to the touch, I remember thinking. It was an unconscious mouth and in that way innocent and sensual. I wanted to kiss it. I remember thinking Gottlieb probably did too.

Her mouth wore dark carmine red lipstick, theatrical make-up. She was lying on the stretcher. They would take her away. Would Gottlieb go too? or would I? The ambulance drivers wanted to know. I didn't know. I looked at Gottlieb. Lola had opened her eyes. He crouched beside her. She was trying to take hold of his hand. Gottlieb, embarrassed, put his hand in his pocket. She went away in the ambulance alone, after I saw them pull a sheet over her face. Gottlieb went with the police.

I can understand my husband's behavior: without making

excuses for him, I know now how he fell for Lola. I know why
he left me. I could prevent it, if I had it to do all over again.
Gottlieb showed up at home three days later. He had made
bail. He let me believe that Lola was dead. He thought he
should run rather than risk facing manslaughter charges.
We did.

In a Vermont resort, off-season boredom and close quarters made us irritable. He pretended Lola had been a mistake, a nightmare. But Lola dead haunted me. She seemed
to me the unbeatable rival. I couldn't compete. I couldn't be
prettier or more magical or have a stronger presence than a
dead woman.

My human mind can imagine the thing that is not, and so
I have hope and goodness. Also, like any Yahoo, worry and
perversion. Somewhere along the way of my life, passion and
death became a happy pair. These were easily confused for
an avid reader of fiction and romantic poetry. After pages of
eloquent argument Edgar Allan Poe concluded, "The death,
then, of a beautiful woman is the most poetic topic in the
world." I was an absurd lover who carried around a dog-
eared Penguin paperback copy of St. Augustine's *Confessions,*
reading at bus stops about love: "It has no future to anticipate
and no past to remember, and thus persists without change
and does not diverge into past and future time." He said
this about Heaven and God. Human and brutal true love is,
miraculous and common, utterly bewildering stuff. Once
while translating a love poem into German for Gottlieb, I
found the word passion gave me *Leiden,* the passion of Christ.
I copied out the term faithfully, thinking, yes, yes that's right,
that's what I meant after all.

Oh, the mind that is capable of such reckless cognitive
leaps, to be able to think A is B. Thus my necrophilia began.
I knew Lola had been a prostitute, working for ritzy escort
agencies with greasy Arabs. Like a poor London girl she'd
done heroin on and off. When I asked him about it he said,
oh she'd been tested, sure, no problem. I asked no more,
eagerly trusting him with my life.

Finally humiliation. I realized that Lola had been his mistress for a long time, perhaps for years of our marriage. All
our friends had known. I had been an actress who'd been

given the wrong script. I kept saying my lines; everyone was laughing. He made a fool of me. He didn't tell me. My world was perverted, slanted, the grooves didn't fit. My judgment was impaired. I listed like a ship half-sunk. If only he hadn't given me misinformation (I'll be home, keep dinner waiting). My understanding had been as faulty as Noriko's. Her false confidence, too, was encouraged by the empirical reality of her husband's behavior (good father, made love every day) and his colleagues' wives, trying to make up for Hiro's indiscretions, who commented at parties, "You and your husband seem so happy, like perfect couple."

Finally, Gottlieb left me in Vermont. He'd been gone for the longest month in my life when he finally called collect. Re-animated, I accepted the charges. Then he told me Lola wasn't dead after all. He was with her in a New York residence hotel. I imagined easily their tawdry room, something like the Hotel Carlton, squeaky bed, thin sheets, no coverlet, flat poly-filled pillows and a sad writing desk at which no more than telephone numbers and suicide notes had ever been scrawled.

She was nuts, he said. She drinks too much, doesn't come home for days. When she does come back, she has rolls of twenties and new underwear. When he insisted she let him make the money, she had a fit, insulted him cruelly, threw his belongings out the window. Clothes all over the sidewalk and street. She was nuts. He wanted to come back to me.

While he was on the phone with me, Lola was listening through the door. She burst in and attacked him with a ceramic table lamp, then a broken bottle. With the same bottle she gouged her wrists and ran out the door. He found her twenty blocks away in a deserted gutter dying. He, rightly, decided to stay with her.

I cried at the thought of my husband with a manic whore, unable to deny her primitive appeal. Having been a prostitute of sorts to Hiro, I can admit the appeal of illicit sex. If I seem obscene with my frankness, perhaps I'm simply overcompensating. I've nursed my infantile and novel perversion into something humongous because (wrongly) I felt alone. I inhabited an empty room, alone and miserable, and expanded, like a balloon in low pressure. If I had company, I wouldn't look as large and ugly, throbbing for a Sexy Death.

Possibly, if I'm completely honest, I can trace my obsession back to pre-Gottlieb days, the first years of life. I had a passion for ghost stories, and at bedtime my father would accommodate me. My favorite was about a girl who had washed up on shore in Mystic with seaweed in her hair, pale, bruised, not breathing. She was revived. Miraculously, she had not drowned with the rest. She didn't know her name, and her boy savior brought her home and tried to help her remember who she was. Presently, the sands in the shoal shifted and the skeletal hull of a wrecked wooden ship was partially uncovered. Divers found records which told her name. They found her parents' remains, fish-eaten bones. They found her own, too. She was a ghost. The story ended. (Good night, Miss Trixie. Now go to sleep.)

I was also fascinated by sirens who tempted sailors to their death. Religious drama appealed to me too: death by immersion, a resurrecting fertility god whom nuns married. Oh, to be a nun, my young heart ached. My idols weren't Chris Evert or Olivia Newton John, but Mary Magdalene and Marilyn Monroe in *Niagara*.

At my twelfth birthday slumber party my girlfriends told me I was prettier with my eyes closed. Later, I fell in love with a photograph of a dead woman that appeared, ironically, in *LIFE*. Many school afternoons, I pulled the book off the library shelf to stare at a chestnut-haired lovely who jumped off the Empire State Building. In the photograph, she is lying face up, atop the car which was smashed on impact. She seems to be resting, looks perfectly composed, in fact, regal. Although her body appears whole, I know inside it is shattered, if not soupy. Her make-up is neat: red penciled lips, precisely arched brows. Her handbag remains on her arm. Nothing seems amiss, except that one of her shoes is gone; this is her only shame, the only wry tinge of vulgarity to the scene. Otherwise, she is impeccably dressed. One has to ask why she did it. For this picture perhaps, this immortal masterpiece of drama.

Stretching in bed on Thirteenth Alley, I often thought of jumping out the window to achieve the immortality of the

LIFE girl. I would leave my bed sheets trailing from the open window, and down below in the salty dirt of the airshaft, among the bent lampshades and dumped kitty boxes, my body in repose would make a lovely picture, black and white and bloodless. So soft and limp and lifeless would be my body, wrapped in the second bed sheet, like a mottled rope. And the neighbors looking into the airshaft would scream— that peculiar I-found-a-dead-body scream—shrill and high, and they would remark later that it looked as if I were just sleeping and say, too, how uncanny my beauty seemed. And while the authorities gather stories and information, the neighbors will make their guesses, speculate. No one will look without guilt mixed with longing at the elements of disgrace to the otherwise aesthetically pleasing death scene: my nudity which they are not amazingly quick to cover, the slightly awkward position of my legs indecently spread, a trickle of blood from the left nostril, and saliva moistening the corner of my open mouth.

Yes, I have felt that too, Lola replies. She stretches her arms, yawning.

I sit quietly and imagine what it would be like if I were dead: A cable is sent: INCIDENT ON LIGHTSHIP *FRYING PAN* BOUND FOR TOKYO STOP CHARLIE DEAN DROWNED STOP CONTACT MARITIME AUTHORITIES FOR INFORMATION STOP. A network of acquaintances will set itself up and they will exchange phone numbers and condolences. Rocco, Hiro and Gottlieb will find each other, meet on the stoop of my apartment, climb the five flights together, Rocco with the spare set of keys. They'll go into my home to tidy up in order to dull the pain for my parents, who are surely at thirty thousand feet and on their way.

They unlock the door, finding Charlie's smell of toasted almond soaked in the fabric of the furniture, curtains, and clothes. It's not as if her death would have extinguished her smell, but it's ironic nonetheless. Her dirty laundry in the bathroom hamper will be repulsively absurd. Things, like her hairbrush, that wait for daily use will annoy. None will dare drink water from a glass in her kitchen. They'll think about the dead girl's muggy breath that still lingers in the closed apartment. When Gottlieb touches a tissue bearing her red lip print, creeping hot vomit will burn his esophagus.

The thought of suicide has finally hatched in the dusty coop of my imagination.

25

The Canal

Around four a.m., I don the dress I was wearing the night we left Club Kiki. I let my hair out of its tie and arrange my locks over my shoulders. I make up my face for the first time in weeks. I want to look perfect when I die, and when I check the cloudy mirror above the sink, I think I do—comic book eyes brighter from exposure to the sun, upturned nose pinkish raw, and rosy cheeks and shoulders. I tiptoe out on deck, with my heels in my hand, to meet Lola and Juan at the railing near the launch. The ship is currently anchored near the entrance of the Tokyo canal, and Lola has agreed to take me through the canal with the motorboat and then return to the ship herself. Juan asks me why I'm all dressed up. "You didn't think I'd make my big exit in a pair of your dirty pants, did you?"

He says I'd be a little overdressed for a fishing dock, that's all.

I don't plan on making it to the dock.

With her usual lack of interest, Lola doesn't ask me why the hell I have to get off the ship all of the sudden. I suppose she assumes I'm mad at Ohno about the Filipino ladies. Juan, the egomaniac, thinking it has something to do with him, grabs my hand as I'm climbing over the railway. "Charlie, I'm sorry," he says. Rolling my eyes, I climb the flimsy ladder down the side of the ship. Juan follows, watching my head between his feet.

Immediately above the surface of the water, a small boat hangs near a platform. Juan lowers the boat into the water and shows Lola how to operate the motor. "Don't turn off the motor when you get to the dock. If it cuts out," says Juan, "you'll have to wait ten minutes before you can try to start it again."

When Lola and I get in, Juan tells us to row about a hundred yards out before starting the motor. We pull away from the *Frying Pan*, which had seemed a fragile tiny thing in the ocean, like a dinghy to passing freighters. Now from this vantage point her proud hull rises out of the water like the Rock of Gibraltar. I feel so small.

Although it's dark as my eyes grow accustomed, I begin to discern the irregular silhouettes of fishing boats, black on navy, floating here and there. I smell pungent bait rotting in the water. We hear foreign voices and exotic laughter. Lola starts the raised motor. She turns the boat around with one oar, drops the motor into the water. After so many weeks of moving so sluggishly, we fly through darkness, berserk, native. The wet wind is cold as we race into blackness, the boat slapping into the waves. Lola maneuvers well, but suddenly a fishing boat comes up in front of us out of nowhere. Lola swerves. Our motor catches on something, but keeps going. "Take it for a while. I'm getting tired."

Lola slows the boat down. When we switch places, the motor stops. "Shit," I say, although I had intentionally turned the key to off. We sit in the nippy darkness, still vibrating from speed.

"Shit," repeats Lola. "Well, ten minutes, and it's fucking cold."

The boat drifts in the direction it had been going. Tentatively, I put a oar in the water, making a gentle stroke. Lola cannot help laughing at our silence and fills it with a leading comment. "When I first met Gottlieb," she says, "he gave me a two-hundred-dollar tip, but that wasn't the thing."

"Two hundred dollars?" I ask, remembering how fucking poor we were in those days. "I guess he wanted you to think he was rich and powerful." Poor Gottlieb. I knew that he had been neither.

"Yeah," she does her best to try to remember what had happened next and then to assign it a meaning I will appreciate. "I called him, and we met near Battery Park." Lola sucks in a sob. "It was pouring rain. We got in a phone booth."

I picture them, the booth, the rain. Where was I that day? At home waiting? Maybe in the rain waiting for him somewhere.

She laughs, wiping under her eye with the back of her hand. "We said nothing really, only small talk. Then I had to run, but before I left I said, 'Just touch my breast once.' He did. He reached inside my blouse and touched me for the first time. I left him with an erection."

He probably called me from that same booth and apologized for being late. He probably even touched me that night and thought of her breasts. Though his actions may have done me no actual harm, it's horrible to think how awkwardly I fitted in to the story. "Aren't you afraid that since he cheated on his wife with you that he'll cheat on you too?"

"You don't understand." Pride, aggravation, and a jabbing ache to be understood push her to make another effort. "It was different with us."

"Did you ever think about the wife?" I ask.

Lola considers for a moment. "No," she says, "I don't think you understand."

There is a long hesitation, plainly tense. A ghost walks over Lola's grave. She shudders. She pulls her arms inside her sweater, letting her sleeves dangle lifelessly. We begin to rock in the counter-crossing wakes of several small boats. "We must have drifted into a traffic lane," I suggest. Suddenly, a few twinkling lights and rushing water grow in brilliance and thunder. A tanker passes within ten yards, its red beams finding us in our little boat, drifting. Someone shouts angrily in an unknown language. Lola begins to row away from the dazzling lights and noisy engines.

I look at Lola as I had that ugly night on the West Side Highway. Then, too, were shouts being hurled at me. Then, too, were red lights playing with my features of disbelief. Lola, the girl in Gottlieb's wrecked car, the prostitute in the play, the dying girl in the gutter, the girl willing to finance my husband's gambling habit by stripping. I think we must have traded places that night, and I've taken her sins like borrowed underwear. Lola, vanguard of the blue cinema, my precursor, I've spanieled her from the initial crash site, through topless bars, hostess clubs, brothels. Driven by a neurotic need to see retake after retake of God's egress.

"Try the motor now," says Lola.

I lurch across the boat and straddle my pretty Lola. I find my hands around her throat, the throat that I'd seen bruised, that I'd kissed, the throat I might have wrung the first time I saw it. When I flip her on her back, I'm delighted by the way her arms and legs flap.

Coughing, she croaks, "What are you doing?" gripping my wrists, trying to struggle free.

"You stupid girl. Don't you know who I am?"

She leers with curled lip, "Of course I do. You're Gottlieb's wife. What do you think I am? A fool?"

I say indeed she is a fool because Gottlieb called me. He wants me back.

Lola shoves me into my seat. She grabs an oar, stands over me, a throbbing vein standing out among the tightened tendons of her neck. Holding the oar like a bat, she takes a wide swing. I duck; she misses, hitting her knee against the side of the boat, almost falling in. This just makes her angrier. With a scream, she brings the sharp side of the oar down on my head. A hot bolt shoots through my skull. I fall forward, slowly. She slumps back in her seat, drops the oar, looks at me with disgust. I put my hand to my head, blood. I look at my red palm and look at her. Slowly I get up, holding the side of the boat.

She looks at me with the plainest expression of boredom I've ever seen—mouth tight, slitted eyes. Then she raises one brow, a look of vague anticipation of what I might do next.

"I'll haunt him for the rest of his life," I say, letting myself fall backward into the water.

Ignoring the initial cool, salty shock, I doggedly swim toward the bottom, with the strange, flappy awkwardness of my gown, trying to get as deep as I can. I hadn't taken a deep breath before jumping, and I try to swim until it's too far to make it back to the surface in time for air. In denser, cooler water, I feel like an ant in hardened sap. Then the line of my lunge curves, and I find myself bobbing on the surface.

"Charlie," Lola screams, and, funny, but I think I hear real

185

concern in her voice. "Charlie." She pokes the oar in the dark water. "Grab the oar." I hear her panicked voice. "Here it is."

But I've already drifted. A merciful current is sweeping me away from Lola's now tiny call. My toe slips free and my left shoe dangles by the ankle strap. I managed a half-hearted dog-paddle, water at my chin.

Lola starts the engine, maneuvers toward the direction of my splash, but the choppy waters bear no trace of me.

Except for distant lights of fishing boats, I swim in clammy darkness. It's just before the dawn. Will I drown before sunrise? My head stings, my arms are already tired, but that's nothing, I'm a long, long way from dying. I still feel the salty smart too keenly. Will numbness come gradually or all at once? I wish I had the courage to pull my knees to my chest, huddle up, inhale water, and sink like a stone. Instead, I wait for exhaustion, for a spasm, a cramp. Oh, all my fascination with dramatic escapades. Drowning is tedious. How very ordinary it is to die. But luckily no one will ever know the prosaic quality of my last thoughts.

In the wake of a passing fishing boat I bob under churning foam. In the distance, the launch speeds back to the ship. Hysterical Lola must be going back for help. By then it will be too late. My arms are now tired. A burning lightheadedness. Dullness spreads throughout my brain cells. Ah, but Gottlieb survives in my mind, a phosphorescent glow of wagging light as I sink.

A convulsion in my chest propels me upward. Against my will, I splash and flap. Give in, I say to my persistent, angry, manic self, give in, let go. And finally, with sheepish-eyed exhaustion I do—although stringy tentacles of doubt attach to every hoary belief, and each gaudy bit of faith. The cool water closes over my head, and I imagine—in the murky clarity of my new resolve—my body, bloated and floating, being tugged at and eaten by hundreds of mad, happy, hungry minnows.

26

Hotel Savvy

Some fishermen found me. With the sunrise, a deus ex machina-like vessel happened by. They dragged me out of the water just as night gave up to a grey morning and found hospitable refuge in my head. As it turns out, I had been paddling in the canal, where a persistent current would have killed me, if not for the several boats that cluttered the waters and ensured my discovery and rescue.

When they found me, my green gown clung to my skin like fish scales. My hair was matted to my face and shoulders, and my bare bosom had fallen out of my low-hanging neckline. It seemed they'd discovered a mermaid, unhappily a dead one, so they thought. "What a catch!" they probably said in Japanese. I was brought on board and laid on the studded metal deck with hundreds of fish flapping frantically around my pale limp body. The four old fishermen stood and admired me until an angry young apprentice, fourteen, pushed aside the cynical old salts and breathed life into me.

My first recollection was this dark-skinned boy with his mouth over mine. His small mouth had teeth crowded into multiple rows like a shark's. I vomited. The rest of the crew laughed, but he was kind and held me tightly against his narrow chest.

The boy, Ryuga, brought me to a dingy clinic in the town, where I briefly saw a doctor who was Ryuga's second cousin.

The doctor said I should take care or I might develop pneumonia. He gave me a prescription, but I have no money to fill it. I don't feel well at all.

For the moment, I'm staying in a so-called "rabbit house." Ryuga's mother, Taco, agreed to take care of me. Taco—a strange name: it means octopus—is thin, like her son, but has fat cheeks. They speak little English, but I do understand that the local legend around here is that I'm some sort of seawitch; the "dead girl," is what they call me in Japanese.

I slept feverishly for three days, only cognizant of a light scraping sound which turned out to be Taco shuffling around the living room in fuzzy slippers. She never picks up her feet.

On the top of my head a purple lump has grown where Lola whacked me with the oar. Taco washed the cut while I sweated and slept on a mat in the living room. She gave me water and watched me.

For three days I have slept on the floor, on a thin futon. But today it was taken from me in the morning and hung out on the porch alongside their own. I could use a few more days to recuperate, because I don't feel quite myself, but I have to give the room over to daily activities. In the nearby kitchen Taco makes miso soup, fish and rice for breakfast. For dinner it's tempura, more fish and rice.

The living room is tiny, but when Taco pushes one of the walls open, the garden outside becomes part of the house. The neighbors, who live five feet away, also have their living room wall open. We can hear their t.v., smell their dinners, and they ours. We all wear kimonos and pretend that we can't see each other.

Yesterday, as I lounged on my futon, passing neighbors were caught staring at me. "Pah," said Taco and shooed them away. She doesn't believe the rumors. Other neighbors, walking from the market, gawked while Ryuga and I watched television. One fisherman's child drew a picture of me with yellow hair and green skin. She came up to the opened side of the house and laid it on the floor and ran away.

The *Frying Pan*, now anchored in the canal, made the local news. The reporter interviewed Mr. Ohno's wife, Satsuki, whom I recognized from that ridiculous drawing in Ohno's bunk. I didn't understand the report, but apparently the grand opening of the casino is imminent. Some interior shots showed the gorgeous gambling rooms. The Filipino girls, appearing in the background, had obviously been cleaned up and prettied by Satsuki. Ryuga watched indifferently, without altering the speed with which he slurped his soup, so I assumed no mention was made of C.D.

I overslept this morning. When I woke I found Taco reading my pulse. I opened my eyes, and she started in fright. I have to go now. Now, even Ryuga is suspicious of me. I am pale and clammy. I do look like death. I have to go now, they say, kneeling next to me.

Where to? I have no passport, no Japanese, no money.

I sit up on the futon with some difficulty. Ryuga and his mother have equipped me with an English/Japanese dictionary and they are equally, though inversely, armed with a Japanese/English dictionary. I flip pages, finding the right words, but I am not able to form a question. Simply repeating the words in various orders doesn't work. Taco shakes her doughy face when I ask, "Cash advance where get?"

Ryuga leafs through the dictionary. They consult each other, then in unison pronounce, "cledit." I check my book under "credit" and find a little character which is said to represent a credit card office. I point to it, and they nod joyfully.

They bring me into town to my alma pater, American Express. Taco wears her fuzzy slippers. I claim to have lost my card, passport. They ask me to provide my account number, my mother's maiden name and my checking account number. After a brief check, the clerk, with impudent trust, gives me cash against my account. Ryuga gives me a leather change purse as a going away present.

Having money means that I can leave. The question is: *dochira e?* Where to?

To Gottlieb, of course. To the *Frying Pan*, where I can attend my own wake like Tom Sawyer. In this respect, things have turned out surprisingly well. I have not cheated myself out of the best part, the aftermath, the wake.

I decide to resurrect on the deck of the *Frying Pan* as Desdemona, Geisha Ichiban. I'll crash their opening night party.

Gottlieb will be in the wheelhouse counting receipts when suddenly he'll see a vision of his estranged wife haunting the bow. I'll be wearing harlot red, laughing with some charming sailor who has just whispered in my ear. I'll glance up, catch Gottlieb's eye and stop laughing.

(Gottlieb runs out of the wheelhouse.)

The sailor starts to introduce me, "Desdemona Dean. It's my pleasure to introduce you to the manager of this exciting casino. Gottlieb"—his mouth waters in terror—"this is Desdemona. Perhaps you've heard of the most sought-after geisha in Tokyo. She's only just arrived and already two clients have committed suicide after she rejected their marriage proposals."

"Are you a demon, or are you my wife?" Gottlieb will put the question flatly to me.

I will say I am both, and he will . . .

I plan to go to Tokyo where I will become, in a matter of days, the most delicious geisha Tokyo has ever had, and then I will visit the *Frying Pan,* as a guest of Ohno's wife.

With Taco's help, I locate the Ohnos in the phone book. The woman who answers the phone says Ohno is not available, but she asks, "You friend of Mr. Ohno?"

"Yes, Desdemona Dean, a friend of Mr. Ohno from New York."

There is a pause while the maid gets Satsuki. "Anything for a friend of Mr. Ohno," she says. "Meet tomorrow Prince Hotel six o'clock."

At first I was suspicious of the ease with which Mrs. Ohno agreed to meet me. But I remember that Hiro had said that in Japan they treat visitors very well. I could expect to be spoiled wherever I went. Indeed Taco and Ryuga have been unnecessarily gracious, poor as they are. I buy them groceries before leaving and they wish me good-bye, relieved of their burden.

On a bus to Tokyo, I watch rather dull scenery, unending apartment buildings of white concrete, like staggered building blocks with balconies, each with an airing futon.

As the bus enters the city, I am impressed with its well-orchestrated arrangement of mismatched structures. Three-

and five-story buildings are clustered together, without appearing crowded somehow. Many buildings have recessed entrances, secret passageways. Buildings wrapped in covered staircases resemble modern art. No orderly row houses here. A modern building sits next door to a thatched roof hut. Tokyo is like a giant coral reef, funky, growing with incongruous twisted structures. New buildings seem about to bud everywhere.

As I exit the last stop, the helpful bus driver tells me to flag down a taxi, the four-door colorful cars. I'm wearing my only dress, the green gown which Taco kindly shortened for me. Stockingless, my legs are goosepimply and naked, so naked. Standing in the center of a meticulously gardened traffic island, I realize I am far too blonde in a sea of dark-haired people. I hail speeding colorful cars. Despite being conspicuous, I'm unable to convince a cab to stop.

Everyone filing in and out of the tall office buildings wears virtually identical double-breasted suits, with matching shirts, even the high-heeled ladies whose skirts hit just above the knee (short calves). Everyone seems so organized, so unified, but me.

Never before have I felt so uncomfortable about my height, my flagrant ways, my overall strangeness. I am now as eye-catching as one could possibly be. Everyone sees me. Everyone looks. I have never looked more in need of a ride to safety than I do right now.

Seeing another orange, white and black car approach, I raise my arm. Slowing, the capped driver examines me and drives on. I try this twice before I realize police also drive colorful cars. Then I see a Japanese man stop a cab by kind of waving it away. The drivers hadn't recognized the meaning of my New York gesture, a torchless Statue of Liberty.

As soon as I imitate the native, a taxi obediently halts. To my surprise, the door pops open by remote control. I get in. A cab scene should go well enough, because my Japanese language tapes helped me rehearse the necessary dialogue.

The driver, wearing spotless white felt gloves, turns and asks, "*Dochira e?*" (Where to?)

So far so good, exactly like the driver of *Japanese For Beginners*. "*Akasaka made onegai shimasu,*" I reply. This phrase involves a meaningless apology and a request to go to Akasaka, the neighborhood Taco said was famous for hotels and hostess clubs.

The driver says, *"Hai"* to my request and pulls into traffic. *"Nihon wa hajimete desu ka?"* (First time in Japan [little girl])? *"Ee hajimete desu."* I admit it is my first time, fearing that he'll probably take the long way now, but this is the response I practiced. My part in the tapes had been a trusting tourist. Next he should comment on the weather.

"Atsui desu ne?"

Yes, it is hot, or at least it was on my language tapes. Actually, today is rather cool. He continues to chat in Japanese, but I cannot follow because he says things my language tapes haven't prepared me for. I continue to reply in agreement. *"Ee hajimete desu."* Yes, it's my first time for this, for that, for everything.

Finally, he drops the virgin off on the neat streets of Akasaka. Having lost the protection of car and driver, again I feel gawky and awkward. In New York, I was conspicuous by choice. Here, being finally incomparable, truly one-of-a-kind, I long for subtly, for camouflage.

I go in pursuit of lodging. While in the cab, I had passed several painted signs which read, "Hotel Savvy." I know of the kind of hotel that calls itself Hotel Something. It's a place for people without reservations, who look in the white pages under "H." It's a place for transients and is usually cheap. Another "Hotel Savvy" sign greets me on the corner. This one is neon, an indication that I'm getting closer. Then I see and follow one with a crooked arrow. When I cross under a highway and pass a Kentucky Fried Chicken, frowning in disdain, I find myself in a shopping/tourist district, lots of shops, booksellers and perfumeries. No further direction from helpful signs. I look at the people around me, longing for help, wishing for the courage to ask directions. I see two people, a man and a woman, apparently co-workers in a nearby pharmacy, both wearing white lab coats, which make them look official, possibly helpful. As I approach, they see each other, bow twice and say, *"Ohio gozaimasu,"* the traditional workday greeting, before turning from me and going into their shop. I linger outside.

A young, good-looking man in an expensive Italian suit looks friendly so I start to ask him. "*Su'masen.*"

I have his attention, half smiling, half annoyed, but for an unknown reason he shoos me away.

I continue to circle the same block, afraid to go in a new direction because I might lose my way. Each time I pass the same shops, I am embarrassed, imagining the keepers saying to each other, "Look, there goes that blonde again."

Akasaka, apparently, is a wealthy district. The men and women on the street appear nice on the surface, like Americans did in the fifties: impeccably dressed, similarly dressed, according to company policy or national policy. Underneath, like Americans in the fifties, they're probably festering with sexual neuroses. The men are dying to accost me, I know, but are too shy. Several dark eyes linger on my bare legs. I try out my Japanese on a passing businessman who had gazed at my eyes longer than most. "Hotel Savvy *wa doko desuka?*" I ask.

He, startled, scurries on without answering.

Feeling tired and rejected, I decide to find a restaurant to get some assistance and coffee. I quickly notice that none of the restaurants has windows. I see small doorways with menus, plastic sushi on display, but I can't see inside. Finally, I muster enough pluck to open a door, but after braving the initial dark threshold I am greeted with a darker twisting passageway. I follow it to a curtained door.

Hiro had given me one such curtain for my own home. They usually bear the name of the establishment and say something to the effect of, "Open, please come in." But I feel blocked by it and retreat.

Back on the street, regretting my cowardice, I resolve to enter the very next restaurant I see. What if they're closed between lunch and dinner? What if the waitress doesn't speak English? Should I merely point at the menu and hope for something edible?

Finally, I find a western-style diner, with windows and an English menu. I order coffee (*Koohii o kudasai*). The waitress says something familiar and waits. I mumble the first thing that comes to mind. It seemed to connect with one of the exercises in the language tapes, probably something about

Victoria N. Alexander

validating my passport or purchasing postcards. Unfortunately, she is impressed and replies in Japanese.

I stop her. "I don't understand." Then I ask, in English, for directions to Hotel Savvy.

"Hotel Savvy?" The waitress crinkles her nose in English. "Why you want that? You American?" She sets the coffee down and charges me five dollars for it. "Hotel Savvy is not good."

"Is it inexpensive?"

"Very cheap," she says and tells me where to go.

I order two refills. Each time she returns   bill and adds to it. The final bill comes to eight hundred and sixty-two yen. After waiting fifteen minutes for the waitress to return for payment, I remember (Hiro had mentioned) in Japan one pays at the cashier.

I find him near the entrance sitting behind a tall counter. I present my ticket and try to find the right amount from the change the cab driver had given me. Flustered by the exotic money, I give the cashier nine hundred and sixty-eight yen. Annoyed, he rejects the extra change, which I immediately drop and have to disappear from his view for a while to pick it up. As I leave, he says, in Japanese, thank-you come again, and I, confused, say yes, it is my first time, using the formal address.

I strike out for the hotel, feeling heaviness from the day's search. I'm still not fully recovered, even breathing has become painful, but fortunately, within minutes, above me, grinning in the electric multicolor visage of Tokyo, is the final sign, "Hotel Savvy," in gripping neon, irritably humming, "Vvvvvt, Vvvvvt."

Here I go, checking in to a tawdry hotel. It all seems to fit. This hotel is meant for me. As I march up the walk to the Savvy, a man stands in my path, saying, "Excuse me."

"Yes," I answer.

"Pencil?" he says.

"Have I got a pencil?" I restate his question, automatically touching the zipper of my purse in order to find him one.

"Japanese boy pencil," he clarifies.

"Japanese," I say reflectively, "boy, pencil, boy, pencil, hmm?"

194

He stands there—timid, glasses, trench coat, schoolboy side-parted hair, cupped hand over his mouth—and secretively whispers, "My Japanese boy is like pencil. You want see?"

Right. Okay. I finally get it.

Walking away I wonder why I refused him. Wouldn't he have given me base and depraved sex?

I go into the hotel and check in. For a hotel with a dubious reputation, nothing seems out-of-the-ordinary, except perhaps me. The other guests seem much more like legitimate housewives and salesmen than I do. "Your bags, Miss?"

"No, sir. No bags."

"I see."

On my way to my room, I pass the maid, who is wearing a surgical mask. I admire her bold hypochondria. Then I remember Hiro mentioned when the Japanese are ill they must wear masks to prevent others from catching cold. How selfless they are.

The designer of my room has dealt with the constraints of Tokyo space in ingenious ways. The bathroom is a self-contained unit, much like one you might find in an airplane or Winnebago. My Japanese tub is small but deep, and it shares a faucet with the sink bowl. The faucet swivels, efficiently servicing the two. It's clear the Japanese know what to do in a tight spot. In New York if there isn't enough room for a full-sized bath, they simply install the tub in the kitchen. The toilet tank is narrow, molded in the corner's shape. In the medicine cabinet, I find soap, a toothbrush, toothpaste, shampoo and several other jars and tubes. One jar is labeled "Hand Cream(s)." The parentheses are theirs.

I also find a samurai robe neatly folded on the bed. For a sleazy hotel, this isn't so bad. It sure beats the Hotel Carlton. I sit down at my tiny desk and correct the grammar on the Hotel Information Guide. "Vending Machine(s) are located on (the) first floor. In case earthquake occurred (occurs) get under your desk."

Here I am in Tokyo, with money and a place to sleep. I have enough toiletries to make myself presentable and one reasonably good dress. Thinking, that was easy, I get into bed. Tomorrow, I will meet with Satsuki and we shall look at my future together. If I'm to become a prostitute, I will have to stop rejecting customers on the basis of bad appearance or poor manners. I must learn not to discriminate. In my long-running fantasy, a crowd of men watch. Someone says, "Yes, that Desdemona, anyone can do it with her: she likes it so. Hey who's next? She sometimes does ten a day."

I roll over, exhausted. I can hardly sleep for the banging in my ear against the pillow. My heart is as excited as a bird's. I have had, for the past week, nightsweats, cold and disturbing. I wake trembling as if from nightmares that hang dimly like a light image on retina. Eventually, I manage, after thoroughly dampening the sheets, to fall asleep.

At ten a.m., the cleaning lady raps on the door. Ignoring the "Do not disturb" sign, she looks in at me, prone on the tiny bed, apologizes and slams the door. I sleep on till one, and finally venture out in the late afternoon in pursuit of "breack fast" (the spelling on the room service menu).

On the way to the elevator, I notice the cleaning crew squatting in the linen closet. As I wait for the elevator, they converge upon my room. Apparently, they couldn't go home until the job in my room was done.

The hotel restaurant is closed until dinner. I can't remember the last time I ate—Taco's bland rice and fish—how I wish I had some now.

Before leaving, I try to apologize at the desk for detaining the housekeeping crew and ask if I could look after my own cleaning.

The old man thinks I'm complaining about the service and apologizes.

27

So Sore Desu

At six o'clock, I sit in the Prince tea room having just ordered a ten dollar cup of coffee. I wanted to be early so Satsuki wouldn't notice my naked legs. (The price of stockings at the local discount store was prohibitive.) I didn't have to tell her what I look like. She'll know me.

When she arrives, a plump woman in a purple suit with limp layered hair, she immediately spots the blonde and advances. Sitting, she tosses her matching bag in a vacant chair, places her elbows on the table, her chin in her palms and looks at me grinning.

More waiters converge on us, handing her a menu and a hot towel, which she only pretends to use and throws aside. I begin to describe my situation: alone and illegal, without friends, virtually ignorant of the language and customs. I was a friend of her husband in New York. Could she help me get a job?

I take a sip of my coffee, she her tea. I compliment her husband's integrity and mention how highly he spoke of her. All the while, she nods, quietly, smiling above her tea cup. Presently, I begin to suspect her English skills. We sit in silence for two sips of coffee. "So," I say, "it was very nice of you to meet with me."

"Hi," she says with a quick nod, and I realize what a noisy American I've been. She hasn't comprehended a word. Embarrassed, I take the bill—she'd had an expensive pot of Jasmine tea—and get up to leave.

She laughs at me, snatching the bill from my hand. She says, "You working as geisha?"

Relieved, I nod.

She had mentioned my name to her husband. He didn't recall, but that didn't matter. "You are beautiful," she says.

With the comical expedience of movie editing, I am soon tooling about Tokyo in an Aston Martin Lagonda, a car whose existence I had only heard of in connection with Prince Andrew. Satsuki at the wheel chats on her carphone. Traffic is heavy, and Satsuki jerks in and out of lane.

I'm woozy. The honking of horns seem less like protests to me than excited sighs. The whole of downtown Tokyo is ecstatic with neon, ten times brighter and livelier than Times Square. She enters a highway ramp at fifty miles per hour, and quickly accelerates. The elevated straightaway cuts through the city. There are few exits, so the traffic moves quickly and smoothly. Adrenaline and wind make my scalp tingle. Lack of food and some fear make me lightheaded, as I enjoy the glamour of Satsuki's speed.

When we exit, I am driven to a side street in Ginza, a narrow brick alley. Satsuki honks the horn, gets out—I do the same. We're greeting by a obsequious small man in a dark suit, the hostess club manager, Jun's Tokyo counterpart. I am introduced as a friend of Ohno. They disappear down a dark secluded staircase. I follow, abandoning the car, doors left open, running. I assume a valet will appear shortly. The stair leads to a glass door, which opens quietly when it senses our approach.

By the door, I notice a pair of brown leather men's shoes, worn and wrinkled with new waxed laces. I hope I can keep my shoes because my American sense of propriety tells me it's wrong to be shoeless. "I can leave mine on, can't I?" I ask as Satsuki slips her wide feet out of her purple pumps.

Satsuki says, "Of course," but she means "Of course you cannot." I step up with a shod foot. "No, no!" she scolds and knocks my shoes off my heels with her big toe. We part the curtain and go in.

So sore desu—so this is it—what a real geisha house looks

like, a dark close room with short-legged rosewood furniture, ornately carved with claw feet and etched foliage winding along the armrests and backs. Silk pillows are tossed about, coral, yellow and red, on the sofas, on the floor, propped against the walls. Thin curtains separate seating areas, and the flowing silk trembles in the smoky air. The hostesses are dressed in kimonos, resembling a collection of vividly colored praying mantises, pouring drinks with decorative movements, wiping the table with fleur de lis flamboyance, choreographed flourish, lighting cigarettes with the grace and production of magicians.

I watch in awe of them. In comparison, a Gigi, an Ultra seems rude and insincere.

The owner of the brown leather shoes, an obese tall man, with swept-back, receding, greasy hair, sits crosslegged at a table, too big to kneel. All the other tables are crowded with guests and hostesses. Satsuki and I join the man. A hostess appears and introduces herself.

Elke speaks a little English. "Satsuki tell me you will be working for her?" She softly giggles, handing me a hot towel. "She is good woman to work for." She closes the curtain around us, without shutting out the quiet feminine murmur of the room. I'm introduced to Satsuki's brother, Suichi. He hands me a gift, a foot-long chocolate bar, and I accept it with reservations. In Japan, Hiro told me, gifts are given freely and reciprocation is expected.

I wonder if dinner will be ordered. Not having eaten all day, my head has begun to ache. Should I sample the chocolate? Satsuki and Suichi start speaking rapidly in Japanese, discussing my future. When Satsuki mentions the *Flying Pan* to her brother, I get butterflies in my stomach. Satsuki explains that everyone in Tokyo is talking about the new strange ship that suddenly appeared in the canal. Suichi purses his lips and nods. A little later, we will all go over to the ship, but first other business. Suichi puts down his sake cup and reclines, eyes closed. Satsuki explains that tonight I will entertain a new client who has just flown in from America. He requested an American blonde. If he likes me, well, he would be here for a month. "He's in the chemical industry," she continues, "an important business for Japanese agricultural. His work is respected."

I assure her I agreed. "I had a friend who shipped potassium," I mention, thinking of Hiro.

"Oh so you know? Maybe some girls don't think fertilizer trade is so glamorous, but on small island is difference between eating and starving." The client is handsome, she says, and wealthy, doesn't have wife. Satsuki smiles and hunches her shoulders in a kind of vicarious excitement. Isn't it lucky that I happened to call?

I agree.

"But he is not here on business this time. Personal troubles. You must be good to him. Customer is king."

Elke hands me sake in a square wooden cup with salt on the side. "Drink up!" encourage brother and sister. They watch; I obey.

Meanwhile Elke, a fastidious geisha, carefully straightens the objects on the circular table, one drink placed at four o'clock, another at six, matches center, just so.

I feel the rush of the sake gone to my head. Carefully, I finish it. Some dribbles out of the strange box down my chin. Elke laughs at me. "American think square cup hard to drink." She suggests I go to the ladies room to check my powder.

The restroom is made of beautiful pale orange marble. The toilet is merely an opening in the floor to squat over. Following Elke's advice, I check my reflection. I'm not wearing any powder, but I agree I look faded. Eyes are glassy. I press my hand against my forehead, like Lola used to have me do to her.

When I return Satsuki and Elke are gone. Suichi explains that Satsuki is meeting with the client. She could vouch for him. He was actually someone her husband knew of in New York. Ohno owed him a special favor. The client would come straight to my room. "Shall we go?"

We get up, I with difficulty, almost falling, but save myself by grabbing his shoulder. Out in the hall, our shoes wait in a neat row freshly brushed and polished. Suichi puts on his coat, grunting softly to himself, while his arms search behind aimlessly for his sleeves until I direct his small hands into the proper holes.

I follow Suichi through a back exit into a cool and empty hotel lobby, fine, opulent and Western. A long-coated valet welcomes us to the Duchess Hotel, a savvy hotel. Nothing like my Hotel Savvy. Suichi smiles and explains Satsuki was horrified and suspicious of the Hotel Savvy, so she made a quick call and had "her man" go over and check me out. My things will be sent to Satsuki's private suite here at the Duchess. "I hope you don't mind," he says and squeezes my wrist.

I gawk at the shiny floors and floral arrangements. Suichi is already strutting through the foyer, his roomy suit jacket fluttering behind him like a sail. I catch up with him. A desk clerk scampers up to Suichi, begs, bows and scampers off. Suichi fans his hand at the row of photographs along the wall which feature the same hotel chain all over the world. He owns them. "Where do you want to go?" he asks.

For one greedy moment I want to write postcards from Hong Kong, Jetta, Singapore, and St. Louis to Rocco, Lola, Hiro, and yes Gottlieb, all of them, but with a pang of delight I remember that I am dead as far as they're concerned, and I have a better surprise.

Suichi says, "Come, Desdemona," and I follow him to the elevator. As we soar thirty stories, while he breathes noisily through his mouth, my head begins to pound. Suichi stabilizes me by grabbing my elbow. "You okay?" I shake my head. "Too much to drink?" I nod, though I'd only had two cups of sake. At thirty, he exits the elevator first and goes down the hall without waiting for me.

He opens the door to an American-sized suite, bath/shower which I'm instructed to use immediately, a full service bar, big western beds and heavy plastic-backed curtains that will block the sun and let me sleep late. He tells me to get dressed—opening a well-stocked closet, selecting a heavily embroidered kimono and tossing it on the bed. After he leaves, I do as I'm told but a little wearily. I'm so tired. I cake cover-up under my eyes to cover the purplish shadows. The end result is a much paler Desdemona with blood red lips and darkly lined eyes. I look almost like a Japanese mask.

I put on the kimono, with ridiculous sleeves and long

annoying flaps hanging from them. Far too tight for *my* chest. I imagine that even Japanese women can't wear these things anymore now that their breasts have been encouraged by hormone-rich Kentucky Fried Chicken. I slip on the recommended pair of elevated sandals and hobble a step or two, wondering how Japanese hostesses do it so encumbered. The whole country seems like a hostess, genuflecting, hoping, serving, wanting to be nice, polite, beautiful, loved. To be loved.

I wrestle out of the kimono, like getting out of a straitjacket. This bit of exertion makes me break out in a cold sweat. Remembering what the doctor had said about my cold turning into pneumonia, I check the medicine cabinet. I find only a bottle of NyQuil. It can't hurt, so take a generous swig.

As I wait for my client, I survey the city from this, my thirtieth-floor window. Satsuki has provided me with a fine view of Tokyo. *Subarashii keshiki desu.* When you look down on the Japanese from the height of a mean American tourist residing in a lofty western hotel, you see their humble secret. Within the frame of neat city blocks, the houses are clustered together in beehive fashion, with no ostensible thoroughfares to give light or view—only small airshafts. A mere fraction of the units face the street. Roofs touch one another on all four sides, hearts and hearths sunk deep.

The phone rings. It is Satsuki. "How are thing?" I tell her the kimono didn't fit. "Then turn off the lightswitch and lie on top of the bed, and don't put anything on: the client will be right in," she says.

Now I feel too warm and decide to take a quick cool bath. As I lie in the tub, steam rises from my goosepimply abdomen. I notice, with mild disgust, blue veins crisscrossing my groin. My teeth chatter as I dry myself, wrap the towel over my shoulders and sit shivering on the edge of the tub. Footsteps approach in the hall, so I drop the towel and quickly lie down on the bed. I have the prickly kind of excitement of a child playing hide-and-seek, about to be discovered. The footsteps pass my door and are gone.

The room is freezing. I must turn down the air conditioner, but my body feels too heavy to move and at the same time weightless.

What seems like hours later, I wake from a wet, sticky

dream. I can't breathe. Rasping, I open my eyes. I vaguely remember walking from the bed to the bathroom. I seem to see the room through a small window or windshield, as if I were operating my body, a mechanical monster, from inside its head. The phone rings. When I try to get it I find I cannot locate up or down, the room spins, the phone keeps ringing. Finally I knock the handset off the cradle and hold it to my cheek. Dim green light from the keypad illuminates my face. It's Satsuki again, saying, "You sleeping, honey? Good. Go back to sleep."

I drop the receiver. So that's how the client wants me, out cold. I realize the drink at the club was probably laced with sedative.

It will be happening soon. A silhouette of a man will stand in the crack of light from the opened door. His eyes, dull red, will wander over my body, long shiny legs, curly ashen triangle, powdered belly, hard swollen breasts, chilled nipples, blonde hair scattered on the pillow, serene, pale face, eyes closed. Hardly a movement of breath spoils the erotic eeriness of the still-life he'll see.

I think I sleep; I feel something touching my body, something firm, warm and weighty on my belly, but I wake and the room is still quiet, dark and cold. Someone fumbles with the door knob. Then the door slowly opens. I try to pick up my head but can't. The door is closed. Everything is black, only a familiar voice.

* * *

Hiro surveys Angel's motionless body with quiet grin. He knew he'd find her like this. The cable from Lola was, as he thought, just another one of Angel's deceits. It hadn't been hard to find her. He recognized her style in her new alias. In New York, when his driver told him she had boarded the *Flying Pan*, he kept tabs on their voyage, even tipped off the officials in Panama. But she managed to make it here. And here she was.

When he learned Angel had jumped overboard and probably drowned he began dreaming, horrible dreams, dreams he enjoyed in a confused way, dreams in which he groped her white, indifferent body. Now it was better to think of her that way. He no longer fantasized about a living, breathing, sympathetic Angel.

Touching her leg, he is shocked by its lack of warmth, jerking back quickly. He grabs her wrist. No pulse? He starts for the phone. No, wait. He puts his ear to her mouth. Some breathing. It's only the drug, perhaps she got too much. He holds a fistful of her hair to his mouth. She doesn't move, and he tosses the lock of hair across her face.

"Angel," he says with drunken sternness, "you sleeping?" As a kind of joke he pinches tender nipple, but Angel remains perfectly still. Sitting heavily on the edge of the squeaky mattress, he considers her lusterless white complexion, her smooth arms and her fragile rib cage that barely moves. He squeezes her cheeks with a forefinger and thumb, opening her mouth. He hears her breathing now, a wheezy sporadic rattle.

He grabs the phone to call the hotel doctor. Emergency. She is dying he thinks. Hotel operator promises to inform Satsuki.

After placing Angel's hands on her chest—a morbid joke, but she deserves it—Hiro steps back to look at her. He takes off his tie and thoughtfully unbuttons his shirt. "You're so beautiful." Groaning he turns away and stares at the blank wall.

His buttoned cuff clings on his wrist. Annoyed, he flings shirt to the floor. Then quickly, he climbs on the bed and Angel, unzips his pants and parts her legs with his knee. He has only a few minutes with her alone. Just in case, he touches her wrist again and is satisfied with the ghost of a pulse. He kisses her slack mouth. She once laughed when he kissed her—the times she wiped her lips.

After searching through his pants pocket for a few crumpled yen notes, he holds them in his hand against her face. Still, she doesn't stir. He turns her on her stomach. With a cupped palm he traces the roundness of her cheeks, then with both hands he parts her buttocks. He presses his thumb against anus, examines it, experimentally slips his thumb in; an involuntary gasp escapes her mouth. Then as he straddles her, he notices her breathing may have stopped, but she is still warm inside. Gradually, rhythmically, he shoves her body up until her head begins to hit the headboard.

28

Gottlieb

Satsuki, accelerating out of a sharp turn, regains control of the car. Beside her, curled up in the passenger seat, is the body of Charlie Dean, half wrapped in a bedsheet—to Satsuki it's Desdemona, friend of Mr. Ohno, a hundred-and-twenty-pound problem, not so heavy, but awkward to carry to the private elevator without being seen and into her car in VIP garage. Thank God her husband will take over from here.

Traffic thickens in the venous streets that lead to the canal. Satsuki doesn't look at the passenger beside her. She stares at the road, soberly waiting for lights to go green. Finally the listing *Frying Pan* comes into view. It is decked out in twinkling, eerie lights, swaying gently.

There is panic on the deck. Several hands are running around while Ohno watches from the pier. Juan shouts to Ohno from inside the forecastle, "We can't use the damn dock rope to pull her. It's rotten. It will give. Just wait for Gottlieb to get here with the cables."

Ohno and two deckhands fasten a rope to a truck on the pier. "This isn't going to work," Juan objects.

Satsuki parks alongside the ship, lowers both windows and gets out of the car. Ohno frowns over his shoulder at the car and its passenger. His body jerks with recognition. "Charlie?" Hurrying to the car, he incredulously regards Satsuki and the body. Satsuki self-consciously conducts herself as if re-hearsed. "It is Desdemona I told you about . . ." but she is cut short.

"Charlie!" Ohno says with unsophisticated delight. Satsuki tries to smile, but cannot. He notices this, checks his inclination to celebrate. He offers a weak explanation to Satsuki. Ms. Dean is an "old friend."

"She's dead."

"She *is* dead?"

The truck engine clamorously roars into action, and the *Frying Pan* is heaved forward and dragged about ten inches.

"The ship's started to come right again," says Juan and warns the men not to try to make her sit completely straight. "We could lose her."

While Satsuki explains the body to her husband, Ohno looks at it calmly. He had wanted to keep her out of trouble. She had been so difficult to talk to, to be intimate with. If not for Satsuki, he might have been more direct, he might have tried to love her. He says slowly, dry-mouthed, "Perhaps it would be better to let Charlie go down with the ship. Come, let's take her inside, Satsuki."

Satsuki backs away from the ship that appears to be sinking.

"No need to be alarmed," reassures Ohno. "We even have time to pull out some of the liquor and equipment."

The rotten rope snaps. The bow begins to sink, and Juan curses the name of Gottlieb.

The much-talked-about, yet unseen, casino manager Gottlieb has failed to provide some important equipment, a pump for the bilge, cables. Gottlieb is not on the *Frying Pan*, or anywhere near the canal, if he is still in Tokyo at all. The only news they've heard from him is secondhand. After one of the Filipino girls disappeared, they found a note on her bunk that said He had come on board in the middle of the night, and they were running off together.

As Juan curses, the angle of the falling beacon changes, and whirling red light scatters across the parking lot. The deck chairs start to slide. One tumbles headlong. Juan throws a chest over the side onto the dock. Some of the deckhands begin to unload some of the liquor. Juan takes a case himself and begins to bring it down the gangplank.

"Forget the liquor. We recovered Charlie's body. Get it out of the car and put it in her bunk," says Ohno.

Juan, noticing the car for the first time, drops the case and runs to look before Satsuki pulls the bedsheet over Charlie.

Lola, dressed in white cotton robe, bolts out of the sinking ship and runs down the graded plank sideways.

Lola shouts, "Where's Gottlieb?"

Ohno still had no word from him.

"Is there a message for me?"

He says, "He's coming soon."

"You don't know when?"

No one has an answer. Frightened, she snaps, "Tell me!"

"Excuse me," says Juan. Lola is obliged to clear the gangplank to let him pass with a bundle over his shoulder. "What difference would it make?" he asks sardonically, shifting his load. "In the end, it's up to us to sink or save the ship." Juan hurries down a hatch.

Lola says to Ohno, to the others, "You mean he really isn't, he doesn't . . ." Her voice trails off. Ohno glances guiltily at the pavement. The ship lists and creaks, beginning to take on water very rapidly. Juan reappears and rushes down the gangplank, shoving Lola to safety. From the dock, the crew of the *Frying Pan* watch as she sinks in the boiling water.